BLIND EYE

MEG LELVIS

BLACK ROSE
writing™

© 2018 by Meg Lelvis
All rights reserved. No part of this book may be reproduced, stored in a retrieval system or transmitted in any form or by any means without the prior written permission of the publishers, except by a reviewer who may quote brief passages in a review to be printed in a newspaper, magazine or journal.

The final approval for this literary material is granted by the author.

First printing

This is a work of fiction. Names, characters, businesses, places, events and incidents are either the products of the author's imagination or used in a fictitious manner. Any resemblance to actual persons, living or dead, or actual events is purely coincidental.

ISBN: 978-1-68433-009-6
PUBLISHED BY BLACK ROSE WRITING
www.blackrosewriting.com

Printed in the United States of America
Suggested retail price $18.95

Blind Eye is printed in Book Antiqua

For *Cate, Nolan, & Teddy*

and

In memory of *Kris Hadrits*

Acknowledgments

Special Thanks to:

Reagan Rothe and his staff at Black Rose Writing
Dave King, design lead at Black Rose Writing
Roger Leslie, editor
Danielle Hartman Acee, publicist
Houston Writers leaders Roger Paulding, Fern Brady, Lynne Gregg
Critique friends Barbara Andrews, Jim Murtha, Connie Gillen, Carolyn Thorman, Bill Ottinger, Mark Pople
My sister, Carole
Tom Williams for cop advice
Gail, Kaye, Myrna, Monica, Wilma, Margaret, Gary, Kristy, Rebecca, my cheerleaders

Blind Eye

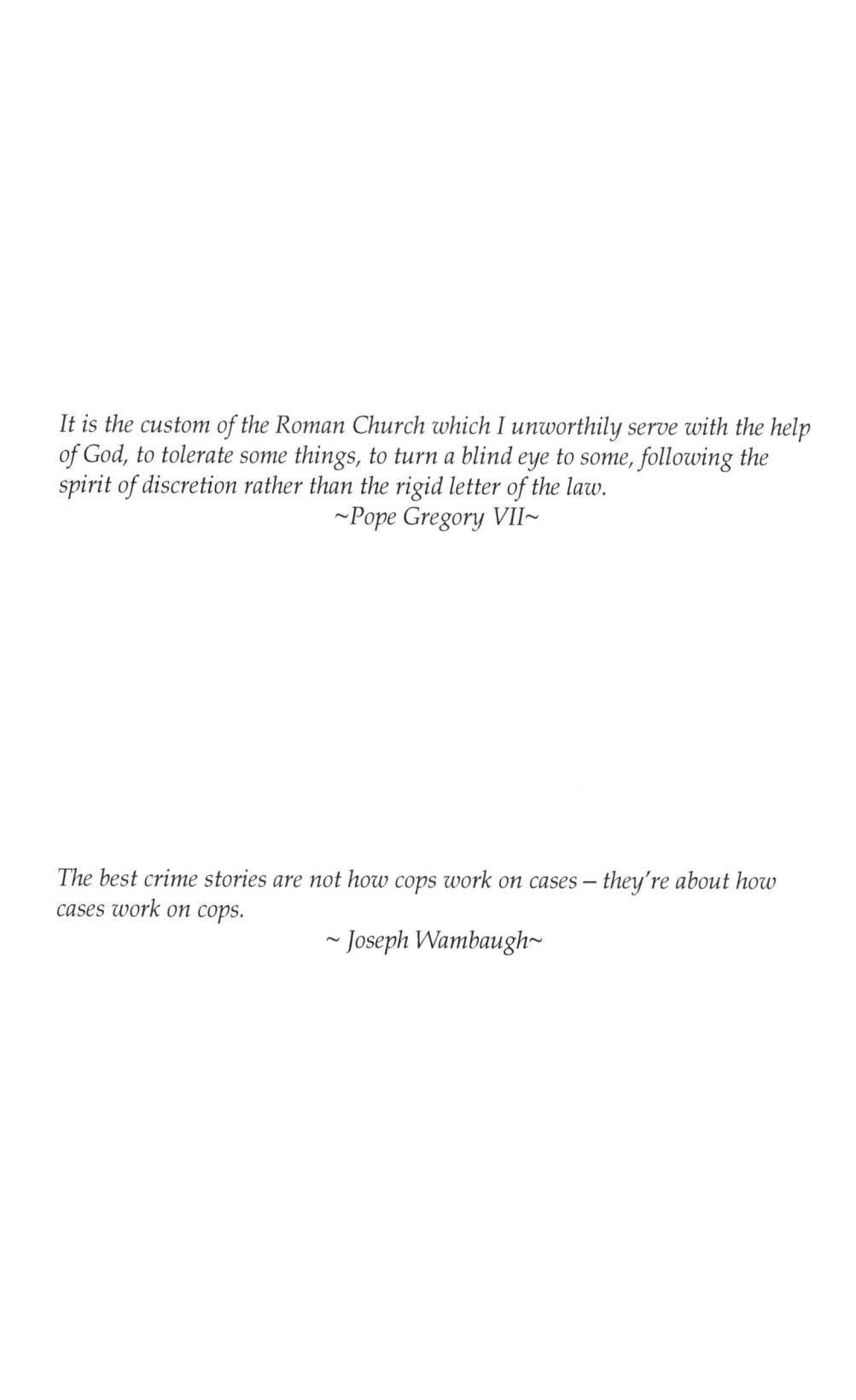

It is the custom of the Roman Church which I unworthily serve with the help of God, to tolerate some things, to turn a blind eye to some, following the spirit of discretion rather than the rigid letter of the law.
  ~Pope Gregory VII~

The best crime stories are not how cops work on cases — they're about how cases work on cops.
  ~ Joseph Wambaugh~

Chapter 1

At first Detective Jack Bailey thought the old lady's murder was a robbery gone bad. Happened often to the elderly living alone. He told dispatch he was on his way to the scene, flipped on the siren, and sped through the morning rush hour traffic toward White Sox Stadium, near the victim's apartment in the TE Brown complex. Jack was familiar with the address, an eleven-story building for senior residents.

When he arrived at the second floor apartment, a young patrol cop met him at the door. "I'm Jeff Lake, Detective."

Jack grunted a makeshift greeting. "What ya got?"

"The old lady must be eighty or ninety, probably strangled. She's in her bed. No sign of forced entry, the place looks neat, but I just got here." The cop pointed Jack to a door off the living room and kitchen. They entered the bedroom; Jack cringed as an odor of human waste assaulted his nostrils.

A stout white-haired woman lay on her back, arms resting at her sides. She wore a plain long-sleeved white blouse and a calf-length navy skirt, fuzzy pink slippers on her feet. The blue bedspread beneath her was stained with brown blotches, but unwrinkled.

The men looked around, not touching anything. Jack noticed tiny burst blood vessels below the woman's eyes. Looked like nail scratches on both sides of the jaw line with light bruising on the neck.

Jeff straightened his cap. "The neighbor next door said the lady didn't show for their morning coffee. She called management, they went in and found her."

"Vic got a name?"

"Yeah, Sister Anne Celeste."

Jack felt a nudge in his gut. "A nun?"

"Yup."

"Who'd want to murder a nun? A priest I can see. Most likely was strangulation. Sometimes there's no marks, but these are pretty clear."

They returned to the living room, a compact, functional space with neutral tones and tiled floors with a small kitchen at the back wall. Well designed for old folks. Jack's uncle lived here years ago; Section 8 housing.

"Detective, CSI is on their way. Call just came in."

Jack nodded. "Your first nun?" The cop looked like a high school kid.

"Yeah, but I've only been on the force two years."

"Tell ya a secret, kid. It's my first nun too. Just hope it doesn't become a habit." Jack snorted. "Sorry, bad joke."

Jeff looked puzzled. "Joke?"

"Never mind," Jack sighed. Damn kid was too young for his own good.

• • • • •

Five minutes later the CSI guys arrived and began the familiar routines Jack knew well after twenty-one years in homicide. Almost eighteen months ago he'd moved back to Chicago from a six-year stint in Richmond, Texas, near Houston. He missed the mild winters, but that was all. The sweltering summers damn near killed him. Now that March was here, hope of spring was in the air.

"Jeff, show me the neighbor's place. I'll talk to her, and you canvass this floor. I'll get my partner and a couple uniforms to assist." He punched in a number on his phone.

"Still think the motive was robbery?" Jeff asked.

"No signs of struggle, but need more details." Jack's instinct told him something was off. The nun looked too tidy, lying in repose. He spoke into his phone for a moment and clicked off.

"Partner's on his way."

They stepped outside the door, heading for the neighbor's apartment when Rich, a CSI guy called out. "Hey, Bailey. Wanna show you something."

Jack turned back, and Rich held out a piece of white paper folded in half. Jack pulled his gloves from his pocket and took the paper.

"Found this under her right arm by the wrist. Weird."

Jack unfolded the paper. In blue ink two names were hand printed followed by numbers, one name atop the other. Startled, he read aloud, "Psalm 27:10 and Isaiah 41:17." Now he was sure it was no robbery. He looked at Rich. "Give me a minute to take a pic."

Jack sat at the kitchen table and took a photo of the verse with his phone. He glanced at Jeff.

"Keep it under wraps. Don't want this detail to leak out." Jack handed the paper to Rich, who headed for the bedroom.

"They're Bible verses aren't they?" Jeff asked.

Jack rolled his eyes. "I'll look 'em up later. Now, let's find the nun's friend."

After knocking on the door of the nearest apartment, Jack was immediately greeted by a thin, gray-haired woman wearing a red turtleneck, tan pants, and brown sensible shoes.

He flashed his badge. "Detective Bailey, Ma'am. Bridgeport PD. May I come in?" He waved Jeff away to start canvassing.

"Oh yes, officer, I've been waiting." She gazed at Jack, then giggled nervously. "I don't mean to stare, but you look like somebody on TV or somewhere. Uh, come on in."

He was used to people commenting on his resemblance to Liam Neeson, fellow Irishman born the same year. Jack was about six feet two, solid build. His thick black hair, generously salted with gray, framed sapphire eyes.

He followed the woman to a brown tweed sofa where they both sat. Same layout as the nun's apartment. Jack took out his pen and notebook, then asked the woman her name and what happened earlier that morning.

"I'm Ida Swanson, I am good—I mean, was good friends with Sister Anne." She cleared her throat. "Oh, it's a terrible shock. I can't believe, such a good person. Who would do this? These things don't happen here." She dabbed her eyes with a white hanky. "It's supposed to be a safe place."

Jack guessed she was in her eighties, but, as his mother would say, 'well preserved'. Her skin was relatively free of wrinkles, and high cheekbones indicated she was once a pretty woman. "Can you tell me what happened from the beginning, Mrs. Swenson?"

"Swanson," she corrected, and Jack nodded. Swedish names; all the same to him.

She repeated the story she told Jeff, interrupted with bursts of sobs. She knew Sister Anne Celeste for over twenty years when they both moved into the complex.

"She taught at Nativity of Our Lord Church since the war. That's World War Two, young man. When she got too old to teach at the school, they kicked her out. That's what they do, you know. Farm them out to pasture."

"So I've heard." Jack was familiar with Nativity, where both Mayor Daleys were alumni. "How did Sister feel about that?"

"She didn't like it one bit. She wanted to be useful, so she went there every day and helped out, you know, like volunteers. She helped with Bingo and in the office, different little jobs, you know how it is."

Jack didn't know, and didn't want to. He'd strayed from the Catholic fold years ago and had no intention of returning. He was the third generation of his family to attend St. Bridget's Church a couple miles away. It closed in 1990, which caused his mother much wailing and lamenting, but the number of parishes was declining all over. Too bad, but Jack didn't lose sleep over such things.

"Did Sister Anne Celeste ever mention a problem with anyone, someone at the church or a neighbor?"

Mrs. Swanson frowned and shook her head. "No, never. Everyone loved Sister Anne."

Not quite everyone, Jack thought. "Did she have family?"

"A niece not too far away, lives in Oak Lawn. They saw each other on holidays. I'll give you her name. We both kept each other's family information just in case."

She stepped into her bedroom and returned with a recipe sized paper. She handed it to Jack and waited while he copied the information.

Jack closed his notebook, thanked Mrs. Swanson, and handed her his card. "Call if you think of anything else. Even if it doesn't seem like much. Sometimes little things turn out to be important."

They walked to the door. She said, "I hope you get whoever did this. Sister Anne was a wonderful human being." Ida Swanson wiped her eyes again.

"We'll do our best, Mrs. Swanson. Be sure and lock up." He heard the bolt turn and the chain slide into place. She seemed like an astute witness. Nothing flaky about that old broad.

When Jack returned to Sister Anne's apartment, his partner, Karl Scherkenbach, better known as "Sherk", stood talking to two patrol cops.

"Hey, Jack, where do you want these guys to canvass?" Sherk was the poster child for his German heritage; tall, blond and blue-eyed, he exuded an air of health and confidence. Wire-rimmed glasses gave him an intellectual presence.

"Start on the third floor, then the fourth. Another uniform named Jeff is doing this floor. You and me will do the downstairs. Not expecting much; all old geezers."

The two cops headed out. Jack said, "Did Rich show you the note they found?"

"Nope." They sat at the kitchen table. Jack opened his notebook and read the Bible scripture titles to Sherk.

"Ah, the Psalms and Isiah, comfort books." Sherk punched in keys on his phone. "Here's the first verse. *When my father and my mother forsake me, then the Lord will take me up.*"

Jack raised his brow. "Figured this would be right up your alley." Guys in the squad laughed off Sherk's propensity for quoting Shakespeare and other literary figures; they told Jack to overlook it, that his new partner was basically a good guy. No surprise to Jack that Sherk was acquainted with the Bible as well.

"The other verse is longer," Sherk said. "Should we analyze after we canvass?"

Jack was fed up with conversations of nuns and Bible verses. "Yeah, let's go."

• • • • •

By noon Jack and Sherk were in the break room at the District Nine Chicago Police Department. The two-story, flat-roofed building is located on Halsted Street, the main north-south road in Bridgeport. Its reddish brown brick walls and drab green entryway and pillars fade into the neighborhood landscape. Sunlight peeked from the clouds, promising a bright afternoon. A typical March day, melting snow, nippy, but a vast improvement from the last few months of freezing-ass cold.

Jack helped himself to coffee and a stale cinnamon roll. He sat across from Sherk at a small table. "No surprise the canvass was a bust."

Sherk took a swig from a can of Pepsi. "Yeah, maybe the others lucked out. Nothing from forensics yet."

"What's your take on the verse?"

Sherk adjusted his glasses. "Obviously, one word is found in both verses, which I'm sure you noted."

Jack was in no mood for well-intended sarcasm. "Come on, Sherk, get on with it."

"Okay, okay. The word is 'forsaken'. In plain English it says when my father and mother forsake me, the Lord will be there for me. The next one from Isaiah means when the poor and downtrodden need help, the Lord will provide for them and not forsake them."

Jack stared at his partner. "Yeah?"

"Actually, Jack, like much of the Bible, the imagery is beautiful. *When the poor and needy seek water, and there is none, and their tongue faileth for thirst* — "

"Spare me, Jerry Falwell, how does it connect to the nun?" Too bad Sherk had to take that literature class in college and annoy everyone in the squad.

"I'd guess the killer was forsaken or abandoned by her, which at this point, doesn't fit with what people say about the venerable sister."

Jack shrugged. "What about the perp? Some kind religious fanatic?"

"Hard to say. I've never encountered this before. We'll ask our esteemed resident psychologist, Daryl Gray what he thinks."

Jack inched back his chair. "Yeah. Need to check out the nun's church, maybe turn up something. Just my luck, get stuck talking to priests. Why don't you go alone?"

Sherk laughed. "I'm Lutheran; can't do Catholic by myself."

He and Jack had been partners since Jack came on board nearly two years ago. Sherk was smart and meticulous, but Jack preferred working with older cops. He resented taking orders from a kid of forty-eight, but once he settled in, Sherk let up on the mentor role. He still annoyed Jack at times; reminded him of Munch from *Law and Order*. Did people still watch the reruns?

• • • • •

After lunch Jack and Sherk parked in front of Nativity of Our Lord on Thirty-seventh Street near Union. The historic church, one of the oldest in Chicago, was built in 1868 to serve the Irish population, many of whom worked at the nearby Union Stockyards. The church was home to both Mayor Daleys, and Jack's family had entered its portals for the occasional wedding, christening, or funeral. His grandfather was a boyhood friend of the elder Richard Daley, and Gramps told Jack and his brothers many a tale out of school regarding the old pals' past shenanigans.

Jack climbed out of the cruiser and gazed at the majestic Gothic stone structure, its steeple ascending to the heavens. "Been a long time since I darkened these doors."

Sherk beside him. "Quite a history, this place. Was designed by Patrick Keely; that's impressive. It was destroyed in the great fire of 1871 and rebuilt a few years later. Renowned for its extraordinary stained glass windows."

"Yeah, I've heard most of that lecture, believe it or not." Was there anything this geek didn't know?

Jack opened the heavy wooden door, and they entered the shadowy narthex, rays of light whispering through small high windows. A waxy sweet odor wafted in the air. Jack took a deep breath and ignored the little voice that told him to cross himself with holy water in the marble font ahead to his left.

Sherk's muffled words broke the silence. "Jeez. This is magnificent."

"Yeah, I guess. You can speak up; this ain't a library." Jack looked around and strode into the sanctuary. Rows of multicolored stained glass windows depicting scenes of the nativity, Madonna and child, the Last Supper, and nameless saints, afforded the only light in the vast space.

Sherk pointed to a prominent window near the middle row of pews. "Look at that, the Archdiocese of Chicago coat of arms."

"Yeah, I know, and talk louder." Jack glanced at the translucent red design of a phoenix against a gold shield topped with a crown of green, blue, and red jewels.

Sherk continued in a low voice. "The phoenix is symbolic of the church arising from the ashes of the great fire, as well as the resurrection of Jesus, of course."

"Sherk, you're gettin' on my last good nerve. Let's find a live body to talk to."

They turned toward the sacristy, and a thin young man wearing black jeans and shirt approached them. He smiled. "May I help you?"

The men flashed their badges. Jack said, "We need to see the priest, Father Jim I believe."

The man cleared his throat. "Ah, yes, officers. I assume you don't have an appointment."

"You assume right," Jack said.

"Yes, well, right this way. By the way, I'm Patrick." The guy appeared nervous. Guess he wasn't used to cops showing up on official business in his place of worship.

They followed Patrick to a side exit which led them outdoors to the education building and offices. They entered, walking past the reception area where two women sat at their desks, heads down, appearing busy with paperwork. When the men reached a closed door half way down the hall, Patrick knocked softly.

Jack heard someone say, "Come in."

Patrick opened the door and led them into a spacious paneled office with two large windows on one side and rows of bookshelves filling the remaining walls. A heavy set older man with a receding hairline sat behind a massive wooden desk. He wore the requisite black long sleeved tab shirt with a white clerical collar. An ornate gold crucifix hung from his neck. He smiled and rose from his chair.

"Well. Who do we have here, Pat?"

"These are policemen, Father." The man looked at Jack and Sherk. "If you'll excuse me, you can introduce yourselves to Father Jim." He closed the door on his way out.

Jack introduced Sherk and himself and showed Father Jim his badge.

The priest continued smiling and offered the men two chairs across from his desk. Jack never felt comfortable with men of the cloth. Didn't trust them. Perhaps from his days as altar boy when old Father Thomas yelled at him for holding the cruet of wine in the wrong hand. Could also be from media coverage after the priest sex scandals emerged in the mid-eighties and reached the national conscience a decade later. At first Jack's mother refused to believe the news stories, but later came to terms with the issue, brushing the whole business under her faux Oriental rug.

Jack sat and crossed his legs. "We need to tell you about Sister Anne Celeste. I'm afraid she was found dead early this morning." He paused. "It appears it was murder."

The priest's hand flew to his crucifix. He gasped. "Holy Mother of God."

Jack sensed something else behind the priest's shocked expression. Wonder what it could be. Jack's imagination?

Chapter 2

The priest's face shone with perspiration. He wiped his brow. "Dear Lord, how? What happened?"

Sherk leaned in. "She was found in her apartment. Cause of death appears to be strangulation. We'll know for sure within a day or so."

Father Jim gasped, turned pale. He crossed himself and bowed his head.

Sherk continued. "When was the last time you saw Sister Anne Celeste?"

The priest hesitated. "Excuse me, but I need water. Would you care for some?"

The men declined and waited while the priest fetched a bottle of water from a nearby table. He took a gulp. "Ah, let's see. I think she was here yesterday or the day before. We can check with Pat. He manages things. Sister and all the volunteers sign in with him."

Father Jim explained that she helped with various tasks, including weekly Bingo, filing, and answering the telephone. He checked a file that verified she entered the Sisters of St. Anne Convent in Chicago for training and was installed at Nativity of Our Lord in 1950.

Before Jack could calculate her tenure, Sherk said, "Wow, over sixty years. Quite a history. When did she retire?"

The priest paged through the file. "She retired in 1985 at age sixty. She's been volunteering since then, but not every day. The last few years she'd come in two, three times a week for a few hours."

"Slacking off, huh?" Jack's voice sardonic.

Sherk rolled his eyes. The priest said, "Excuse me?"

"Nothing. Tell me about her, Father. What was she like, how did she get along with people?"

"Very friendly, outgoing lady. I started here three years ago, and everyone held her in highest regard. A compassionate, faithful servant."

Yeah, look where it got her, Jack thought. "Can you think of any reason someone might want to harm her?" He studied the priest and noted a twitch in one eye.

"Oh, mercy, heavens, no. She was loved by everyone." He took another swig of water.

Doth the good padre protest too much?

"Father, we're well aware of confessional privilege, but if you know anything, if Sister—"

"I can't comment on that, Detective, ah, Bailey is it?"

"Yes, Jack Bailey. I know the law, Father, but sometimes if someone's deceased—" He figured the priest wouldn't budge, but why not try.

The priest pushed back his chair. "Are you Catholics, Detectives?"

Sherk shook his head. Jack said, "I was brought up in the church, but—" He let the sentence hang in mid air.

Father Jim sighed. "I see. Then you know the sanctity of the priest-penitent covenant." He eased himself from the chair. "I need to contact Sister's niece, Molly Winters. Has she been notified?"

"Not yet. Heading that way now." Jack knew the clergy often accompanied officers for notification of kin, but he preferred to see the niece without the padre.

The priest looked at his watch. "Oh dear, I'm afraid I'll be late for a meeting if I come with you. Perhaps if we hurry." His voice trailed off.

Sherk said, "I'm sure Ms. Winters will need your comfort, Father Jim, but maybe you would prefer to see her when you have time to spare. You'll need to meet with her regarding funeral arrangements, I assume." Good ol' Sherk to the rescue.

"Yes, yes, of course. I'll plan to visit this evening. Oak Lawn isn't that far." Father Jim cleared his throat. "I recollect hearing somewhere that Sister was sort of, ah, a shirttail relative of a former priest here, oh, maybe in the seventies. Somehow connected with Molly, but can't recall how." He scratched his head. "The old brain can't remember a lot of things these days."

"A lot of that going around." Sherk said.

Jack scoffed. Still in his forties, his partner wouldn't know squat about aging.

They said their goodbyes to Father Jim and exited the building. Jack wondered if the priest's memory was as muddled as he'd claimed. Bet he remembered plenty.

"Don't see much sense in talking to church people at this point," Jack said.

"I agree. Sister was a saint. Loved by one and all. Likewise, with the niece no doubt."

They climbed into the cruiser and headed for 90 south, then 94, exited on 20 and drove west to Oak Lawn, a middle class suburb a few miles south of Midway airport. Traffic wasn't heavy yet; just wait an hour or two.

Jack parked in front of a neatly kept one-story red brick house with white trim. The neighborhood was over forty years old, established with well-maintained yards and plenty of trees. Random patches of snow clung to the grass, but spring was around the corner as Jack's mother said. At least the sun was out. Nice to wear light weight jackets and ditch the parkas, gloves, boots.

Sherk rang the front doorbell. A dog yelped from inside. They waited. A voice called out, "Who is it?"

"Bridgeport Police." They held up their badges at the peephole.

The door opened halfway, and an attractive, fifty-something woman looked anxiously at them. "Oh God, is it Aunt Anne? She lives in Bridgeport."

Jack said, "Molly Winters?"

"Yes, that's me."

"We need to talk to you. May we come in?"

She let the men inside and shooed a medium-sized tan dog of blended heritage down a hallway. "Go lie down Bruno. It's fine." The mutt plodded off.

Jack said, "I'm Detective Bailey, this is my partner, Detective

Sherkenbach. We won't take much of your time."

Slim with light brown hair, the woman wore fitted jeans and a lightweight yellow sweatshirt. She led them through the entry into a tidy living room furnished in neutral tones. The words, 'nice ass', passed through Jack's brain.

Molly gestured toward the sofa. "Did something happen to my aunt?" She sat in a beige arm chair next to the sofa. Wringing her hands, she leaned forward.

Jack said, "I'm afraid we have bad news, Ms. Winters." He waited a couple seconds. "Your aunt was found this morning in her apartment. She couldn't be revived. We're very sorry."

Molly's hand flew to her throat. "Oh my God! A heart attack? Did she fall?"

Sherk leaned toward her. "Ms. Winters, I regret telling you this, but your aunt appears to be the victim of a homicide. That is, right now, we think she may have been— ah— strangled."

Molly gasped. "What? You can't mean—she was—somebody killed her? My aunt? That can't be." She held her face in her hands and sobbed quietly.

This was never easy. Worst part of the job for most cops. "Can I get you some water?" Jack asked.

"No. No thanks." She stared into space. "I can't believe it."

Sherk told her details of what happened earlier. They sat in silence.

Jack said, "I know you're still in shock, Ms. Winters, but can you think of anyone who might have wanted to harm your aunt?"

"Oh, God no. Everybody loved Aunt Anne. Everybody." She paced back and forth between the furniture. "Maybe a robbery? Someone broke in?"

"It didn't look like forced entry," Sherk said. "When did you last see her?"

"Um, about two weeks ago for my mom's birthday. They were sisters, Mom turned eighty-two last month. She lives in Beloit, Anne and I drove together, stayed the weekend." Molly stopped pacing and sat on the edge of the chair. "Oh, God, how will I tell Mom—

murdered? This is like, like the twilight zone or something."

"You sure you wouldn't care for water?" Sherk asked. "I'll go in the kitchen and— "

"No. Hell, I need a drink. I shouldn't, but—" She got up and turned toward the kitchen. "Want to join me?"

Jack was tempted, but knew better. He and Sherk waited while she disappeared in the kitchen. A minute later she returned with a glass of red wine. "Wish I had something stronger." She sat and took a hefty drink.

"Did you notice any change in your aunt's mood, state of mind lately?" Jack asked.

"No. She was always cheery, maybe slowing down a little, but she's, ah, was eighty-seven." Molly took another drink. She spoke slowly. "But, now that I think about it, after dinner last Christmas she and I were talking alone. I'm a lapsed Catholic, but she never poured on the guilt. Anyway, I said I should confess my sin of gluttony for stuffing myself, can't recall the details, but she said something about herself and confession. Damn, I can't remember."

"So you think the topic of confession pertained to her directly?" Jack's interest piqued.

"Yeah. Yeah, I do. I know I kidded her, saying, 'Oh, Anne, you've never done anything wrong in your whole life. What, do you confess you burned the toast?' Then she looked at me, kind of a sad smile. She said sometimes not doing something—She closed down after that, like something unpleasant drifted through and then she was back to her old self."

Jack started to rise. "Thanks, Ms. Winters. Here's my card. Call if you think of anything else."

Sherk said, "We spoke with Father Jim. He'll be contacting you about arrangements."

Molly led the men to the door. "Thanks. He was good to Anne. She was the oldest volunteer there."

The men said their goodbyes and strode toward the cruiser. "You thinking what I am?" Jack asked.

"Think so. Sin of omission. What did the good Sister fail to do?"

Chapter 3

The next morning Jack awoke groggy and unsettled before the alarm buzzed. Images of Jack's fifth grade teacher, Sister Petrina, infiltrated his brain, part of fractured dreams where sheep grazed and priests leaped out of confessionals. Were the damned nightmares snaking their way back in his life? He'd done well since his move from Texas; couldn't face a recurrence of PTSD symptoms. He knew he wasn't cured, but still—

Boone, Jack's large yellow dog of questionable ancestry, lumbered across the floor and nuzzled against the pillow.

"It's okay, boy, might as well get up." Jack thought about Sister Petrina as he headed for the shower. Mean old battle ax; a firm believer in corporal punishment, and the sting of her ruler on Jack's knuckles remained etched in his memory. At least his nieces and nephews were spared the rod of present-day nuns, lucky kids.

The phone rang as he emerged from the shower. Who'd call this early except to deliver bad news? He wrapped a towel around his waist, retrieved the phone from his nightstand, read the caller ID. Crap. He tapped on speaker mode. "Hey, Ma. What do you want so early?"

"Jacky, is that any way to talk to your old mother? Listen, I read about the nun in the paper. Do you know anything about that? Sister Anne Celeste. You know, I think I remember her. She was about my age." His mother finally took a breath.

"Yeah, Ma, got wind of it yesterday." At times he wondered why he'd moved back to Chicago.

"How did it happen? The paper didn't give a cause of death. It said—"

"Ma, we don't know yet. I gotta go. Some people have to work, you know." He finished toweling off.

"Don't get smart with me, mister. I've worked damn hard my whole—"

"I know, I know, fingers to the bone and all that. I'll see you in a couple days for dinner like we planned. Have a good one, Ma." He hung up before she could utter another word. He imagined her "humph" as she hung up. At this hour, he visualized her dyed henna hair still in curlers, bathrobe tied around her ample waist.

Half an hour later, Jack arrived at the station. He shivered as he stepped from his car. A whiff of burning logs drifted into his nostrils, reminding him of promised snowfall. The air felt frosty, the sun hidden behind puffy clouds. Jack heard forecasts of possible late winter storms, but with April two weeks away, he hoped for the best. He'd had enough winter with long days of no sun. No wonder folks were depressed. Next winter he'd consider vacationing in the south. Not Texas. Too many ghosts remained in Richmond. That door must stay closed.

He greeted the gray-haired cop at the front desk and made his way down the hall toward the bull pen, a large drab room which housed detectives, patrol cops, CSI guys, and office assistants. Rows of interior windows alongside the door were covered halfway with open mini blinds, enabling everyone in the hallway to gawk inside and see who was where. This annoyed Jack and his colleagues; felt like a fish bowl.

An aroma of fresh coffee floated through the air as he reached his desk and grumbled good morning to Sherk, whose desk faced Jack's. Cops of various shapes, sizes, and gender stared at computer screens or bustled about, phones buzzed, keyboards clicked.

"Morning, Jack," Sherk said. "The sarge wants to see us about the nun case. Any further ideas before we grace her with our presence?" Sergeant Daisy LePere ruled over her detectives with an iron fist, a fact Jack's co-workers warned him about his first day on the job.

"Figured the bitch in heels would wanna bust our balls about it." Jack sat and rearranged stray papers on his desk. "Couple things about the case first. I think we need to find out if there's been allegations against priests at the Sister's church back in her day. And who was the shirttail relative the padre mentioned? We'll ask Molly Winters after the shock wears off."

"Yeah. As we said yesterday, Sister Anne may have been part of a cover up." Sherk rose from his chair. "Let's go face the dragon lady."

Jack reached for his stained White Sox mug. "Need coffee first."

He trudged to a table beside the far wall and filled his cup, then they headed toward Daisy LePere's office down the hall from the bull pen.

The door was open, and they walked in. "You wanted to see us?" Sherk asked idiotic questions at times.

LePere looked up from her desk. "Good morning, Detectives. Close the door, have a seat." Her smile looked forced. Tall, blond, and willowy, she appeared to be in her mid-thirties Although her blue eyes and high cheekbones were eye-catching, staff members found her offensive and difficult; no one admitted she was, by traditional standards, a pretty woman.

The men obeyed orders and sat in two chairs across from her tidy glass-topped desk. The room was small, but uncluttered. Pale yellow walls held framed certificates along with photographs of lions and cheetahs from a safari vacation with her father, according to the grapevine. She allegedly acquired the sergeant's position through family connections. Jack didn't know details, just hearsay. Why a rich bitch would want the job was beyond him.

"What's your plan with the nun?" Old bag didn't beat around the bush. She wore her usual uniform of tailored dark pants with a white long sleeved shirt, a colorful silk scarf draped around her neck. A coordinated jacket hung on the coatrack by the door.

Sherk said, "We'll talk to Sister Anne's niece again about a possible family connection to a priest, review surveillance tapes from the apartment, inside, outside, and get the tech man to research former priests at Nativity for allegations." Jack preferred to let Sherk do the talking when they dealt with LePere. Didn't trust himself to keep a lid on.

She squinted. "You think this might be priest abuse?" She looked at Jack. "Cat got your tongue, Bailey? What's your theory?"

Jack shrugged. "Could be abuse connection with the Bible verses. We're checking financial, phone, the usual records, but not expecting anything remarkable." He didn't tell the battle ax more than he had to. Times like this he longed for his old job in Texas where he ran the investigation.

"Okay, go back to the church. Talk to more people. Squeeze the priest on anything she kept personal, a possible confession, even though he'll claim confidentiality. Do the job you were trained for." She waved them toward the door.

Jack felt his blood pressure rise. They did this crap yesterday. Useless busy work. Typical of the broad.

Sherk said, "All right, we'll revisit the church, but I don't think it'll—"

"I do the thinking around here, Sherkenbach." She turned to her computer. "And next time bring me some evidence."

"Yes, Ma'am." Sherk tipped an imaginary hat.

"Have a nice day, Sarge." Jack hoped she caught the sarcasm.

"It's Ms. LePere to you. And close the door behind you."

On the way to their desks, Sherk said, "Don't let her get under your skin, Jack. Not worth it."

Jack growled. "One of these days, Sherk, pow, she's flyin' to the frickin' moon."

Sherk sniggered. "'Come not between the dragon and her wrath.'"

Jack harrumphed. "*Hamlet*, I suppose."

"*King Lear*, and I misquoted. It's actually 'his wrath,' not hers."

"Whatever." Jack turned on his computer. "Wanna take another look at surveillance while I get the research goin'?"

"Sure, and then we can go back to the church per the dragon's orders."

Jack rose and headed across the room where a thirty-something man sat staring at his computer sreen. Gary Calvin was the department go-to computer geek, who worked his magic tirelessly and modestly. The guy was beyond smart; a genius at least.

Overweight with curly red hair, his uniform of choice was raggedy jeans and t-shirts inscribed with pithy sayings.

He looked up as Jack approached. "Hey, Bailey."

"Got a job for you, Calvin. Top priority. Stop whatever you're doing."

"Yeah, you and half a dozen other people tell me the same thing. What is it?"

Jack examined the words on Calvin's shirt: *I'm Here to Help your Ass – Not Kiss It*. "Great turn of phrase."

"Ha, my mother gave it to me when I moved back home."

Jack groaned. "Sure hope you're kidding."

"I am. Now, what's beyond your computer skills that you're bothering me for?"

Jack explained the nun's case and background needed on the church and priests. "I wanna find any hint of allegations, and if so, who attended the school during the time the priest in question was there. Looking for about fifth to ninth graders."

Calvin brushed his hand through his wavy locks. "Gotcha. Not my first priest investigation." He waved Jack to leave and began tapping his keyboard.

Jack threaded his way across the room to his desk. He called Molly Winters and asked about her aunt's family relationship to a former priest. He jotted down notes as he listened. "Thank you, Ms. Winters. By the way, has Father Jim called?"

He paused. "Good. I see. Well, keep us posted when you know what time the Mass will be."

Within ten minutes Sherk arrived and sat down. "Nothing on surveillance, Jack. Tapes ran from early evening to yesterday when first responders arrived. Suppose the perp could've snuck in earlier. Just the usual looking people. The desk clerk saw nothing."

"Crap. Hoped something might show up. Not the best security, but for an old folks place, it's not bad."

Sherk said, "Nothing was visible on the front street, but the cameras don't cover more than about a fourth of the block either side. Even less in the back."

Jack frowned. "I got Calvin on the priest research. Talked to Molly Winters too. Found out the nun was related to a former priest. Ready for that story?"

Sherk flipped his notebook open. "Go ahead."

Jack read his notes. "Sister Anne's sister is Molly's mom, Lila. She marries a Jon Murphy, whose cousin, Joe, is a priest at Nativity in the seventies some time."

"So Sister Anne's brother-in-law had a cousin who was a priest at Nativity when she was there," Sherk said. "Not exactly kissing cousins. Guess it could be significant."

"Too early to tell. Let's head out to the padre's. A waste of time, but it'll keep the ol' biddy off our ass."

Sherk glanced at his watch. "Time for a break. We can check out the new coffee house across the street. Made for cops."

"You kiddin' Sherk? I heard that's a tea room for bored soccer moms."

"Au contraire. The Jackalope Coffee and Tea House caters to all clientele, including men of our station, no pun intended. Their specialty is a delicacy called 'puffs of doom cream puff.'"

"Cream puffs? I rest my case." Jack said.

The men donned jackets from the cloakroom near the door and headed out of the building.

They strolled across Halsted Street and approached the coffee house near the corner of Thirty-second. Splashy colored images were painted on the windows with large lime-green and orange letters above the doors spelling 'Jackalope.'

"Gotta admit, it doesn't look like a prissy tea room," Jack said as they entered the establishment. He was glad only a few customers were seated about. Didn't like crowds. He spotted a table near the far wall. "Let's sit there. Be by ourselves."

The men shrugged off their jackets and sat across from each other. Sherk gazed at the décor. "Quite a place. Sandwiches and soup too, Jack. We'll come here for lunch some time."

Jack pointed to a rabbit-like head with antlers mounted on the wall. "Is that supposed to be a jackalope?"

Sherk chuckled. "Suppose so. Looks like a combination jackrabbit and antelope. You may know the jackalope is a mythical creature peculiar to North American culture."

"Do I look interested?"

A young girl with pierced ears and nose arrived and took their orders of black coffee, a cream puff for Sherk, an apple fritter for Jack.

"Shit. Hide your head," Jack whispered.

Sherk turned and looked toward the door.

"I said hide." Jack bowed his head, studying his hands.

"Well, if it isn't my two top detectives hard at work serving and protecting." Daisy LePere and Captain Chub Nesbitt approached the table. Jack looked up; wanted to wipe that oily grin off her face.

Sherk started to rise. "Taking a quick break, Ma'am. Good morning, Captain."

"At ease, Sherkenbach. We won't stay," LePere said.

"Good morning, Detectives," Nesbitt said. "Don't get a chance to see you very often."

Thank god for that, Jack thought, although Chub Nesbitt was a decent guy; better than LePere. A sturdy black man in his sixties, Nesbitt stood over six feet tall and dressed with impeccable taste. He had a large square face, and was amiable to all.

Jack nodded, wanting to bolt from the place.

"We'll let you get back to work now. I'm sure you're busy planning strategy for your case." LePere gazed at Jack and turned away.

"Good to see you guys," Nesbitt said. He led LePere to a table across the room.

"Simmer down, Jack. I can see your blood boiling." Sherk snickered.

The waitress appeared carrying pastries and steaming mugs of aromatic coffee.

"Mmm, look at this." Sherk eyed his huge crusty blob of a cream puff. He picked it up and bit off a chunk, then returned it to the plate. Thick, yellowy filling oozed from the bite mark onto the dish. "Ahhh, wunderbar."

"You got the German sweet tooth, Sherk." Jack wrinkled his nose at the ravaged puff or whatever it was, opened his mouth and devoured a chunk of apple fritter.

He glanced at LePere and Nesbitt who were ordering from the waitress. "LePere can't afford calories; the bitch could stand to drop ten pounds." He wasn't about to admit her weight looked average for her height.

"I'll bet she has coffee or tea," Sherk said. "Don't let her irritate you."

Jack grunted. "Just our luck we run into them. This place is too close to work."

"You need to practice your social skills." Sherk took another bite. "Anyway, we should get the forensics report back this afternoon, maybe autopsy if we're lucky."

"Won't be anything new," Jack mumbled. "A waste of time going back to the church too. At least the padre might know when the nun's funeral will be."

"You planning to go?" Sherk polished off his pastry.

"Yeah, we should. See who's there. Perp may show up." Jack didn't buy that old cop's tale, but who knew?

Chapter 4

The rest of the day, a total bust. Father Jim was no help, claimed he knew nothing more than yesterday. Sister Anne Celeste's funeral Mass was scheduled for next Tuesday morning at 10:30. The priest's parting words were, "Precious in the sight of the Lord is the death of his saints."

"Ah, the Psalms," Sherk piped up. "One hundred fifteenth I believe." Frickin' show off.

Father Jim smiled. "Close. One sixteenth."

After they left, Jack said, "Thought you knew your Bible, Sherk."

"Yes, I slipped up on that one."

They wandered through the education building, looking for anyone new to interview regarding Sister Anne. No luck. Each person repeated the same sentiment: the nun walked on water. Eager to leave, Jack hoped he'd seen the last of Father Jim and his church. Then he thought of the funeral. Maybe the case would be closed by then. Fat chance.

Back at the station, Jack and Sherk dined on a makeshift lunch of vending machine baloney sandwiches, Fritos, and Sprite. Seated at his desk, Jack unlocked the bottom drawer, looked around, and twisted the cap off a flask of Jameson. Surreptitiously, he splashed an ounce or two into his Styrofoam cup of soda.

"I saw that, Bailey," a raspy woman's voice croaked behind him. "Gonna get caught one of these days."

He sighed, took a swig. "Want a taste, Velda?"

A stout woman in her sixties sidled up to him. "Too early for me. But let's meet at the pub after work, my treat."

Jack smiled at her. "Got plans today, but sometime real soon."

She rolled her eyes, permed gray curls held rigid. "Sure, that's what they all say."

Dressed in a tan pantsuit which would look attractive on a taller woman, Velda Vatava, known as the general of the bull pen, was confident no one could run the department as well as she. Assertive and efficient, she fancied herself among the brass, even if her salary did not reflect that status. She reminded one and all she was an organizational guru.

"She's a glorified secretary, but doesn't know it," Sherk had told Jack his first day on the job two years ago. "A stickler for rules, but get on her good side, and she'll ignore them. Get on her bad side, and watch out. A couple guys transferred when she made their lives miserable."

Jack remembered the day Sherk introduced her. Jack held out his hand. "Velda Vatava. That's quite a name. What is it? Polish? Czech?"

"Gettin' close. Hungarian." She beamed as if proud of her heritage. "Most people have trouble pronouncing it."

"Not me," Jack said. "Actually it's kinda poetic." A word seldom used in his vocabulary.

"Ha!" Sherk said. "You want to hear poetic, tell him your middle name, Velda."

Her cheeks turned pink. "Oh all right. It's Veronica."

"Velda Veronica Vatava," Jack said. "Sounds like a nursery rhyme or something."

She'd tittered along with Sherk. "Actually, that's what Sherk first said. Like that children's writer, Shel Silverstein. Sherk even started writing a poem about it."

"Velda, we could wax poetic all day, but we have work to do."

Since then, Jack remained on Velda's good side, even though she was often a real annoyance. He knew enough to play the game.

Jack took another drink. "Got something important, Vatava?"

She handed him a file folder. "Always important, Bailey. I got this from forensics on the nun murder. Autopsy report should be in tomorrow morning."

Jack opened the file. Maybe she'd leave if he looked down to read it.

"Have a good one, guys." She turned and strolled away to bother another cop.

"Here, take a look." Jack handed Sherk the file. "Tell me it's good news." Scanning the report, he said, "Nothing earthshaking for now. They found a couple partial prints on the nightstand plus synthetic fibers around her shoulders and neck. Fibers and DNA will take a couple days at least. May find a match. 'Hope springs eternal,' Jack."

Jack groaned. "Enough with your Shakespeare."

"Alexander Pope." Sherk said.

"Take your word for it." Jack polished off the remainder his sandwich and guzzled his drink. "Perp must've worn paper booties, no footprints. Shows some smarts. Let's see if Calvin found anything."

They tossed their napkins and cups in a trash can and made their way to Gary Calvin's desk. He looked up from his screen. "You're in luck, guys. Found some flaws in the otherwise lily-white reputation of Nativity of Our Lord back in the seventies."

Sherk and Jack, on either side of Calvin, stared at his computer. The geek clacked away, bringing up various lists and charts. "Here we have sex abuse allegations brought against a Father Daniel McGarvey in 1973 and 74. Couldn't find out who instigated them, but he left for greener pastures soon afterward. Died in the late eighties." Calvin glanced at the detectives. "You know they covered up the sins of the fathers, so to speak, by shipping them off to other parishes out of town."

"Right," Jack said. He recalled when the *Boston Globe* broke the story of that city's priest abuse scandal. "What about former students?"

Calvin reached for a file on his cluttered desk and handed it to Sherk. "You guys can go over these names and ages. No one showed up in the data base, so if your theory stands, your perp doesn't have a record."

"Why am I not surprised to hear that? Thanks, Calvin." Jack followed Sherk to their desks where they each perused enrollment lists during the time of Father McGarvey.

"At least no complaints against Father Murphy, the nun's distant relative," Sherk said.

"None we know of." Jack knew anything was possible.

They skimmed the lists of students, focusing on fourth through eighth grade boys. Jack thought he recognized several last names, even though he attended another Catholic school ten years earlier than these boys. Perhaps familiar names from intramural sports back when Bridgeport was smaller and personal.

Nothing on the lists jumped out at Jack. "We're spinning our frickin' wheels, Sherk. I've had it up to here."

Sherk nodded. "I agree. Until we get something from autopsy and DNA, we might as well put the good Sister on the proverbial back burner."

They turned their attention to other matters, namely their never-shrinking stack of paperwork. Before long, Velda reappeared at their desks.

Jack looked up. "Back so soon?" Thought he was rid of her for the day.

She ignored his question. "Got a call from Nancy at the *Herald*. She wants an update on the nun. The *Trib* and *Sun-Times* called too." She held her spiral notebook open. "I'm ready when you are."

"Why the interest from those people?" Sherk asked.

"The murder of an elderly nun is news, particularly when robbery or money isn't the motive. Besides, generations of Bridgeport kids had their knuckles rapped by her," Velda said.

Jack informed her they had nothing new to report, and kept mum regarding the Bible verse as a calling card left by the perp. After she hurried off with her usual air of self-importance, he said, "Thank god."

"You doing okay, Jack?"

Jack was surprised. "Yeah, why?"

Sherk shrugged. "You seem a little irritable."

"That's what I am, Sherk. Nothing new." At least he hoped that was the case.

True, he felt restless lately. He should go out more. His life lacked substance and satisfaction; times like this when a case headed south. What was he missing with the nun? The answer must be in the Bible verse. The bastard's playing cat and mouse. Thinks he's smarter than we are.

Jack couldn't sit still another minute. "I'm callin' it a day, Sherk. See you tomorrow."

"Sure, Jack. Going to your mom's for dinner tonight?"

"Naw, that's tomorrow. I think she's gonna play cupid, but don't ask."

Chapter 5

Jack could easily walk the six blocks home, but in winter he was too lazy. Didn't feel like hoofin' it today, even though the exercise would do him good. Clear his head. Sure hoped he and Sherk could nail Sister Anne's murder since it was gaining press coverage. Closing a big case would look good on his career-ladder record, such as it was.

He lucked out and found a parking spot on the street a few doors from his duplex. Boone yelped when the front door key jiggled in the lock and Jack came in.

"Hey guy, 'wass up?" He ruffled the big dog's fur. He noticed Boone sleeping more lately, although he always barked and jumped when anyone arrived. No need for an alarm system with him around.

After changing into sweats, Jack spent an uninspired evening drinking Guinness, eating leftover pizza, and streaming reruns of *Inspector Lewis*. He wondered what Molly Winters was doing tonight. Maybe after the case closed, he'd call her. Then again, maybe not.

• • • • •

The next morning passed without incident. After another lunch of vending machine sandwiches and Sprite enhanced with a shot of Jameson, Jack called the medical examiner.

"Right, I'll hold for a minute, but this can't wait," Jack said. He knew the ME was busy with other cases, but the autopsy report on Sister Anne Celeste should be ready by now.

It took Jack awhile to get used to the ME, Dr. Hal Araki, and his Japanese accent. His given name was a mile long with all consonants, so he'd shortened it to something people could pronounce. The man wasn't big on personality and wore a perpetual scowl on his large square face, dominated by a substantial black moustache. At first Jack struggled to ignore his father's voice in his head cursing the 'goddamn Japs, got us into war.' Now things were better; Jack respected the ME's work and ignored his foul humor.

Impatient, Jack planned to hang up when he heard Araki's voice. "Hal, thanks for answering. Calling about Sister Anne—"

Jack looked at Sherk, pen and notebook ready. "Right, strangulation. What kind of ligature?"

After a minute Jack said, "Okay, Hal. Don't worry, I'll read it thoroughly this afternoon. Thanks. A pleasure, as always." Jack tapped off the phone.

"Think he got your biting sarcasm?" Sherk asked.

Jack shrugged. "Let's say I think we understand each other."

By five o'clock Jack and Sherk had reviewed reports from Hal Araki and the crime lab. Jack was ready to call it quits when Daisy LePere phoned him and summoned the partners to her office.

Her door was ajar; Sherk knocked. "You wanted to see us?"

"Is that a question, Sherkenbach? Come in. Take a seat." LePere wore a pale pink silk blouse with her usual black pants. She sipped from a white mug.

The men sat across from her tidy desk. She gazed at them. "Well, what's new on the nun case?"

Sherk began. "We spoke with Dr. Araki and he verified what we suspected. Sister Anne Celeste died from ligature strangulation. Fibers and bruising indicate some kind of fabric was used, like a scarf or necktie."

LePere nodded. "Signs of struggle?"

Sherk shifted in his chair. "Minimal. Skin cells were under three fingernails. Several short strands of hair not belonging to Sister Anne were on her neck and clothing. DNA from the skin and hair aren't in the database."

"Damn," LePere said. She looked at Jack. "You have anything to add, Mr. Silent?"

Jack had something he'd like to add, but he'd get canned if he said it. "Partial prints they found weren't in the database either, surprise, surprise. No analysis on the fibers other than the scarf or necktie theory. No other remarkable fibers were found. So there we are, Sarge."

"It's Ms. LePere, Bailey. Why do I always have to remind you?"

"Senior memory lapses." Jack smirked. "Or maybe my mother dropped me on my head when I was a baby."

"No comment. Watch your attitude." She rose and started for the door. "Carry on with looking into the nun's history and go to the funeral. The perp may show up. Look for a single man who doesn't look like a friend of the nun's."

Brilliant idea, Sherlock, Jack thought. "Yes, Sarge. Oh, sorry— Ms. LePere." Jack exited the office, Sherk on his heels.

They headed back to their desks. Jack said, "Yeah, we'll look into the nun's history. How does that bimbo keep her job? Oh yeah, family connections."

Sherk shook his head. "She's more to be pitied than censored."

"Enough of your Shakespeare. Besides, I don't feel sorry for her."

"Actually it's a song by William B. Gray. An old saloon song. Have you heard of Mae West?"

"Come on, Sherk. I've been around the block a few times. Once my ma got loaded and did a pretty decent impersonation of old Mae."

"Wish I could have seen that. At any rate, I don't think the sarge is a happy woman."

"I don't give a damn, I'm outta here. Wish me luck. Dinner at Ma's tonight."

"Ah, yes. Maybe you'll meet someone interesting."

"That's what I'm afraid of. See ya later." Jack made his way to the coatrack, retrieved his jacket and cap and headed out the building.

He drove down West Thirty-second Street from the station until he reached Aberdeen Avenue six blocks away. He managed to find a parking space a couple houses from his duplex instead of the usual circling the block and down the alley to carports allotted for residents. He missed having a garage like the one in Texas. Well, can't have everything.

Jack's neighborhood was an older working class area with homes, duplexes, and apartments in a row with little space between them. Trees lined the streets and sidewalks, with the residences a few feet away. No front yards here; three steps from the street and you were at the front doors.

Unremarkable looking, the building was dark brown with tan window trim. Nothing you'd look at twice, but the place had been updated with decent tile floors and attractive kitchen countertops and appliances. He was lucky to find the house, thanks to his brother, Tommy. He not only had been a lead for the Bridgeport detective job, but steered Jack to the residence. He hoped Tommy would be at his mother's for dinner tonight so he wasn't the lone man for the dreaded matchmaker event.

• • • • •

It was still light out when Jack left the duplex and drove toward his mother's house. No snow yet, but an iciness filled the air. Jack turned left when he reached Racine Avenue and headed south. The community had changed since his move to Texas over seven years ago. Like many large cities, enclaves like Bridgeport had become diverse and trendy in certain neighborhoods. The Bridgeport Art Center, a repurposed warehouse, boasted several galleries and a sculpture garden. Along with upscale shops and restaurants, many residents called the area a "happening place."

Jack was painfully aware of these sites because of Karen. She introduced him to a world of art and travel when they began dating. The loss of his wife and young daughter, Elizabeth twelve years ago haunted him to this day. Karen would approve of the neighborhood changes if she were— Jack forced thoughts of his wife and child back into the darkness.

He turned left onto Thirty-eighth Street, then hit Morgan and took a right. The Bailey family home was located short of Pershing Road, the southern boundary of Bridgeport. An older neighborhood, its rows of homes and tree-lined streets were well maintained and many had been updated. The three-level house was dark green during Jack's childhood; now its current façade featured gray siding with ivory window trim. A new white picket fence surrounded the tiny front yard, where three steps led to a small porch. Two gray wooden chairs sat on either side of the shiny black door. Tommy worked hard to maintain the place; always was a good handyman.

Jack parked down the street and let himself into the house with his own key. An aroma of pot roast and onions wafted in the air. "Anybody home? I'm hungry," he called out.

"Coming," a shrill voice answered.

Jack removed his cap and jacket, and before he could toss them on a chair in the entry, Maureen Bailey scurried in. "Not there, Jacky. Hang them in the closet." She lowered her voice. "We have company."

"I thought I was," Jack said.

"Don't start with me. Come on in," she whispered. "And be nice."

Maureen's most prominent feature was her bright henna hair, which she insisted was the exact color it was when she was a child. At eighty-eight, she was feisty and active, with few of the aches and pains common to those her age. Medium height and hefty, she took time with her grooming and make-up, which resulted in her appearing ten years younger.

"You look nice, Ma. Who you trying to impress?" Jack took in her forest green turtleneck and long black vest over loose black pants.

"Shush. I said behave." She led Jack through the entry way by the stairs into the living room. Unlike the avocado shag carpet from Jack's childhood, hard wood covered the sitting and dining room areas. Vintage end tables and an armoire contrasted with updated chairs and a sofa.

An attractive middle-aged woman dressed in a brown tweed pants outfit sat on the burgundy colored sofa. Her dark hair in a layered blunt cut framed her oval shaped face. She smiled at Jack as she started to rise from the sofa.

Maureen said, "Oh, stay seated dear. It's only Jack. Oh, I mean—" She grabbed Jack's arm. "Jack, I'd like you to meet Bonnie Ames.

Bonnie, my son, Jack." Maureen beamed as if proud of her accomplishment.

Jack took Bonnie's outstretched hand and smiled. "Nice to meet you, Bonnie." He could turn on the charm when he wanted to.

"Jack, I've looked forward to seeing you. I've heard so much about you from your mom."

"Guilty as charged." Jack joined her on the sofa a comfortable distance away. He leaned back and crossed his legs. He felt a guilty sense of relief that Bonnie was nice looking, in his opinion anyway.

Maureen hovered about like a hummingbird. "Would anyone like something to drink before dinner?"

Bonnie said, "A glass of red wine would be nice."

"Your usual, Jacky?"

"Yes, Ma."

Maureen scampered away, and Jack felt the burden of awkward silence. Just the two of them. Alone. Damn, he was out of practice.

Chapter 6

"Don't worry, Jack." Bonnie leaned toward him. "My mother's the same way. The main reason I agreed to show up is your mom said you look like Liam Neeson."

Jack waited. "And?"

"And what?"

"Do I look like him?"

"I can see the resemblance, but you look older and wiser."

"Actually we were born the same year. He must be wiser though."

Jack shifted on the sofa and faced Bonnie. "Do you live in Bridgeport?"

"Close by. McKinley Park. I'm a coordinator at the hospice clinic branch of Mercy Hospital, a little west of the lagoon. I live a couple miles north of there."

Maureen bustled in with drinks. She handed Bonnie a glass of Merlot and Jack a tall mug of Guinness.

"I've known Bonnie's mother for years. Knew her from St. Bridget's back in the old days before it closed." Maureen sat in a chair near the sofa. "Oh, what a sad day that was. Mayor Daley was married in that church and— "

"Ma, don't wanna be rude or anything, but— "

"I know, I know." Maureen took a sip of Jim Beam from a highball glass. "I won't bore our guest."

"It's okay." Bonnie smiled. "My mom feels the same way about St. Bridget's. She found a new church in Palatine when she moved there a few years ago."

Jack took a swig of beer. He wondered if they'd yak about churches all night. He restrained himself from glancing at his watch.

After ten minutes of small talk, Maureen said, "I think dinner's about ready. Let me go check the pot roast. Jacky, come and help."

Bonnie shifted on her seat. "I'll be happy to help, Maureen."

"Oh no, dear, you're our guest. Jacky will just carry things to the table." Strands of red hair stuck to her forehead. "Whew, it's warm in here."

They hustled about in the kitchen; Maureen ordered Jack to carry the pot roast, salad, and bread to the dining room table, all set with white linen tablecloth and napkins. Jack noticed the good silverware surrounded pink depression glass plates, cups, and saucers.

"Why all this, Ma? You're not entertaining the queen."

"You hush. I told you, be nice."

Dinner passed with compliments from Bonnie about the lovely table setting and tasty food. She was gracious; Jack thought the meat was overcooked and the potatoes and carrots soggy.

After cherry pie and coffee in the living room, Maureen insisted she wanted no help cleaning the kitchen and Jack and Bonnie should stay put.

Bonnie grinned. "I guess we ought to do as she says."

"Yeah, no arguing with her." Jack turned on the sofa toward Bonnie. "You're sure being a good sport about this."

"It's fine. I've actually enjoyed myself. Your mom's very, ah, interesting."

"Gotta humor her to survive around here," Jack gulped drained his coffee.

"You know, Jack, my single friends and I started an un-date agreement when we were fixed up with someone. We say we'll go for coffee or a drink, not dinner, and see if we want to pursue things."

Jack was confused. "Sorry, I'm not following. Out of practice."

Bonnie laughed. "It's a way of appeasing the person who fixed you up, with no pressure to follow through. The point is to see how things go in a non-pressure situation. Then if there's no call within a week from either party, no hard feelings."

Jack raised his brow. "Sounds like a Seinfeld conversation."

"I think it is." Bonnie drained her coffee cup. "I'll take charge here. Let's meet somewhere for a drink after work, see what happens. Again, no pressure, it's not a real date."

"Okay, I'll give it a shot." This was weird, but made sense for some reason. "When can you meet at Shinnick's Pub for a pint?"

"Now you're catching on. Some time next week works for me."

"Tuesday is Sister Anne's funeral. We can toast the good nun later on."

Bonnie nodded. "Oh yes, I wondered how the case was coming along, but I know you can't discuss it. The paper says still no leads?"

"That's about it," Jack said.

"Tuesday sounds good. After work's fine for me. Should we meet at Shinnick's around five thirty?"

"Sure, it's a date. I mean an un-date."

Jack reached in his pocket for his wallet. He handed Bonnie a card, while she dug hers out of her purse.

"Ah, exchanging phone numbers. That's nice." Maureen ambled into the room. Jack suspected she'd been eavesdropping. Was a perfect entrance.

"Don't get excited, Ma. Too old to give ya grandkids."

"Oh, hush. What will Bonnie think? Talk like that."

"Don't worry, Maureen." Bonnie chuckled. "My mom's just like you."

An hour later, Jack walked Bonnie to her car. She took his hand. "No pressure for a goodnight kiss either. I had a great time. See you Tuesday."

Jack leaned toward her and kissed her lightly on the lips. "Thanks, Bonnie. A very relaxing time for a mother-match-up."

They said goodnight and drove home in their separate cars, darkness surrounding them.

• • • • •

Maureen called Jack bright and early to drill him on his impression of Bonnie and their plans to meet. "Ma, keep this up, and I'm moving back to Texas."

Throughout the weekend, Jack thought about Bonnie. Although she was attractive with a fun personality and sense of humor, he doubted he was ready for a relationship now or maybe ever. He didn't buy into the 'meant to be' crap. His track record with women was dismal. A romantic interest a couple years ago ended in shambles. No one could ever hold a candle to Karen, and it was unfair to compare her to any woman he met.

This week he and Sherk needed to haul ass on the nun's murder. If the long-ago priest abused a kid, he'd be old enough now in 2012 to seek revenge. They'd take a closer look at the list of students from Father McGarvey's time. Maybe something would pop out. Can't have the good citizens of Bridgeport afraid to go out at night.

Chapter 7

Less than a mile away from where Detective Jack Bailey was pursuing his investigation, a faded thirty-something man named Donald Sowder wandered through the world avoiding attention at every turn. In a movie, he'd play an accountant perhaps, a sales clerk, a computer nerd. His medium brown hair parted on the side lay flat on his small round head. He wore thick wire-rimmed glasses, too large for today's fashion. Average build, average height, he dressed in mostly brown or tan clothes. A witness would be hard pressed to describe him. Just what he wanted. What he relied on.

Donald strolled along Thirty-seventh Street seemingly unnoticed by anyone, always his plan. Story of his life. No one ever gave him a second glance. He blended into the woodwork, the scenery. Like a chameleon. Invisible.

The mid-morning sun melted the last remnants of snow. Winter's end lifted his spirits, and he felt relieved he wasn't working his tedious job until next week.

He reached Union Street and turned right, stopped, and gazed. There it was in all its glory. He hadn't seen Nativity of Our Lord Church for years. Donald felt compelled to see it today. He was exhilarated, but kept his face void of expression.

The old nun's demise had been easier than he thought. Actually, quite simple. Everything worked according to plan. Last Wednesday night, easy access to her apartment; the girl at the desk bought his story, no problem. He rode the elevator right to the apartment.

After he rang her bell, Sister Anne Celeste called out, asked who was there. Must've looked through her peephole. She said she recalled Donald's name and let him in. His heart hammered when he saw her face. She hadn't changed except wrinkles crinkled her face; she'd added a few pounds. Did she look guilty? He couldn't tell. Surely she remembered.

Funny how she offered him tea. Like nothing had happened. He declined the tea. She was interested in his life. *What did you do after high school, Donny? I heard you went to college here in town.*

She nodded when he said he'd dropped out of Columbia after a year. He had no direction. No goals. So he attended tech school, got into computers like lots of guys. Been working at Midway Airport for years. Nothing exciting of course.

Her milky eyes penetrated him. How could she forget — unless he wasn't the only one. Oh god. Hope there weren't more. He felt dizzy. Needed water.

Afterwards he barely recalled the words Sister choked out. Asking his forgiveness. Too late. Damage done. He snuck out the apartment unseen. He felt energized, high when he reached his car two blocks away on Wells Street. No one would notice a gray Toyota at the end of a high school parking lot beside several other sedans and a black pick-up.

A blaring horn interrupted his reverie. "Watch it, asshole," the driver yelled.

Donald jumped back on the curb. Crap, can't afford attention. Must be careful. He wandered along Union past the church. "I got you back," he whispered as he gazed at the stained glass windows of martyred saints glimmering in the sun.

Reaching the next block, he crossed the street to Shinnick's Pub. He could use a pint; too bad they didn't open until noon. He kept walking, turned onto Pershing, and wandered to his car parked alongside a convenience store.

He wished there were a decent movie playing. Getting lost in a dark theater always appealed to him, but nothing other than crappy films these days. Nothing like Poe's stories. The best. 'Nevermore'. Was proud of his collection of Edgar's short stories. The beating of the old man's heart.

Yesterday Donald ran errands: grocery shopping, visiting his mother in the human warehouse as he called it, even though it was a decent place for what it was. What a bother. She hardly knew who he was; still he didn't want her to die. Not yet. His old man had put her there. Forget that history, Donald told himself.

He took I-55 south toward the airport and his dismal apartment. One of these days he'd move. But he had plans to carry out before going anywhere.

What would he do without computers? He could discover anything. This afternoon he needed to put the final touches on his plans for the next project. He already knew what Bible verse to use.

Chapter 8

Early Monday morning Jack's phone rang, piercing his slumber. He raised his head, squinted at the clock, 5:04 AM. Shit, now what?

"Bailey," he croaked, and then listened. "Fuck. Does Sherk know?"

Jack hung up and punched in Sherk's number. Waited. "Yeah, I know what time it is. Dispatch called. They found another body. Sounds like the same perp. Call ya back with the address when you're half awake."

Within half an hour, Jack had showered, dressed, filled Boone's food and water dishes, snatched a stale caramel roll, and tramped out the door. Darkness surrounded him as he made his way down the block to his car. He tightened his jacket collar around his neck to offset the cool breeze.

After climbing in the car, he called Sherk, told him the address, and entered it in the GPS. Firing up the engine, Jack wound his way out the neighborhood, headed west to I-55. Too early for heavy traffic. Shouldn't take over twenty-five minutes.

He raced south on the freeway in the direction of Midway Airport. Ten minutes later he passed the terminal signs and exited on Highway 171 driving east and then south. He slowed down at Resurrection Cemetery, turned right, arriving at a one story ranch style house in an older neighborhood. Two patrol cars sat in front, lights flashing. Jack pulled up, parked, and stepped into the cold, brisk air. He hurried up the sidewalk to the front steps.

A uniformed cop was securing the perimeter with yellow crime tape. Jack mumbled a good morning, donned his gloves, and opened the front door.

A familiar looking young cop stood in the entryway. "Hello, Detective Bailey. We meet again."

"Yeah, Jeff? You were at the nun's place last week. Where's our vic?" A musty, moldy odor pervaded the air. Jack glanced around the drab living area. Looked like an old folks' home from days gone by with its tattered olive green sofa, chair, and one pole lamp.

"He's in the bedroom this way." Jeff led Jack down a dim hall. They reached a room at the end and walked in. An overpowering stench of urine hit Jack's nostrils before he spotted the body lying face up on the bed. At least it was urine, could be worse.

"Same position as the nun," Jeff said.

"You the first one here?"

"Yeah, Finch, the guy outside, came the same time. Front door was unlocked, doesn't look like a scuffle."

Jack studied the man on the bed. A young guy, perhaps in his twenties, dressed in a long sleeved ragged blue shirt and faded, torn jeans. A pair of white tennis socks with holes in the toes covered his feet.

"Wonder what killed him? No signs of bruising like the nun's, no blood visible so far." Jack peered close to the deceased's right wrist. "What's this? Another message from the almighty?"

Jeff approached the bed for a closer look. "Yeah, it barely shows. Bet it's another Bible verse."

"You're a quick study, kid. I should wait for the tech guys to see the note, but hey, it's here, ready to fall off the bed. Just take a peek." Wasn't the first time Jack bent the rules.

He eased the edge of the paper from underneath the plastic-looking hand until the note was freed. Same kind of white paper as Sister Anne's, folded in half. Jack opened it and read aloud. "It were better for him that a millstone were hanged about his neck, and he cast into the sea, than that he should offend one of these little ones. Luke 17:2." Looked like the same blue ink printing as the first note. Only difference was the verse was written out rather than just the title.

"What do you make of that?" Jeff asked.

"Had to have been there. I don't see a millstone and he didn't drown in the sea." Jack folded the paper and carefully returned it to its rightful place under the hand of this soul who perhaps offended a little one.

Jeff's half-smile looked excited, hopeful. "Looks like we have a serial killer on our hands."

"Sorry to disappoint ya, kid. Gotta kill three or more. But don't give up. My hunch tells me the future holds promise."

He instructed Jeff to call in two guys and start canvassing the neighborhood. After Jeff left the room, Jack heard the crescendo of a wailing siren, squealing brakes, a car door slamming. He waited in the bedroom for whom he hoped was his partner.

"Good morning, Jack." Sherk hurried into the room and unzipped his jacket. "Cold out there."

"The Bible thumper strikes again." Jack waited while Sherk took in the crime scene.

Sherk bent toward the corpse's right hand. "There's the tell-tale note. What words of wisdom doth it impart?"

"Dunno. Wait for the tech guys."

"Come on, Jack. I know you better than that." Sherk removed his glasses and cleaned them with a handkerchief. Only guy Jack knew who used a handkerchief.

"If you must know, something about a millstone around the neck and drowning in the sea comes to someone who offends little ones."

Sherk raised his eyebrows. "I'm impressed at the paraphrasing, Jack. It pretty much nails our theory of Sister Anne turning a blind eye, and this one was no doubt a sin of commission in the eyes of our perpetrator."

Jack's phone buzzed. He answered and listened while Sherk studied the body, careful not to touch.

A minute later Jack said, "That was dispatch, more info about the call on the body. Was anonymous, one of those disposable phones. Caller said to check out this address for a dead body. Wouldn't give a name. Male voice, no accent. Caller's last words were 'vengeance is mine, saith the Lord,' so that explains why I heard right away it's the same perp as the nun's."

Sherk said, "But from the looks of it, the guy could've died a natural death. He's young for a heart attack, but it happens. Wonder how the perp got him and Sister Anne in bed with no signs of struggle or dragging the body into the room."

Jack thought a second. "Obviously well planned. We're dealing with one smart son of a bitch. Covers his tracks. Do you think he has some ties to the clergy? A former pastor, youth group leader, something to explain the Bible verses. We should look into cults and crap that attract religious fanatics. Maybe he thinks he's God, ridding the world of evil."

"That's it, Jack. This latest note reinforces our suspicions."

Jack heard the front door open followed with muddled conversation. "Good, CSI's here." He heard a woman's voice in the hall. "Hell— LePere," he said to Sherk.

Rich, the CSI guy, strode into the room with two other men behind. They looked like ghosts in their white garb and immediately shooed Jack and Sherk from the room.

"See you back at the station," Rich said as he and his men kneeled down to retrieve equipment from their black bags. "I'm sure you did nothing to contaminate the scene."

Jack held up his gloved hands. "You know me, Rich."

"Only too well, Bailey."

Daisy LePere appeared in the doorway. "Enough idle chatter, men. Get to it. Bailey, Sherkenbach, let's go."

Dressed in her usual dark pants and black jacket, she turned and paraded into the living room. She gazed at the men. "I hear it's the same perp. All we need, a serial killer on our watch."

"Sarge, you know he's one vic short of serial killer status." Jack smirked.

"Don't get smart with me, Bailey. You know damn well what I mean. We can't afford any more murders, especially connected to the nun, whose funeral is tomorrow, I might remind you."

Sherk cleared his throat. "We'll keep the connection out of the press. We'll treat it as an unfortunate coincidence that a second murder occurred so soon after Sister Anne's."

LePere ran a hand through her blond waves. "Two murders in one week—less than a twelve-mile radius. I forget the last time that happened in Bridgeport. Maybe never." She wound her Burberry scarf around her neck and made her way to the door. "Go get this guy. Do your damn job. By tonight I hope."

Jack looked at Sherk. "No problem, Sarge. We're on it."

"Ms. LePere to you."

Jack rolled his eyes. He and Sherk followed her out the door. When she walked beyond earshot, Jack said, "What do ya think? By six or seven o'clock we'll close the case?"

"No reason not to," Sherk looked amused. "We'll get Gary Calvin on it first thing."

Jack climbed into his car as his partner headed toward his vehicle down the block.

• • • • •

Traffic thickened as Jack traveled north toward the station. He didn't know a better route, so he told himself to relax and think. No identification on the vic, but shouldn't take long to find the homeowner's name. Calvin will check the sex registry list, might get a hit. Maybe the perp left something else besides hair and fiber; something solid. Dream on.

The station buzzed with activity when Jack wandered in thirty minutes later. Cops bustled up and down the hall, keyboards clacked, people chattered on phones. Jack grabbed coffee from the kitchenette area. Nothing to eat. Damn, he was starving. Could use a couple donuts.

He made it to Gary Calvin's desk. "Calvin, need you to check—"

"Good morning to you too, Bailey. If it's the address on Arbor Lane you refer to, I have it here." He flipped through several papers with his chubby hand.

Jack bent closer to Calvin's shirt. "First things first. Gotta read today's words of wisdom." Jack silently read, *I'm only responsible for what I say, not for what you understand* printed on the geek's black shirt. "That must refer to me. That's cold, Calvin."

"Ha. Frankly, you understand better than some old geezers."

"Thanks, I guess. Where's that ID?"

Calvin handed Jack a paper. "The house is owned by Louise Welton. Her husband died five years ago, house is in her name. She has several children who live out of state. I was ready to look on sex registry when I was rudely interrupted."

"You read my mind," Jack leaned over Calvin's shoulder to see the monitor as he typed away on the keyboard.

A moment later Sherk appeared. "Know anything yet?"

"Workin' on it," Jack said. "What took you so long?"

"Some people drive within the speed limit."

"A-ha," Calvin exclaimed. "Surprise, surprise. Looks like Bruce Welton is your guy. Louise is his grandma. He's living with her, and guess what—he's on the registry. I'll dig around for more, get back to you."

"Thanks, Calvin. Good work," said Sherk.

"Nice someone appreciates my efforts." Calvin stared at Jack.

"Always good talkin' to ya, Calvin."

Back at their desks, Jack and Sherk updated their notes on their computers and spiral notebooks. Jack felt comfortable using paper and pen rather than his phone or pad. He still identified with the old school, and besides, his fingers were too large to manipulate touch screens for more than a couple minutes.

After twenty minutes, Jack grew impatient for Calvin's report. "Should be ready by now." He looked at Sherk. "I'm gonna ride his ass."

As Jack pushed back his chair, Calvin arrived with a file in hand. "Happy reading, guys."

"Thanks." Jack took the file and watched Calvin lumber away.

Sherk listened while Jack paraphrased from the report. "Bruce Welton is, was twenty-five, high school education. Sprung from Stateville two months ago, had to register as a sex offender. He gave the Arbor Lane house as an address, owned by his grandma, Louise.

He's employed as a maintenance worker at the Home Depot on Larpenter.

"How long was he in the penitentiary?" Sherk asked.

Jack studied the paper. "Two years. Before that he was custodian and groundskeeper at Willard Charles Elementary on Roberts Road. Seems several parents complained, and one stuck. Settled out of court, the prick pleaded guilty." Jack looked at Sherk. "Vic was a six-year-old boy."

Sherk bit his lower lip. He had a son the same age.

"Don't quote me, Sherk, but it's a damn shame we're supposed to catch the killer. I'm ready to pin a medal on him."

Chapter 9

Jack knew he needed to separate the case from his personal feelings, but knowing and doing were two different ball games. He understood why pedophiles were prime bait in prisons. Let em' have a taste of their own medicine.

He scribbled notes. "Let's head out to Home Depot. See what we can dig up on Welton. We'll grab lunch after."

Sherk untangled his legs, ready to leave. "Sounds good. Calvin can track down the grandmother."

Twenty minutes later they arrived at Home Depot on Larpenter, a side street several miles from Bruce Welton's house. Jack parked the cruiser in front of the sprawling retailer, and he and Sherk emerged. The sun glimpsed around silvery clouds, but the air felt sharp.

They entered the store, tracked down the middle-aged store manager, and followed him into a small office past rows of refrigerators. In no mood for social niceties, Jack asked about Bruce Welton.

"Let's see here," Phil Rhodes said as he pulled a file from a steel cabinet next to the wall.

He sat at his desk; Jack and Sherk remained standing. The guy's phone buzzed, and he spent the next couple minutes justifying the price of two-inch nails. Jack clamped his jaw. Wished the jerk would hang up already.

When Rhodes finally turned his attention to the file, Jack sighed with relief.

"Bruce Welton. Started two months ago. I don't know him very well. Seems nice enough. Works the warehouse back there." Rhodes looked worried. "What's the problem?"

Jack studied him. "Welton was found dead this morning. Might be foul play." That was the story for now.

"Oh god," Rhodes said. "He was so young." He wiped his forehead.

"Yes he was." Sherk cleared his throat. "When was he last at work?"

Rhodes thumbed through several papers. "Was scheduled yesterday until five o'clock. You'd have to talk to the department supervisor to see if he was here. His name's Conrad Jones. He should be around. I'll give him a call." Damned if the guy's phone didn't buzz again. Jack exhaled loudly.

Rhodes answered. "Lemme call ya back." He punched in numbers on his cell. "Yeah, Conrad. Got two men who want to talk to ya." Silence. "Right. Letcha know."

Rhodes turned to Jack. "He's in the back unloading. You wanna go there, or meet him here?"

Sherk said, "We'll go there. Thanks for your help."

Following Rhodes's directions, Jack and Sherk made their way to a mammoth warehouse; stacks of boxes of all shapes and sizes rested on shelves and sections of the floor.

"Rhodes doesn't know the truth about Welton unless he's a damn good actor." Jack side-stepped a box of lightbulbs in his path. "Wonder how he got the job."

"The law on hiring felons is a slippery slope. It depends on state laws which can change. Many variables present themselves, like the severity of— "

"All right, man, I get the point. Calvin can research your slippery slope."

"Agreed." Sherk indicated a far wall with sun shining through a large opening. "The loading dock's over there."

Several men were lifting, shoving, and carrying boxes from the platform into the warehouse. Jack approached a tall black guy pointing to a washing machine wrapped in packaging material. Two other men eased it from a dolly onto the floor at the end of a ramp.

"We're looking for Conrad Jones."

The man beamed, white teeth flashing. "You found him."

"Can we talk privately?" asked Sherk.

"Go ahead," he told his co-workers. "Be back in a minute."

He led Jack and Sherk to a quiet spot in a corner. Sherk pulled out his notebook. "We're here regarding Bruce Welton."

Jones told them Welton was a quiet sort, didn't socialize with others, did an adequate job, was strong for his medium size. He clocked out yesterday at 5:15 P.M. and was scheduled to work today from 8:30 to 5:00, but didn't show. Jack felt certain Jones didn't know Welton's history any more than Rhodes.

"He was a milk-toast kind of guy— you know what I mean?" Jones glanced around. "I take it something happened to him?"

"Found dead in his apartment this morning. Possible foul play." Jack coughed. "Have to ask, where were you yesterday between five thirty and five this morning?"

Jones looked surprised. "Me? Oh, ah, at home with my wife and kids. Was here till seven, stopped at the Jewel for a few groceries and then home."

Jack nodded. "Okay, that's it. Here's my card if you think of anything else."

Jones took the card. "Yeah. Too bad, young guy like that. Something off about him, now that I think about it. Can't put my finger on it though."

If he only knew, Jack thought as he and Sherk turned to leave.

Back in the car, Jack started the engine. "I wanna stop by the morgue and bust Araki's balls on the autopsy. We'll get lunch later. He might be cutting Welton open even as we speak."

"That image whets my appetite." Sherk, a man of dry wit.

"How many autopsies have you witnessed?" Jack backed out of the parking space and traveled toward I-55.

"Two. As you know, I have a habit of becoming unavailable as an attending detective for the occasional equivocal case we encounter."

Jack harrumphed. "Yeah, noticed that. Not my favorite part of the job, but thank god the department isn't hardass about a detective witnessing every one."

"I wonder how many Miss Daisy has seen."

"None I'm guessing. I'm sure the bitch is lying in wait for us. We should stay away as long as possible. Maybe a long lunch at the pub."

"Sounds good. Let's eat first, Jack. We'll call Dr. Araki when we're done."

"Okay. I'm hungry. Shinnick's?"

"Fine with me."

Traffic was light, and they reached the pub in twenty-five minutes. Jack parked on Union Street down from Nativity of Our Lord Church. The lunch crowd was thinning out, and Jack chose a booth near a large window.

Shinnick's, a Bridgeport icon established in the 1880's, was once frequented by both Mayor Daleys. Original tin walls and ceiling still remained, with huge white columns and ornate molding showcasing the interior. The Shinnick family still owns the pub, once a haven for politicians whose photographs decorate the walls, guarding secrets of Chicago public servants, not all of whom were entirely scrupulous.

Jack strolled over to the traditional Brunswick bar and ordered two pints of Guinness from a balding, overstuffed bartender. "How's it going, Charlie?"

"Not bad, Bailey. Your brother was in here yesterday, maybe day before."

Jack shrugged. "You see Tommy more than I do."

Charlie filled two tall mugs and handed them to Jack. "Say hi to Sherk for me."

"Will do. Don't take any wooden nickels."

"Ha. What century are you from, Bailey?"

"Can't get my gramps outta my head." Jack carried the beers to the booth, where he and Sherk raised a toast to whoever snuffed out Bruce Welton.

After their lunch of thick cheeseburgers, fries, and cole slaw, Jack paid the tab; the men waved goodbye to Charlie and ambled to the car.

Jack climbed into the driver's seat. "Ate too much. Time for a nap."

Sherk stretched his long arms. "Yes, great idea. That was indeed a hearty repast."

"Yeah, filling lunch too." Jack glanced at Sherk. "Gotcha."

Jack tapped in Araki's number on his phone and listened. "Not till then? We're tied up. I'll send Gonzalez or Kennedy. Later." He tapped the phone off. "Damn, Araki's starting autopsy at three. After that lunch, I changed my mind. Kennedy likes that crap. Let him go."

"Fine with me. Let's go to the office, update Kennedy, and check with Calvin." He flipped his notebook open and rattled off his to-do list.

Jack drove down Pershing to Halsted, and arrived at the station in ten minutes. On the way to their desks, they stopped at Gary Calvin's desk.

"Got what you needed, boys." He held up a file in his chubby paw. "Ask and ye shall find."

"Receive, Gary. Receive," said Sherk.

Calvin eyed him. "Huh?"

"Ask and ye shall receive. Find is relative to seek and ye shall find."

Calvin ran his hand through his ginger hair. "You're killin' me, Sherk."

"He gotcha, Calvin." Jack guffawed and tramped away.

"You're welcome, Bailey," Calvin called.

"I know. I'm the one makes your job interesting," Jack answered.

Sherk stayed at Calvin's desk and asked him to research Bruce Welton's felony status as an employee at Home Depot. "Thanks, Gary, we'll check later."

Jack called Kennedy and updated him on the Welton case. The younger detective was eager to leave the office and attend the autopsy.

Sherk sat across from Jack at their adjoining desks. "Here's the file. Enlighten me."

Highlighter in hand, Sherk took the papers and skimmed several pages before summarizing the contents for Jack.

Nothing earth-shaking, except Welton's grandmother, Louise, was in Florida, where she wintered every year with her sister in West Palm Beach. She told Welton she expected to return to Chicago the end of March, next week. She'd been gone since November, but signed papers for her grandson to live in her house. Welton moved in on January 30. A cousin had checked on the house twice a week the previous two months. Calvin obtained this information from Louise Welton's realtor.

"Okay, so the scum had the place to himself," Jack said. "Who knows what shit happened in that house. We need to call the old lady. Did she truly know her own grandson? And what does that make her?"

They'd soon find out.

Chapter 10

It was a toss-up who would call Louise Welton to inform her of the death of her grandson, who she may or may not be aware was a registered sex offender; specifically, a pedophile. Jack reached for his pocket and fished out a quarter. He tossed the coin in the air and covered it with his hand.

"Call it, Sherk."

"Tails."

Jack lifted his hand. "Two outta three."

"Afraid not, Jack. Let me know what you find out. I'm going for coffee."

Jack moaned and tapped in Louise Welton's number.

Oddly, she didn't seem shocked or upset at hearing about the untimely demise of her grandson.

"I always wondered about that boy. Something strange about him. Too quiet." Louise's voice crackled and she coughed frequently. A smoker? "Always wondered if he was on drugs. His brother got hooked on cocaine or heroin, can't recollect exactly, but it was bad."

"Did you worry about him staying at your house?"

Louise hesitated. "Not really. My son Paul, who's Bruce's uncle, told me he'd check on the boy every now and again. He's the one, got Bruce the job at Home Depot. My Paul's some kind of supervisor or something at the store in Naperville. Then there's my other grandson, Bruce's cousin. He checked on the house before Bruce moved in."

"I see." Nothing more to glean from this conversation. "That's all for now. I assume you'll notify your family."

"Oh yes. Bruce's mom, who knows where she is. Left years ago, but his dad in Minneapolis will be upset. Just know he will."

Jack thanked the woman for her time and hung up. Guess Grandma was in the dark about her grandson. Perhaps a good thing.

Welton's uncle must've known the score. Helped his nephew out by somehow getting him in at Home Depot, keeping the sex offender part under the radar. Depending how the case progressed, Jack might end up tracking down the uncle. He'd worry about that later.

Velda Vatava's sudden appearance interrupted Jack's thoughts. "Almost time for happy hour, Bailey. Where's your flask?"

He looked up and spoke in a sing-song cadence. "Velda Veronica Vatava, vhat a vonderfully strange-sounding name."

"Hey, that's Sherk's poem. He still hasn't finished it." Velda's burgundy colored pants suit with a loose-fitting long jacket accentuated her stout figure. Her black flat shoes didn't help the image.

Jack eyed the thick file folder in her stubby hands. "Got something for me? Tickets to the Blackhawk's game?"

"Ha, you crack me up, Bailey." She handed him the file. "A gift from your pal Ms. LePere. Pertinent information on updates of various and sundry penal codes which all cops should memorize. Read it and weep."

Jack groaned. "Be sure and tell her—never mind, you don't use that kind of language."

Velda laughed. "Try me sometime, Bailey. Try me." She turned and swerved to miss bumping head-on into Sherk.

She grasped his arm to steady herself. "Hey, guy. Just quoting your poetry." Velda cackled and marched on to somewhere important.

"Should I ask?" Sherk sat at his desk and faced Jack.

"Nah. She just dumped a pile of red tape bullshit on us to peruse and file away."

"What did Bruce Welton's grandmother have to say?"

Jack relayed his conversation with Grandmother Louise while Sherk drank his coffee.

"Nothing further to do, Jack. In all probability the woman doesn't know the truth about her grandson. Too late in the day to question the parents of the boy Welton abused."

Jack ran his hand through his once black hair, now flecked with gray. "Yeah, I'm heading out. Calvin should have a report tomorrow about Welton's prison record and how his uncle finagled the Home Depot job."

Sherk drained his mug. "Calling it a day. Past five o'clock. Time to relax."

As luck would have it, Daisy LePere approached the minute Jack rose from his chair. Her bleached hair was pulled back into a bun at her neck, not a strand out of place. Gold hoop earrings dangled in the breeze. "Going somewhere, Detectives?"

Jack held up his arm, looked at his watch. "Yeah, Sarge, we've put in a full day. Happy hour time."

"Ms. LePere to you, Bailey. What's the latest on the Welton case?"

Sherk said, "We don't have cause of death. Welton was a registered sex offender, lived—"

"I know that much, Sherkenbach." She gave him a withering glance and turned to Jack. "Anything new?"

"We'll get on Araki's ass tomorrow for the autopsy. Forensics should have something by noon. We'll question further connections to Welton tomorrow."

"What's wrong with now?" LePere sighed. "Never mind. I'll expect a progressive report tomorrow afternoon. Do your job, fellas." She turned and traipsed toward Gary Calvin's desk and spoke to him.

"There she goes, busting Calvin's balls, poor guy," Jack said.

"Let's get out of here before she thinks of something else to encumber us with." Sherk gathered his phone and briefcase.

He and Jack made it to the cloak room, retrieved their jackets, headed down the hall, and left the building.

Jack breathed in the frosty air, a relief after the oppressive mood in the station. He said good night to Sherk, climbed into his old Beemer and headed home. His fridge needed replenishing, but he couldn't face the extra effort to stop at the mom and pop corner store on the way. His thoughts meandered back in time as he steered along the streets of his youth. Dusk cast shadows on the landscape as an image lurked on the edge of his mind. A date he wanted to forget loomed ahead in less than a week.

When he unlocked the back door, Boone trotted up to Jack and yipped a greeting. The days of the big dog going into a frenzy at Jack's arrivals were long gone.

"Hey, boy. Ready for a walk?"

Boone barked twice in response as Jack fastened a collar and leash around the thick, furry neck. The huge mutt loved his walks, although he no longer pranced or tugged at the leash as he'd done in his younger years.

Jack enjoyed walking Boone in weather like this, pleasantly cool, unlike the bitter cold of previous months. Cleared his mind to think.

Lately, Jack felt time slipping away, his world moving too fast. Not that life overflowed with excitement or activity, but memories of better times grew increasingly distant. He dreaded the phone call he knew would soon come from his mother. She'd remind him of the date next Saturday, March 28. As if he could forget.

• • • • •

After scarfing down a gourmet dinner of frozen pizza with two bottles of Guinness, Jack reclined in his favorite brown leather chair. As if on cue, the expected phone call arrived. He glanced at the caller ID. Maureen Bailey.

"Yeah, Ma. What a surprise."

"Don't get smart, Jacky. You know why I'm calling."

He knew, all right. Five days from now would be the anniversary of his late wife, Karen's birthday. Twelve years later, the day was no easier to endure, mainly with Karen's mother, Beth, reminding him each year of their annual gathering at the gravesite, which included the grave of his daughter, Elizabeth. Age five, and robbed of her life along with her mother on a trip to Ireland. Would the pain ever end?

"Okay, just the facts, Ma'am." He couldn't hack hearing every detail of his mother's conversation with Beth, who had rubbed the Bailey family the wrong way from the get-go.

"Of course, you know this Saturday is Karen's fiftieth birthday, and—"

"For god's sake, Ma, Karen happens to be deceased. It's not gonna be her birthday. It would have been. Just tell me what the old queen bee wants."

"Don't take your foul mood out on me, young man. I'm just the messenger. Next time I'll tell her to call you. See how you like talking to her."

"All right, all right."

"We're gonna meet at the cemetery at one o'clock and lay flowers. Then we're invited to their house for coffee and dessert. Think you can manage that?" Her voice dripped sarcasm.

"Christ, I don't wanna deal with them at their house. Bad enough being around them at the cemetery. Tell her I can't make it. I got a department meeting at two o'clock."

"Ha," Maureen said. "That's a lame excuse. You don't work on Saturdays and they know that."

"Ma, I'm sick of her riding my ass about this. Every year it's the same thing, and then there's Elizabeth's birthday in the summer."

"It won't be so bad. Laura will be there this year."

"Guess that'll be the best part." Jack had always liked Karen's older sister who lived in Denver. She'd helped Jack through his grief after Karen's death by talking with him over drinks well into countless nights.

"Okay, Jacky, you come over for an early lunch and we'll go together. Maybe Tommy will come too."

"How 'bout Jenny?" Jack's sister lived with her husband and family several blocks from Maureen's house.

"Maybe. I'll find out."

Jack sighed. "Yeah. Gotta go." Too much family drama. "See ya, Ma."

"Wait a minute. When are you seeing Bonnie again?"

Shit. He'd forgotten. "Tomorrow night, Ma. I'll call the next day and give you all the sordid details."

"Goodbye, Mr. Smart Aleck."

Jack sighed. Seeing Karen's family two or three times a year was a real burden. He'd never liked Beth, who looked down her nose at Jack and his family, giving him the distinct impression he wasn't good enough for her daughter. Despite Karen's denials, he knew otherwise. He could hear her laughing. *Oh, Jack honey, don't be silly. Mom likes you a lot, she knows you're a wonderful man.*

He'd never forget the first time he met Karen's parents in their pricey brick house in Park Ridge, a Chicago suburb a cut above Jack's Bridgeport roots. Stewart Buckley, a successful corporate lawyer, was welcoming and warmer than his wife, Beth, who Jack found distant and reserved. She grew a little friendlier after the wedding, but he never cared for the woman. Times like this he wished he were back in Texas.

Boone plodded over to Jack's chair and put his large snout on his knee. "How you doing, big guy?" He ruffled the dog's furry head and ears. "Big day comin' up. Let's call it a night."

• • • • •

Jack tossed and turned, but sleep eluded him. He thought of Sister Anne's funeral tomorrow. Wished Sherk would go alone, but LePere wanted two sets of eyes on the look-out for possible suspects. Since the Bible thumper was no doubt a wack job, maybe he would show up at the church. Then there was his un-date with Bonnie at the pub tomorrow after work. How would that go? So far, he liked her pretty well. No dynamic chemistry knocked him off his feet, but you can't have everything. Not like twelve years ago.

Chapter 11

Tuesday morning Donald Sowder awoke in a good mood. Glad he signed up for a vacation day so he could stay home from his miserable computer job at Midway Airport. Yes, this was a special day. He stumbled out of bed, pajama bottoms sagging below his waist. Was he getting too skinny? No appetite lately.

Shuffling to the kitchen, he noted his dingy apartment didn't depress him for once. The gray unadorned walls seemed brighter, the threadbare tan sofa inviting. He measured coffee and water, turned on the pot. As a strong chicory scent filled the air, he felt hungry for a change, so he fried a couple eggs and toasted two slices of bread. Eggs sizzled in the pan, the edges turned brittle and brown. With a spatula he scooped them from the pan and placed them just so on the plate. Piercing the bright yellow center with a corner of toast, he watched as the gooey liquid streamed over the white part and onto the dish. He sopped up the runny yoke with the rest of his toast. Cooked to perfection. Umm.

Donald smirked as he devoured his remaining breakfast and slurped coffee. Getting rid of that scum Bruce Welton was easier than he'd thought. Easier than Sister. He felt proud of the research he'd done. Not everyone could accomplish such a task, although sex registry lists were public nowadays. And rightly so.

He felt great empathy for the little boy Welton abused. The prick most likely got what he deserved in the slammer. Poetic justice. How do you like it, asshole?

Wouldn't it be great to see the cops' reaction when they find out what killed Welton? Bet they're scratching their heads on this one. No sign of struggle; Welton had done exactly as ordered. Trudged into the bedroom without a peep, lay down on his bed. Guns talk. Nice little Ruger LC9. Never used it. Bought it two years ago for protection. Chicago's claim to fame: gun violence.

His method of ridding the world of Bruce Welton? Sheer genius. People think it's easy to bump someone off. Not so. Takes careful planning. He wasn't sure how his plan formulated, but he knew when.

Two years ago he'd stopped in to visit his mother when his younger sister showed up, freaking out because the vet put down her favorite horse. She worked part-time at the Circle C Ranch ten miles south off 294.

Ignoring her ranting and tears, he experienced a lightbulb moment.

"Must take a strong dose of medicine to put down a horse," he'd said.

His sister had sniffed, told him to piss off, and continued bawling to their mother.

Later, Donald googled the appropriate anesthetic, and figured he could order it online.

It took him six months to think about the idea. Always was indecisive. He'd finally ordered the drug, and two weeks later it arrived; he patted himself on the back for his brilliance.

Donald wondered if the cops received the autopsy report yet. God, he wished he were a fly on the wall when they heard the news. Bet that Japanese medical guy never saw the drug used before, not on a human anyway.

Too bad Donald's cleverness didn't pay off in a real job. With his brains, he could've been a doctor or scientist. Shown the playground bullies of his childhood a thing or two. *There goes Donny Sowder puss. Donny Sowder smells sour.* The taunts refused to release him.

But he was ruined, damaged long ago by that—never mind, don't go there. Keep it in the past. Stay in the now. Seek justice after all these years. *When it is finished, bringeth forth death.* The book of James. Hit the nail on the head.

Blinking himself back to the present, Donald sat at his old Formica kitchen table. Gotta get going. He rinsed off the egg-crusted plate and silverware, and placed them in the dishwasher. Next, hit the shower. Had to ready himself for the morning's event.

• • • • •

Exhilarated as the steaming water poured over him pinpricking his smooth flesh, Donald breathed in deeply. He lathered his face with Yardley Lavender soap for men. Soothing fragrance.

Would the detectives in charge be at the funeral this morning? He should be able to spot them. No worries, they wouldn't notice him. He knew how to play it smart, play it cool, blend into the woodwork. He was Mr. Average.

After much deliberation over the past week, he'd decided to visit Sister Anne Celeste one more time. Later this morning. Render a proper good bye. Have the last word.

Chapter 12

Daisy LePere was lying in wait for Jack the minute he sauntered into the bull pen the next morning. She stood erect, arms crossed over her gray silk blouse.

"I got a message from Hal Araki. He wants you to call him about the autopsy report on the Welton murder."

Jack threw off his jacket and hung it on the rack. "What's the rush, Sarge? Why didn't he email it over?"

"Ms. LePere to you, Bailey." She led Jack to his desk. "He found the cause of death somewhat curious. First time he's seen it. Hal wanted to tell you or Sherkenbach before sending it."

"Why? Afraid we're remedial readers?"

"Lose the attitude, Bailey. Just call him." She turned and strutted away.

"Wait. Did Araki tell you what killed Welton?"

"Just call him."

Jack punched Araki's number as Sherk arrived and eased into his chair. Jack tapped on speaker mode and pushed the phone toward Sherk.

Araki answered. "About time. Who's this?"

"Bailey, and Sherk's listening in."

"Velly intah-restink, Detectives. You want to hear?"

Jack retorted, "No, I'm calling to ask you to tea. Come on, Araki."

"Okay, okay. Your young Mr. Welton was killed by an injection given in the left side of his neck. Just a pinprick, hard to see. That's why you missed it."

Jack scoffed. "I didn't miss it. I didn't do the exam, CSI did."

"I know, I know. Just meant you meaning the, how you say,

everyone."

Sherk nodded. "The collective you. Go on, Hal."

"Someone injected somulose, precisely known as secobarbital or cinchocaine. I ascertained they used 120 cubic centimeters." Araki paused.

"Is that supposed to mean something?" Jack asked. "We're not frickin' scientists."

"Sorry, Detectives. In layman's terms, the drug amount used on Welton was enough to kill a thousand-pound horse."

Sherk raised his eyebrows.

Jack said, "Jesus, doc. Where would someone get that? Steal it from a vet?"

Araki smirked. "You catch on quick, Bailey. I got DNA samples from clothing and the body. Am comparing them to your nun's murder. Ready tomorrow if we're lucky."

"I assume this somulose is used to euthanize animals," Sherk said.

"Ah, another sharp-witted detective. I think your assumption is correct, but check with vets. I'd ask around clinics, see if anyone is missing the drug."

"Thanks for the heads up on how to do our job, Doc," Jack said. "We'll get on it."

Araki scoffed. "I'll email the report over. Talk later."

Jack hung up. "Enough drugs to kill a horse. Guy left nothing to chance."

"We have two hours before the Sister's funeral. Do you want to question Welton's victim's parents or call veterinary clinics?"

Jack rubbed his forehead. "I need coffee. Let's get Calvin to pull up contact info on animal clinics in a twenty, thirty-mile radius. Check horse stables too."

"I'll get the parents' numbers from Gary. If they live close by, we could talk to them, then go directly to the funeral."

"What's your mad rush, Sherk? We can see them after the funeral." Jack hated dredging up painful memories for parents or anyone. He knew too well how that felt.

Sherk shrugged. "Fine. We'll wait. I sense your hesitation."

"Oh, so you're Freud now? Oh yeah, forgot you Germans are smarter than all of us."

"Austrian."

"Huh?"

"Freud was Austrian, Jack. Born in Vienna. His family was fortunate to escape—"

"Enough of the history lesson, dude. Not in the mood."

Sherk held up his hands in mock defeat. "Let's get coffee."

Jack reached for his stained White Sox mug and followed Sherk to the break room. "Hope they have donuts."

• • • • •

After sloshing their coffee down with a couple stale vanilla wafers, Sherk and Jack stopped at Gary Calvin's desk. The pudgy man wore a gray sweatshirt with black letters.

"Gotta read the shirt first," Jack said. Hunched over his keyboard, Calvin looked up and stuck out his chest to show the front of his shirt.

"Quite clever," Sherk laughed as he read the words, HARVARD LAW, and halfway down the shirt, *Just Kidding*.

"And I thought I didn't have a life," Jack said. "How much time do you spend online ordering your duds?"

Calvin swept his red mop behind his ear. "Lots of time, Bailey. But hey, look at all the chicks I get."

Jack looked around. "Don't see any."

Sherk said, "We could engage in witty repartee all day, Gary, but duty calls. What can you tell us about the parents of Welton's victim?"

"They're both at work now, off at five-thirty. Said they'd be home by six. Here's the info." Calvin handed Jack a post-it note. "I told the mom you had some information to talk about, so she's expecting your call."

"Thanks," Sherk said. "By the way, how hard would it be to order somulose used to euthanize animals?"

Calvin raised his bushy eyebrows. "Interesting. That used on

Welton?"

"Yeah," Jack said. "Any ideas?"

"I'd say a geek could do it, order the drug online."

"You got time to call vet clinics in a thirty-mile radius? See if anyone's missing the drug?"

"Sorry, Bailey. LePere has me on a robbery case. Know what I have to dig up by— "

"Save the sad story, Calvin. Catch ya later."

Jack and Sherk returned to their desks and divvied up the task of calling veterinary clinics within a thirty or forty-mile radius of Bedford Park, the area where Welton's murder occurred. Jack hated doing crap like this. The time dragged by, and the result from calling thirty-two clinics was zilch.

Sherk stood and stretched. "It's time to leave for the church. I presume you have a tie to wear."

"Tie? Are you kiddin' me? This ain't a state dinner."

Sherk reached in a side drawer and took out a red tie. "You should always respect the dearly departed, Jack."

"Sherk, you're killin' me. You're the kid here. Those old school rules are down the toilet. You see people dressed like bums at a funeral Mass." Jack didn't know that for sure, but damned if he was going to worry about a frickin' tie.

Ten minutes later they arrived at Nativity of Our Lord Church, Sherk sporting a tie, Jack tieless. They parked behind the vast gothic structure and climbed out of the car.

"A lot of people coming," Jack said. "Folks the Sister's age usually don't draw a big crowd. Their friends have kicked the bucket already."

"In keeping with everything we heard, her popularity follows her even in death."

"Very poetic, Sherk."

Jack led the way through massive wooden front doors. A waft of incense and burning candles reached his nostrils, causing a lurch in his gut. Old habits die hard, no pun intended. Resounding chords from the pipe organ filled the air as mourners wandered toward their seats, most genuflecting toward the altar before they sat.

Avoiding the font of holy water in the entry, Jack led Sherk to an empty pew in the back below the watchful gaze of a woeful-looking saint depicted on one of the multi-colored stained glass windows illuminating the church.

Jack glanced around at the group of congregants, young, old, fat, thin, men, women, a fair number of canes and walkers. No one caught his attention as a possible perp, but he'd keep his eyes open.

Five minutes later, everyone rose as six pallbearers wheeled the flower-laden rosewood coffin down the aisle and left it at the altar. Father Jim sprinkled the casket with holy water and then sauntered around, swinging his incense burner over the deceased and muttering Latin words of scripture.

"The good Sister is having a Requiem Mass," Sherk whispered to Jack.

For a Lutheran, Sherk knew a lot about Catholics. Always said he should've been a professor.

The priest's scripture readings brought back unpleasant memories of Karen and Elizabeth's funeral. Jack's former in-laws had insisted on a memorial Mass, and Jack had grudgingly acquiesced. The verses from John and Timothy rang as hollow today as they had twelve years ago. *In my Father's house are many mansions...* Yeah, right.

After another gospel reading, a male soloist sang *Ave Maria*, which always gave Jack goose bumps. He never tired of the haunting strains of its poignant melody, carrying him back to childhood days with his family in St. Bridget's Church. The one pleasant memory he harbored.

"I'm impressed." Sherk leaned toward Jack. "The singer is an excellent tenor."

"We'll be sure and tell him that."

Father Jim's homily was the usual brief sermon of encouragement, enhanced with Sister Anne Celeste's highly esteemed attributes. "She devoted her life to Christ, and is now in His hands, to live in His house and serve Him forever."

Jack questioned those words. Didn't the poor woman deserve a rest after a life of service?

Before the Eucharist, the soloist sang *Prayer of St. Francis*. Jack's mother would've approved.

As family members approached the altar, he noticed Molly Winters, Sister Anne's niece, standing beside an older woman and two teenagers. Molly, attractive in her black dress, wore a small dark hat perched atop her brown shoulder-length hair. Was it lighter than when he met her last week? Must be in her fifties, and she still looked damn good. Jack planned to speak to Molly after the service, offer his condolences. For whatever reason, she sparked his interest.

More people rose and walked to receive communion. Jack looked at Sherk. "Before you ask, no, I'm not having my sins washed away today."

"I didn't think so, Jack. Only those in a state of grace can participate. How long since your last confession?"

Jack smirked. "Don't make me cuss at you in church, Sherk."

Communion seemed to last for hours, and finally the congregation rose and sang *How Great Thou Art* as Sister Anne made her last journey down the aisle and out the doors of the church toward her final resting place somewhere Jack had forgotten.

People gathered in the Narthex waiting to walk across the church grounds to the fellowship hall for refreshments and to pay their respects to the family.

Jack maneuvered his way through groups of people to reach Molly Winters, who was engaged in a conversation with an elderly man. When the old windbag finally shut up, Jack caught her eye.

"Hi, Ms. Winters. I met you — "

"Yes, I remember. Detective Bailey. Thank you for coming." She had an alluring smile.

"My partner — " Jack looked and saw Sherk greeting someone halfway across the vestibule. "Anyway, we wanted to pay our respects and keep our eyes out for any — " Didn't want to talk about the case now. Not the time nor place.

"That's nice of you, Detective. Are you staying for refreshments?"

"Afraid not. We need to get back to work." He would rather be alone with her. He'd keep her number handy.

Sherk approached them and greeted Molly. "Your aunt's service was lovely."

"Yes, she would've approved, and been happy to see so many of her friends."

The detectives said goodbye and waved to Father Jim on their way out. He was busy chatting with a middle-aged couple, and Jack didn't want to hang around. Had his fill of idle chatter for one day.

"Let's split up and meander our way out," Sherk said. "Last chance to case out the crowd."

Jack doubted the perp would have the balls to go for lunch, but who knew. They ambled their way around clumps of people standing about, and met at the doorway.

"I noticed several ordinary-looking men in the church, but didn't see them in here." Sherk put on his jacket.

"Yeah, mostly old guys. Maybe a few younger ones, but nobody stuck out."

As they emerged from the church, Jack squinted against the sun but shivered in the crisp air. He climbed in the driver's seat and started the engine.

Sherk took out his phone. "Okay to meet the boy's parents at six-thirty today?"

Jack grimaced. "I guess." He listened while Sherk called and made the arrangements.

They arrived at the station and were nearing the door when Jack stopped. "Fu--"

"What's the problem, Jack?"

"I forgot about my—meeting later on."

He hadn't told Sherk about his non-date with Bonnie tonight at Shinnick's. If he bailed on her, she'd never believe he had to work.

"You wouldn't mind going alone, would ya?"

Sherk followed Jack into the building. "No, but the dragon lady will object."

"Screw her. Look, Sherk, if you must know— "

"Hold it, Jack." Sherk gave a half smile. "I never asked. Far be it from me to intrude in your personal affairs."

They reached their desks after shedding their jackets in the cloak room.

Jack sat and sighed loudly. "Aw, what the hell. Remember the dinner last week my mother roped me into? Got set up, and I'm meeting her tonight. She says there'll be no strings, just have a drink, talk without my ma's big ears around."

Sherk looked curious. "Interesting, Jack. One never knows what might ensue. Yes, I'll do the interview and leave it up to you to explain to Ms. LePere if it comes up."

"Not a problem. And no questions from you tomorrow."

Sherk faked a poker face. "Questions? The last thing on my mind."

● ● ● ● ●

The afternoon plodded by with no new reports on the Bruce Welton case. Forensics should be in by the end of the week. Restless, Jack left at 4:30. He'd be early for his meeting with Bonnie. Fine with him. Fortify himself with a Jameson or two before she arrived.

Shinnick's was half empty when Jack walked through the door. When the hostess approached him, he requested a booth in a far corner. A bored looking waiter sauntered over to take the order.

"There'll be someone else coming, but I'll have a double Jameson while I wait." Might as well get loosened up. He wondered what he was doing, what the real purpose of this meeting was. Did he want a relationship, and if so, what kind? Just friends? Someone smart to talk to? Sex? Had to admit, he missed that. Hell, he didn't know.

Jack stared at his phone screen so he'd look preoccupied. He felt conflicted about meeting Bonnie rather than Molly. There was chemistry with Molly, but he felt he should give Bonnie a chance. Two women on his radar screen. Either feast or famine.

The waiter brought his drink. "Anything else?"

"Nah. I'll wait for my friend."

The minutes dragged on. He wondered what they'd talk about. She must know his past, what happened twelve years ago. Their mothers had known each other for years. He felt pressure building up inside as if this were a real date. He felt the urge to bolt, but forced himself to stay put. He glanced at the entry door. Blotted sweat from his forehead. Oh, God. The time had come.

Chapter 13

Bonnie walked through the door and glanced around. Jack caught her eye, swiped at his forehead again. He waved to her. She skirted her way around tables and customers toward Jack. They greeted each other with hellos and an awkward half-hug.

Sitting across from him, Bonnie shrugged out of her tan leather jacket. "How's it going, Jack?"

"Pretty good." Jack looked around for the waiter. "You hungry?"

"No, I'll just have a glass of Merlot."

Jack nodded, wondering what to say. "How was your day?" How original.

Bonnie smiled. "Fine. And yours?"

Thank god the waiter came and took their orders. "She'll have a glass of Merlot. A Guinness for me."

The waiter took the empty shot glass and walked away.

Bonnie tucked one side of her dark hair behind her ear. A diamond earring twinkled in the light. She wore a black sweater with a red print scarf. "Are you comfortable with this situation, Jack?"

He tried to relax. Took a deep breath. "What's your job again?"

She told him about her hospice position at the clinic a few miles away, how later in her career as an RN she became interested in end-of-life nursing.

"Sounds depressing." Jack wished the waiter would hurry with their drinks.

"That's what a lot of people think, but in the last twenty years, it's become a whole new field in medicine. In our culture, we're so afraid of death and dying, and my job brings the conversation out in the open." She paused. "Sorry, Jack. Listen to me, lecturing like a professor."

"No worries." His phone vibrated, but he stopped himself from grabbing it.

The waiter arrived with their drinks. After he left, Jack held up his mug of beer for a toast. "Here's to non-dates and end-of-life conversations." What a dumb ass thing to say.

Bonnie smiled and clinked her glass with his. "Cheers."

She took a sip. "Look, Jack. I'll be honest. I know about your wife and daughter in Ireland. Everyone from here knew when it happened. I'm sure it's the last thing you want to talk about, but just let me say, I'm so sorry." She took another drink of wine. "I just wanted to mention it and not avoid the subject like it's the proverbial elephant in the room."

"Yeah." Jack cleared his throat. "A lot of people don't want to bring it up, and you're right, I don't talk about it. Even though it's been a long time—"

"I know, Jack. You've heard a hundred times how there's no timeline for grief. I just wanted you to know that I understand." She waited. "Not that I know what it's like."

The room turned hot, stifling. Jack's face felt like it glowed with sweat. He took a deep breath. He wanted out.

"Thanks, Bonnie." He cleared his throat. "This case I've been on, the nun's. You know about that. It's not going anywhere." He guzzled his beer. "You didn't hear that from me, but things aren't that great now." He was babbling. God, why had he come here?

Bonnie folded her napkin in half, then in fourths. "It's okay. We don't have to dwell on that. How's your mom doing? And Tommy and the rest?"

"They're good." Jack managed to update her on his siblings, how their kids were, all safe topics.

Fifteen minutes inched by with benign conversation. Jack drained his beer, and waved the waiter away when he interrupted them asking about another round. Bonnie said she needed to leave. Jack signaled the waiter back for the check.

She put on her jacket. "It's okay, Jack. No pressure. Excuse me if

I'm out of line, but I don't feel you're ready for anything serious now."

Jack sighed with relief. "I don't know what to say. I guess I agree. Nice we can be honest."

Bonnie beamed. "That's the beauty of the non-date. No expectations."

After Jack paid the tab, they strolled into the chilly blackness.

He walked Bonnie to her car. She unlocked the door and climbed in. "If you ever want to just hang out and talk, Jack, you know where to reach me."

"Sounds good. I'll do that." He knew he never would.

Watching her drive into the night, he was glad that was over. He felt bad he wasn't engaging and interactive. But he couldn't fake it. Bonnie's a nice woman. He hoped she'd find someone to make her happy. He just wasn't that someone.

• • • • •

Driving to work the next morning, Jack felt sluggish. He'd tossed and turned all night from dreams of running through green fields toward something he needed. Then explosions. Reds. Oranges. Yellows. Anger lighting the sky. He thought the nightmares were over. Maybe last night was a fluke. Wouldn't happen again. He hated the thought of repeating the PTSD therapy from his past.

He walked into the bull pen where Sherk sat gazing at his computer. Maybe they'd get the forensics report on the Bible-thumper case this morning.

When Jack reached his desk, he muttered, "Gonna get coffee." He found his mug amidst the mess of papers cluttering the surface.

"Good morning to you too, Jack. I'm fine, thank you." Sherk grinned.

"Too early for sarcasm, dude, not to mention cheerfulness." Jack left for the break room.

He managed to avoid talking to anyone and returned with a steaming mug of coffee emitting a strong hazelnut balm.

Sherk leaned back in his chair. "Did you have an enjoyable evening?"

"What about your promise not to ask?"

"Au contraire, Jack. A promise I did not make. After your directive not to ask about said evening, I stated it would be the last thing on my mind. However, it—"

"Pow, Alice, to the moon—" How he put up with Sherk was beyond him.

"All in jest, Jack, all in jest."

Jack flipped open his notebook. "Ready for an update on your meeting last night, assuming you made it there without me." Curious whether Welton's vic's folks knew about the murder.

"The boy's parents were cooperative. Their names are Dick and Jane Ryson."

Jack scoffed. "I'm surprised they weren't running after Spot."

"Pardon?"

"Oh yeah. Forgot you learned to read in Munich. Never mind."

Sherk explained the Rysons had been notified when Bruce Welton was released from prison. They heard about the murder on TV. Sherk didn't ask them to relive the situation with their son, but the father seemed nervous, clearing his throat frequently. Neither parent had a strong alibi of their whereabouts the night of the murder. Jane said she was home with their two boys helping them with homework and did not leave the house until Monday morning. Dick excused himself to get water, and returned saying he'd been to Jewel for groceries, stopped at a Burger King for a quick dinner, and then home by nine or so. Jane corroborated his statement.

"What about pets?" Jack thought about the drug used to ice Welton.

"They have a large yellow dog, similar to Boone. A Labrador of some kind I'd say. No one in the family has a connection to horses."

Jack flicked his pen back and forth. "Did you see the kid?"

"Yes, he and an older brother were in the room momentarily before trotting off, their devices in hand. Seemed like nice, ordinary kids."

Jack closed his notebook. "Looks like zilch there. We'll check the dad's alibi if nothing solid comes up."

"What's on the agenda today other than hiding from Ms. LePere?"

"We should pick Gray's brain about the Bible thumper."

"There's a pun in there, but the wording escapes me at the moment."

"Huh?" Jack frowned. "Oh, like brain gray matter…give it a rest, Sherk. Since you're so witty this morning, you call him."

"Of course, there's Gray's Anatomy, the classic textbook, not the TV—"

"Call the guy already."

Maybe Daryl Gray, resident psychologist, could help. A retired FBI agent, he was known for his profiling expertise.

Sherk made the call, paused, and hung up. "The good doctor is out of town and is expected back tomorrow."

"Damn. The lab's dragging its ass on forensics too." Jack thought for a minute. "We should look at Welton's prison contacts. Maybe somebody got sprung about the same time, and that somebody had it in for a pedophile. His DNA would be in the system though. We can worry about the Bible verse connection later."

"We know mistakes happen in labs, rare as they may be. I'll ask Gary to provide information on Welton's record in Stateville."

"Yeah. Maybe we can go to Joliet and talk to people. Find out Welton's social life in the pen."

Sherk agreed. "Yes, it would give us a break from the station. It's about an hour from here. We could take in the scenes of the city."

"A real thrill. Nothing in that town but the old prison."

"Actually, Jack, there's an interesting old theater in the downtown area. Al Capone used to patronize the place."

"You sold me, Sherk. I'm game."

It might be a good escape. A welcome relief, mostly since Saturday was descending on him. The day he'd have to face Karen's parents at her grave.

Chapter 14

The next day dragged by with no critical information on the Bible thumper. Jack ditched the idea of the Joliet trip as a waste of time. Instead, Sherk phoned a staff member at Stateville regarding Bruce Welton's tenure in the pen. Seems the guy kept to himself as much as one can under the circumstances. The CO said when possible, staff separates sex offenders from other inmates for their own protection. Welton stayed out of trouble except for occasional incidences in the yard where confrontations occurred with several Latino prisoners. One of them named Al Vendez was released the same time as Welton. The CO gave Sherk Vendez's parole officer's contact information.

Jack slurped lukewarm coffee. "I dunno, Welton might have pissed off Vendez, but a motive for murder? I doubt if a low life sleaze ball has the smarts to get ahold of that drug to clip Welton for bein' a pedophile."

"I tend to agree. Our killer seems intelligent enough to cover his tracks, not to mention using Bible verses to send a message. A rather intellectual touch to his MO."

"Wish we'd get the damn forensics report. It's the weekend. Sick of waiting."

The bull pen thinned out; people leaving for the day. Jack was ready to leave when Sherk said, "Here she comes."

Daisy LePere walked through the door and glanced around, seeming to notice the number of cops and clerks vacating the room. She wore her standard dark pants suit with a pink silk shirt. Traipsing over to Jack's desk, she asked, "What's the latest on your case?"

Jack said, "Still waiting for forensics. Sherk found out about Welton's life in the pen before release. Same 'ol, same 'ol."

LePere sighed. "Well, Sherkenbach, enlighten me."

He explained Bruce Welton's prison life and his conflicts with Vendez.

"You need to check him out, even though, in your infinite wisdom, you might not think he's a viable suspect." She stared at Jack.

He stared back. "If forensics comes up with a match, of course we'll bring him in. But we'd know by now. Vendez's DNA would've shown up in the system after the nun's murder."

She scoffed and swept back her bangs. "Presuming the same person murdered both." She hesitated. "Keep on top of it." She turned on her heels and left in a huff.

Jack set his teeth on edge. "What a pain in the ass."

"Do you think it's safe to leave? Our work is done for today." He untangled his mile-long legs and stretched.

"Yeah, the bitch is gone. Let's get the hell outta here." He was eager for a relaxing evening with Boone.

• • • • •

Friday morning Jack sat at his desk, hot coffee and glazed donuts on hand when Velda Vatava breezed through the doorway, her gray pantsuit matching her hair. She handed Jack a manila file

"Here's a present for you, Bailey. You can thank me later."

"Don't tell me. Forensics?" He opened the folder.

"See? Said it was a present. You owe me. I'll collect at Shinnick's tonight."

"Sorry Vatava. Busy, but maybe my cohort in crime can spring for a drink."

As if on cue, Sherk walked through the door. "Did I hear my name mentioned?"

Velda beamed. "You sure did. Bailey volunteered you to buy me a drink tonight in return for the many favors I do for you guys around here. Case in point, the forensics report you've been waiting for."

"Ah, Velda with the wonderfully poetic name. I'm afraid I have a previous engagement this evening. We need to meet another time."

"Yeah, yeah. Just like all men. Make promises they never keep." Velda turned to leave. "By the way, your boss won't be in today."

"Sarge? Ha, she must have a hot weekend planned." Jack scoffed.

"Try to contain your disappointment. See you guys later." Velda glided out of the room.

Sherk eyed Jack's donuts. "I'll be back in a minute. Give you time to peruse the report."

Jack read through several pages in the file, zeroing in on essential information. He devoured his first glazed donut and brushed crumbs from his shirt onto the floor.

Sherk returned to his desk. "I'm all ears, Jack."

"Nothing we didn't expect. Same killer for both murders. Perp's skin cells from the vics' throats and hair fibers match. Not in the system. A long shot that the Vendez creep would've done Welton and not the nun, but now that's settled."

"So we can look at Bruce Welton's relatives. They could give us his friends' names. The uncle who got him the Home Depot job is worth pursuing. Still need to figure the nun connection."

"Yeah, but I like the boy's parents or maybe another family. Did we ever find out about anyone else's kid he messed with?"

Sherk shook his head. "Nothing's on record, but you can rest assured he abused more than the one boy."

"Yeah. Nobody came forward after Welton's murder got in the papers. Guess people are too embarrassed or something. Maybe they're afraid they'll be suspects." Jack reached for his buzzing phone, held it to his ear. "Hey Daryl. Glad you called. Put you on speaker for Sherk."

"Good morning, guys." Daryl Gray's voice boomed. He'd make a good bass in an opera. "I've looked over the information on your so-called Bible thumper, and came up with a general summary. You guys have been around the block a few times; you already know most of what I'm gonna tell you."

"That's fine, Daryl." Sherk opened his notebook, pen in hand. "We value your expertise in these matters."

"First, as you know, he needs another vic to be an official serial killer. Bound to be a third murder, maybe more depending if or when he's caught. I'll call the killer 'he', since women serial killers are rare. This guy's smart, educated, tech-savvy. Your ordinary white guy, thirties or forties, nice looking or average. Looks harmless— gets him past doormen, clerks, and so on, with little hesitation."

"Okay, what else?" Jack drained his coffee.

"Hold on, Bailey. Need some water. Talking to you makes me thirsty."

"Take your time, Daryl. We have no immediate plans," Sherk said.

"Here goes, guys. Your killer isn't a run-of-the mill serial. His motive is to rid society of pedophiles. Stems from his own probable abuse as a kid. I'd say the good nun either hurt him or witnessed someone else doing it, most likely a priest. The nun turns a blind eye, and the boy wonders all these years why she didn't do anything to help. Sees it as the ultimate betrayal. Not just the priest, but the eminent Sister Anne turned on him as well. All speculation, of course."

Sherk paused from his notes. "What's your opinion on the Bible verses? Is the killer being satirical, or mocking the scripture since he's clearly breaking the law of man and God?"

Jack frowned. What the hell was he talking about?

"You may be correct, Sherk," Gray said. "It's clearly a sign of his intellectualism, and you'd think he'd be disillusioned on religion after his treatment by the clergy. Hard to say how he truly feels about religion or if he believes the context of the verses he's left. At any rate, he could have narcissistic characteristics like thinking he's smarter than everyone else, especially cops like you."

Jack raised his brow. "Yeah, I get the idea he's playing cat and mouse with us, the smartass prick."

"By leaving his calling cards with the body, he's seeing if they'll be made public. So far it's been kept under wraps and should continue that way." Gray cleared his throat. "That about sums it up, guys. I'll email you the report. Or you're welcome to come up and get it. It's lonely up here on the top floor.

Jack scoffed. "Poor guy, have to put up with the brass and your private luxury john."

"You saying I'm not the brass, Bailey? Don't bite the hand, and all that."

Sherk chortled. "Thanks, Daryl. We'll wait for your report."

Jack clicked off. "Let's go get the perp now that we know what to look for."

Sherk ignored the sarcasm. "I think we need to revisit the student rolls from the time of Sister Anne and the priest accused of misconduct. Even if nothing came of the allegations on that particular priest, it doesn't mean he was innocent."

"Yeah, it started with the nun, gotta be somebody who went to school during that time. A good project for you. Let me know what you find out." Jack rose from his chair.

"It's not even lunch time, Jack. Thinking of vacating the premises?"

"You bet. I need to go home and feed Boone. Neighbor's out of town and can't take care of the mutt."

"Is that a fact? I think you can devise a more imaginative excuse than that."

"'Oh, what a tangled web we weave'. See, you ain't the only one who can quote Shakespeare."

"Sir Walter Scott."

"Huh?"

"Sir Walter Scott, Jack. His work is the origin of the quote you sited."

"Get outta here. Gotta be Shakespeare." Jack knew he was wrong. Can't argue with Sherk, that pain in the butt.

"Don't feel bad. Many people misquote the tangled web. It sounds as if it could be Shakespeare, but Sir Walter Scott wrote in his play—"

Jack threw up his hands. "Okay, okay, save the lecture. I was wrong, you're right, happy now?"

"I wouldn't go so far as to say that, but—"

"Sherk, you're drivin' me frickin' nuts. I'm outta here." Couldn't wait for a shot of Jameson.

• • • • •

During the night Jack tossed and turned, dreaming of explosions and green fields. He awoke early Saturday morning feeling like an iron fog enveloped him. Boone slept on the floor beside the bed.

"Oh god," Jack groaned. Karen's birthday. Wished he could forget. Rubbing his eyes, he struggled to sit up. He stumbled into the bathroom and splashed cold water on his face. When he looked in the mirror, an old man stared back at him. Eyes were black sockets, head like a misshapen pumpkin.

He staggered back to bed, but sleep stubbornly steered clear of him. Half an hour later he sat up, looked at Boone. "Okay, Buddy, might as well get up, face the day."

The big dog gazed at Jack with soulful brown eyes as if he reluctantly agreed.

• • • • •

Emerging from the shower, Jack heard his phone ring. He figured it was his mother, so he let it go to voicemail. Undoubtedly wanted him to come over for lunch before the ordeal that awaited him. He finished toweling off, threw on sweats and an old sweater, fed Boone, and brewed a pot of coffee.

He sat at his small round kitchen table and scarfed down a couple dry muffins from the corner bakery. After carrying his mug of coffee to the living room, he sank into the leather sofa and checked his phone. Of course, his mother had called. Forced himself to call back.

"What took you so long to call?" Maureen Bailey chirped.

"Caught me in the shower, Ma. What's up?"

"You know what's up, Jacky. Are you coming for lunch? Tommy and Jenny'll probably be here."

Earlier, Jack decided to pass on lunch, but if his sister and brother were there, he wouldn't be stuck alone with his mother.

"I dunno. Got a lot to do. They going to the cemetery?"

"Just talked to Tommy yesterday, and he's going. I'll call Jenny now and see about her."

"Okay. Guess I'll see you around eleven thirty?"

"No, that's too late. Come at eleven. I'll tell the others." Maureen took a breath. "Actually I should make a brunch since it's a little early. I could cook bacon and maybe some pancakes—"

"For god's sake, Ma, give it a rest. Just a baloney sandwich, who cares?"

"Don't get fresh, Jacky. I'll make what I want to. You just get here at eleven. Bye."

Jack sighed and hung up. The woman was George Castanza's mother.

Boone whimpered when Jack rose and returned to the kitchen. "Come on, guy, let's go for a walk."

The sun poked out behind puffy clouds in a sky of powder blue. The air felt cool but comfortable. Perfect sweater weather for the end of March. Small patches of gray snow were scattered on the ground. Jack liked the older homes and tree-lined streets of the neighborhood. Had that small-town vibe. Didn't feel like part of Chicago. He took a deep breath. Felt energetic for a change, which amazed him. A sharp contrast from his usual gloom and doom.

Boone plodded along beside Jack, stopping to sniff the grass, bushes, fire hydrants, whatever was available. Birds tweeted like piccolos in a symphony. Several blocks later, the big dog slowed his pace.

"Okay, Buddy, let's head back." Too bad his life wasn't as great as the weather.

His phone buzzed as they approached his duplex. He stopped, read the screen, and tapped it on. "Yeah, Jenny." He led Boone up the sidewalk and listened to his sister tell him she'd be at their mother's for lunch. "See ya, gotta get Boone in, on a walk."

He punched off the phone, put it back in his pocket, and unlocked the front door. After unclasping the dog's collar, he tossed him a milk bone treat.

Jack couldn't wait for today to be over. Dreaded seeing Karen's parents. Her father, Stewart Buckley, wasn't too bad for a rich white guy, but the mother was a different story. How Karen turned out so nice was beyond him. For the umpteenth time, he thought, 'Why did I leave Texas?'

Chapter 15

By 12:30 Maureen's lunch was over. Tommy offered to drive his silver Chrysler Pacifica since it was comfortable for four people. They headed out of Bridgeport toward I-90 and exited north for the twenty-minute drive to Park Ridge. Maureen sat in front with Tommy, Jack and Jenny in back.

"Smooth ride, Tommy." Jack leaned back in his seat. "Lots of leg room."

"Yeah, gets good gas mileage for a bigger car. How's your Beemer holding up? That thing's gettin' old."

"Runs like a top." Jack turned to Jenny who was gazing out the window. "Glad to hear Nolan's going to law school. Getting into Loyola, smart kid. Runs in the family. Tell him congrats from his old uncle."

Jenny looked pleased, dark wavy hair framing her oval face. Her eyes were the same clear sapphire blue of the Bailey family. The only girl of five children, Jack once thought of her as a tattletale pest, but now he considered her a loyal friend.

"Come around more often, Jack— Nolan likes to see you."

"Yeah. Guess Cate's doing fine."

"She's been looking into colleges already. Maybe Loyola or Northwestern. Hoping for a scholarship."

Jack clenched his teeth. Elizabeth would be seventeen now as well, a junior in high school this fall. He forced himself to look out the window, gazing at stores and unadorned buildings of Chinatown to the east.

They drove without chatter past the outskirts of Lincoln Park. For once his mother wasn't yakking about the weather, local news, her

Mahjong group.

Several minutes later, Jack spotted the tops of distant buildings in downtown Chicago to the east. "That must be Sears Tower."

Tommy glanced out the window. "Willis Tower now."

"Yeah, keep forgetting."

Maureen scoffed. "It'll always be the Sears Tower to me. Don't know why they have to change the names of things. Like the White Sox Stadium will always be Comiskey Park. Now we're supposed to call it Cellular? That's just plain stupid, if you ask me."

Jenny laughed. "Nobody asked you, Mom, but they should."

Tommy shifted the visor. "Yup, Willis was the tallest building in the world, now second I think."

Maureen asked, "Well, what's the tallest then?"

Jack said, "The one in Dubai. Can't pronounce the damn thing."

Tommy said, "Starts with a B, Bunj Kalifa, something like that."

"Whatever." Jenny rolled her eyes. "We'll never get there."

"Your kids might." Jack said. "We sound like a Seinfeld conversation."

Jenny laughed. "Who played George's mother, can never remember."

"Dunno," Jack said, "Ma was gonna audition for the part, but she never got past central casting. Scared off the guy when—"

"That's enough, smarty pants." Maureen turned to face Jack. "I'll have you know I could've doubled for Maureen O'Hara in those days. I was named after her, and I always—"

"Really? We never heard that before." Jenny patted her mother's shoulder. "Shouldn't she be dead by now?"

"Jennifer, don't be smart like your brothers. Of course she isn't dead. She's my age. No surprise we're both alive in 2012."

Tommy snickered. "Yeah, you were born the same year, that's why you were named after her. Didn't know O'Hara was a famous baby actress."

"You can all just go jump in the lake. I get no respect around here. Especially on today, Jacky."

"Oh, Mom, Karen would have a good laugh along with us." Jenny looked at Jack.

"I think so, Ma," he said. "She'd rather we're happy than a bunch of sad sacks."

They were quiet for awhile. Signs for O'Hare Airport popped up west of the freeway as they approached exits for Park Ridge. Jack's stomach wrenched at the sight of the familiar area he'd rather forget.

Five minutes later they wound through neighborhood streets shaded by large maple and oak trees, elaborate two-story brick homes set back from the street. Slowing down, they entered the landscaped grounds of Cooney Funeral Home's vast cemetery. The older section, housing the graves of Karen's relatives, was bordered by large green shrubs and trees. Flat landscape turned into small grassy hills, narrow roads curved around various-sized gravestones.

Tommy's car crawled along until it reached a cluster of several tall pine and fir trees. He parked behind a silver Phantom Rolls Royce gleaming in the sun.

"Looks like 'ol Stewart sprung for a new Rolls," said Tommy emerging from his car with his family.

"Yeah, looks like a 2012, not the wreck of the used '08 he had last year." Jack never saw the appeal of Rolls, with their boxy-looking hoods, but Karen's father had driven a Rolls forever, according to her. Jack referred to the ostentatious Spirit of Ecstasy hood ornaments as the Flying Nuns. His used Beemer surpassed the Rolls in looks, no question.

The fresh air smelled of pine under a cloudless Wedgewood sky; birds sang of spring's arrival. Maureen glanced at the treetops. "What a beautiful day. Just perfect for Karen."

The rest murmured in agreement and meandered around marble markers to join three people standing near two headstones of pale lavender splashed with black.

A thin older woman in a charcoal pantsuit held out her arms to Maureen. They gave one another a stiff, awkward hug. "Oh, Maureen, it's been too long since I've seen you."

Maureen's smile looked forced. She smoothed her short bottle-fed hair. "Hi, Beth. Good to see you."

Beth Buckley greeted the others, while her husband Stewart and daughter Laura waited their turn to say hello. Karen's family had that rich, useless look about them, a line Jack thought of from a Julia Roberts movie. Beth looked like she just stepped out of the spa, with a new haircut, highlights, blow-dry, mani, pedi, and Lord knows what else.

Laura's long straight hair was highlighted like her mother's. Wearing a beige silk pants outfit, she bore a slight resemblance to Karen. They had the same auburn hair, and Jack wondered why Laura ruined it with blond streaks. She smiled and touched Jack's arm, then gave him a quick hug.

"Good to see you, Jack. Wish we could meet in other circumstances."

"I know. Glad you could make it. How are things in Denver?"

"Good, Dan and kids doing fine." Laura turned to say hi to Jenny.

Jack shook hands with Stewart, whose smile showcased white teeth and matching hair. In his cotton polo shirt and khakis, he looked like he just stepped off the Mayflower with a desirable tee time awaiting him.

Beth placed her usual floral arrangements of white and yellow roses by the gravestones; white for Karen, yellow for Elizabeth. Jack never brought flowers except when he came alone on their anniversary.

Reading the inscriptions on the markers was never easy for Jack. Karen's stone with angels in bas relief on either side of the epitaph:

KAREN ELIZABETH BAILEY
Beloved Daughter, Wife, Mother
March 28, 1962 – August 15, 2000

A smaller gravestone in the same shiny black and lavender sat next to Karen's. Above the inscription a marble cherub depicted a child with long hair and flowing dress. Jack forced himself to read the words remembering his daughter:

ELIZABETH MAUREEN BAILEY
Beloved Daughter, Granddaughter, Niece
August 31, 1995 – August 15, 2000

Songbirds mocked Jack's sorrow. The group was silent by the graves, then some began to wander among other markers. Now and then he caught a trace of subtle floral perfume from Beth or Laura, maybe both. Who cared. He noticed the grass, green and lush. Why did cemeteries appear well-maintained and landscaped? Their residents didn't know the difference. People spend big bucks on the dead so they'll feel better about themselves.

Hard to imagine what Karen would look like at age fifty, and Elizabeth, seventeen. Maureen's voice interrupted his thoughts. "Beth says we can go to her house when we're ready. We'll leave you here for a minute, Jacky. Take your time."

He always hated this part of the ritual, when they left him at the graves, assuming he'd want to be alone with Karen and his daughter. He figured he had to man up and do it. A soft breeze soothed his face; he wanted to talk to those he still loved, but the lump in his throat damn near choked him. Times like this, grief ate him alive. Would it ever get better? Highly doubtful.

Chapter 16

As along as he could remember, Donald Sowder knew he was different. Maybe it was his small frame. Maybe his dad yelling at him for striking out in Little League. Maybe his classmates calling him 'Little Donny Sowder Puss'. Pound someone into the ground long enough, he becomes weak. Vulnerable. Just ripe for the picking. Ripe for the eminent Father. Then it happens. But it remained buried in Donald's mind. He willed himself to live in the present, stay out of the past. Concentrate on today. Now. In his crappy apartment.

After devouring a breakfast of fried eggs and toast, Donald carried his dishes to the sink and poured a second mug of coffee. Bitter, strong odor filled his sinuses. He inhaled deeply and trudged into his lifeless living room and sank into the shabby sofa. Gulping coffee, he placed the cup on a worn end table, reached for the remote, changed his mind, and replaced it on the armrest. The gray walls were barren. The matching tan couch and chair, threadbare and stained, should be tossed out, but Donald hated the thought of replacing them. Too much time and energy. Besides, who cared. No one ever visited.

He slouched back and looked straight ahead toward nothing. At least it was Saturday, and he could escape his tedious job and tiresome co-workers. His boss, a major headache as well, forever explained directions as if Donald didn't understand the first three times.

Rising from the sofa, he then wandered to the window, pulled open the drapes, and gazed out. Looked like a nice day. Guess he should visit his mother. Sure dreaded that. Diagnosed with early Alzheimer's, she was stuck in a nursing facility, thanks to his father.

She wasn't missing in action yet, but he didn't want to deal with her. Cramped the old man's style of bowling and drinking beer with his cronies. Lucky for him a buddy knew that Goldpine Home was affordable and a decent place compared to other warehouses for the elderly.

After pouring himself a second cup of coffee, Donald sat at the rickety kitchen table. His thoughts wandered back to last Tuesday. The nun's funeral had gone without a hitch. Confident he had blended into the woodwork, he surprised himself by joining his fellow mourners in their walk to the altar to receive communion. He'd gazed straight into the priest's eyes when he offered the Eucharist. *I'm not in a state of grace, Father. A mortal sin. If I burn in hell, I know another of your brethren who will be right beside me.*

Earlier when Donald entered the church, the smell of candle wax and incense made his stomach turn. Taken aback by the large number of people, he slipped into a pew and sat beside two elderly men, one resting a hand atop a cane leaning against the seat. Donald halfway greeted the old gent and bowed his head in mock prayer. Seconds later, he glanced around at the congregation and was surprised to see many middle-aged and young people. Guess Sister Anne was well-loved by everyone she met. If they only knew.

Donald was not about to attend the reception and lunch after the service; didn't want to push his luck remaining anonymous. Heading for the front door, he kept an eye out for anyone who looked like a cop working the case, who thought killers show up at their victims' funerals. Good luck with that. He'd glanced at a tall guy who looked like an actor from a TV show or somewhere, couldn't place the name. Everyone else looked ordinary. No worries. Donald could keep one step ahead of the police. They weren't as smart as he.

A white-haired usher by the door, reminded people of the reception. Donald pointed to his watch, shook his head. He'd had enough holy bullshit that morning to last him forever.

• • • • •

Donald blinked himself into the here and now, drained his lukewarm coffee, and wondered how to fill his day. He'd wait until tomorrow afternoon to visit his mother since she attended chapel services on Sunday mornings. She didn't realize the non-denominational worship wasn't Catholic. Guess Alzheimer's kept her happy in that regard.

An hour later, he drove his gray beat-up Toyota northeast on I-55. He'd decided to wander around Oz Park since it was sunny with temps in the sixties. Located in Lincoln Park area, Oz was built in honor of Frank Baum, who wrote the classic novel while living in Lincoln Park in the late 1800's.

Fascinated by the book and movie as a young boy, Donald visited the park several times a year, admiring the towering life-like sculptures of Dorothy and her friends placed amongst winding paths shaded by maple trees and deep-colored foliage. Maybe those pink flowers, whatever they were called, would be in bloom.

After fifteen minutes, he exited onto I-90 and headed north. About seven miles later, he turned onto 64 and meandered through tree-lined residential neighborhoods until he reached Webster Street and found a decent parking place in the main lot. Donald got out of the car and made his way toward the central path, ambling toward whatever lay ahead. Dressed in a long-sleeved tan shirt and jeans, he felt comfortable and invisible.

A small boy walking ahead with his parents turned to admire a poodle sporting a purple leash, strolling with its owner. The kid wore thick glasses, striking a painful chord in Donald. He usually ignored children, but the boy reminded him of how he'd looked in grade school. He could still hear the taunts: *Hey, Buddy Holly, like your glasses with mason jar lenses.* Ha ha. Clever assholes. Maybe he should go after them next, after scraping pedophile scum off the earth. Doing the Lord's work, he was. He knew the Bible verse by heart for his next undertaking, no pun intended.

Chapter 17

After suffering through an hour of dessert and small talk at the Buckleys', Jack leaned back in his seat as Tommy drove home. Thank god the graveside visit was over for another year.

Maureen turned around in the front seat. "Well, Jacky, that wasn't so bad was it?"

He sighed. "No, Ma. Loved every minute. Like when you spilled your coffee on prissy old Beth's white tablecloth."

"Ha. That woman poured too much in my cup. On purpose, you can bet. Always has to have the upper hand. Another way of showing she's above me."

Tommy laughed. "Yeah, she was above you, Ma. Standing right over you pouring coffee."

"Very funny. I have such clever children." Maureen sat straight in her seat.

Jenny said, "So you're sure it was a Freudian slip of the hand?"

Everyone chortled except Maureen. "I don't know why I bother with you kids. Next year you can go by yourself, Jacky. I don't need Beth Buckley in her fancy house and fancy neighborhood. How her husband and daughter put up with her, I'll never know."

"Guess I should thank you all for going with me," Jack said. "I'll bring you back next year except for Ma."

Maureen harrumphed. "Fine with me. Don't see why she had to show off and serve that truffle. You'd think— "

"Trifle, Mom, trifle." Jenny touched her mother's shoulder.

Jack added, "She didn't serve us fungus, Ma." More chuckling.

"Quit laughing at your poor mother. How did I raise such smart alecks?"

Tommy glanced at Maureen. "Ma, truffles are like French mushrooms, some kind of fungus. High-end restaurants serve them."

"Truffles are fancy chocolates too, Mom," Jenny said. "Easy to get mixed up."

"Okay, enough." Maureen paused. "Jacky, did I tell you about the box of your father's I found? Tommy looked through it, so it's your turn now. Thought you boys might want some of the stuff in there. I'll give it to you when we get home."

"What's in the box?" Jack asked.

"Looks like a bunch of papers and pamphlets from the war. Never saw it before till I was in the basement looking for an old postcard from my aunt. Looked high and low for it, and found this box way back behind where the old coal bin used to be. Anyway, I— "

"Okay, Ma, I'll look at it." He doubted he'd want anything from his old man's box of junk, but he'd humor his mother, take it home, keep it a week, then give it back. Didn't want more clutter in his house.

• • • • •

The rest of the weekend dragged its weary feet. Sunday evening Jack looked at the battered-looking cardboard box Maureen had foisted on him yesterday. The box, on the kitchen floor by the back door, emitted a musty odor which hung in the air. He sighed and decided to tackle it tomorrow. No doubt boring military documents. No hurry.

• • • • •

The next morning, Jack ran into Gary Calvin walking into the station.

"Bailey, you're here early. What's the occasion?"

"Nah, my usual time, you're the one half an hour late."

"Whaa— " Calvin stopped and glanced at his watch.

"Gotcha!"

"Don't confuse the guy who does you favors." Calvin held the door open for Jack, and they walked into the bull pen. "By the way, heard they found a body last night."

"Hell no. How did you find out already?" Last thing he needed was another murder. Jack shrugged out of his windbreaker and hung it on the coatrack. He followed Calvin to his desk. Sounds of clacking keyboards filled the air. The cop sitting nearby used too much musk aftershave. Jack resisted the temptation to enlighten the guy.

"How soon you forget, Bailey. I know what's going on before dispatch does." He booted up his computer. "That's why they call me president of the geek squad."

Jack didn't know if he was serious or flinging the bull. "That ain't all they call ya, but you don't wanna know."

Calvin cleared his throat. "Everybody likes me, if nothing else, for my shirts." He puffed out his chest. "Just got this yesterday."

Jack leaned in to read the red shirt's black printed words: *If you need Help, just Ask.* Underneath in smaller letters: *Someone else.*

Jack groaned. "Who makes up those lame ass sayings? Sixth graders?"

"I thought you wanted to hear about the murder." He glanced around at cops milling about talking and drinking coffee. "Between you and me it's not your Bible verse guy."

"Let me guess. No Bible verse with the body."

"Elementary, dear Bailey. Scene doesn't fit the MO of your killer. Other vics weren't shot. Anyway, outta our district. North Lawndale called it in, so no worries."

Jack stood. "Now ya tell me. Had me goin' for a minute. Catch ya later."

He reached his desk and grabbed his discolored coffee mug, when Daisy LePere sidled up to him. He got a whiff of her rose perfume. Couldn't stand the stuff.

"Sarge. Just off to get coffee." He knew he was trapped.

"Ms. LePere, Bailey." She wore a pale blue silk blouse under her black pinstriped jacket. Her blond hair pulled back in a knot. "You may be interested to hear there's another murder victim. Happened last night."

"Heard already. Glad it's not in our territory."

She looked taken aback. "How do you know that?" Her blue eyes blazed.

"I have my sources." He gave a half smile. "But I never reveal them."

"Lose the smart ass attitude, Bailey. You may find it interesting that the victim was a minister at a Congregational church in North Lawndale. But no Bible verse found, so it doesn't sound like your perp."

Jack told himself not to scoff. "Gee, Sarge, you'd give Sherlock a run for his money. Now if that's all of your fascinating deductions, I'll get— "

"Bailey, I'm this far from writing you up. I've already talked to Nesbitt about your attitude."

Jack knew Captain Chub Nesbitt didn't give a rat's ass if Jack called the sergeant 'Sarge' or not. Daisy LePere was the person bothered; the woman was a ball-buster and out to get any man who stood up to her.

Jack nodded. "Anything else?"

She ignored the question. "Yes, Bailey. Do you have a brilliant theory on why someone would murder a pastor?"

"Maybe he didn't like the sermon." Jack shrugged.

"Not funny." She turned to leave when Sherk arrived at his desk. He looked at LePere and nodded. "Good morning."

She glanced at her phone. "You're late, Sherkenbach."

Jack glowered. "Didn't know we had to punch in."

"No, but maybe we should think about installing a time clock for the rank and file."

"Sorry," Sherk said. "One of those mornings." He reached for his coffee mug.

"Just don't make a habit of it." LePere stomped away.

"Aye aye, Captain Bligh," Jack muttered.

She turned and faced Jack. "Excuse me, I didn't hear that."

"Nothing, just hoping they'd have donuts today," Jack said, and watched her march away. "Let's get coffee, Sherk. Looks like you could use some." He studied his partner. "You look like shit. What's up?"

Sherk stood and followed Jack toward the break room. "Didn't get much sleep last night."

"Why not?" Jack wasn't used to seeing him tired and down in the mouth.

"Nothing."

They filled their mugs and helped themselves to cardboard-looking sugar cookies. When they returned to their desks, Jack said, "Don't wanna pry, but you're not your usual cheerful annoying self. Juss sayin'."

"I suppose I have to tell you sometime." He stared at his cookies.

"Is it Erica?" Jack recalled Sherk mentioned his wife wasn't feeling well lately.

A patrol cop wandered over and interrupted with a question. "Anything new on the Bible thumper case?"

"Nothing new," Sherk answered. "We have some ideas, but no progress at the moment."

The cop shook his head. "Too bad. Hear about the vic from last night?"

Annoyed by the intrusion, Jack turned to his computer and clicked on his keyboard, hoping the guy would get lost. "We'll keep you posted."

"Right." The cop sauntered away.

Jack quit typing and looked at his partner. "Well?"

Sherk glanced behind him. No one there. "We got some bad news yesterday. Erica has—" He cleared his throat. Jack said nothing. "She's diagnosed with—" His phone buzzed.

Jack's jaw clutched in irritation as Sherk read the screen. "Gotta take this."

Jack waited while his partner carried on a one-syllable conversation. Looking haggard, Sherk hung up. "That was Erica. She heard about the next appointment already." His vacant eyes stared straight ahead. "Awfully early for the nurse to call."

Jack felt a pit in his middle. "Jesus, what is it?" Sherk's face turned gray. His hand shook as he lifted his mug and took a sip of coffee.

Looking at Jack, he pushed his hair from his forehead. "Ovarian cancer."

"Oh, Christ, Sherk. Sorry." He couldn't think of anything else to say.

"I'll tell you more later. Not telling anyone else yet. Still a shock even though we knew it might happen."

"I gotcha. Mum's the word." Jack remembered his mother talking about a relative with what they called female-type cancer, but he knew nothing about it. Never been interested in medical stuff; he was forced to hear too much disease information when his father died of lung cancer years ago.

Sherk stood. "I need more coffee."

Jack watched his partner shuffle away, head down.

• • • • •

By eleven o'clock Jack neared the end of his paperwork. He perused the student lists from Nativity of Our Lord school from 1973 through 1975. Father Daniel McGarvey was the priest during that time when Sister Anne Celeste taught fifth and sixth grades. Allegations against McGarvey were never proven, but he was reassigned to a parish in Indiana within several months.

Sherk looked up from his desk. "I'm done with my perp search. Shouldn't take long to question Bruce Welton's uncle in Naperville. How about an early lunch, and then we can visit the uncle."

Jack stood and stretched. "Yeah. The school list can wait. Naperville about an hour from here?"

"Not much longer. I could use the drive."

"Okay, we're outta here." Good to get away for awhile. Maybe Sherk needed to talk.

They made their way to the coatrack and pulled on their jackets. Velda Vatava approached them. "Trying to make a quick get away, Bailey?" Her brown pants outfit failed to camouflage her stout figure.

"Damn. Almost made it." Jack eyed the stack of file folders she carried. "That better not be for us, cuz we ain't stayin'."

Velda looked at Sherk. "How did a nice guy like you get stuck with him?"

Sherk gave a half smile and shrugged.

She studied him. "Why the long— "

She glanced at Jack, who noisily cleared his throat. He frowned at Velda and shook his head.

Nodding, she said, "Well, gotta go. See ya later." She smiled and strolled away.

Several cops milled about, some heading out the door. Jack and Sherk walked down the hall toward the side door to the parking lot. Outside, the air was nippy; the sun tucked away behind billowy gray clouds.

"I'll drive," Jack said, and unlocked a cruiser. "You got the contact info for Welton's uncle?"

"I do." Sherk climbed into the passenger seat. "I think it's better not to call him first; he should either be at home or work. Let's head out and stop for lunch on the way."

Jack agreed. Usually it was better not to notify possible witnesses or suspects beforehand. Get a truer picture when they don't have time to prepare.

Driving to Thirty-first Street, Jack turned left and exited onto I-55 west toward Naperville. He punched in the address of Home Depot where Bruce Welton's uncle worked.

"May be a waste of time talkin' to this guy. What's his name?" Jack asked.

"Paul Welton. I'm curious how he finagled getting Bruce the Home Depot job. Hard for registered sex offenders to find employment."

"Thank god for that." Jack slowed down for construction signs. "Worst part of the job."

"What's that?"

"Going after perps who do us all a favor by bumping off scum like Welton, not to mention drug lords, gang bangers, on and on."

"It's hard to do sometimes. When my cousin was a resident at Cook County—got awakened at all hours for gunshot vics and wounded junkies off the street."

"Yeah, been thinking a lot lately. Don't know how long I'm gonna last at this job."

"Jack, you say that every week. I wonder what lies ahead for my family."

"I'm sure once you know more—" Jack let his voice trail off.

"We have an appointment with the oncologist tomorrow to discuss Erica's treatment." Sherk brushed his hair from his forehead. "I haven't had time to request a half day."

"Don't worry, I'll cover for ya. Won't let LePere get wind of it."

Sherk sighed. "I'll have to tell her sometime."

"Not necessarily. I got a plan."

Chapter 18

"I'm sure you have a plan, Jack." Sherk sighed. "I'm listening."

"Don't tell the old bag. Go to the cap. He'll be cool with it, won't go through the paperwork bullshit."

"I don't know about going over her head." Sherk turned to face Jack. "Isn't that against regulations?"

"Maybe in a bigger department, but we're a small division. Tommy worked under Nesbitt back in the day, and he said to take all the time he needed when our old man got sick. Besides, LePere doesn't have the balls to argue with her boss."

Sherk sighed again. "Maybe so. I'll give it some thought and deal with it later today."

They rode without talking, passing gray concrete buildings, shopping centers, truck stops, and signs to Midway Airport. Jack yawned. "See any place for lunch?"

"Not yet. Getting hungry?"

"Always hungry, you know that." Jack wondered if Sherk had an appetite. He remembered after Karen—don't go there. He told himself to stay in the present.

Twenty minutes later, Jack exited onto I-355 and drove north into Naperville. He spotted a Jolly Roger's Kitchen in a shopping center. "Roger's okay? Got good burgers."

"That's fine." Sherk's voice flat.

• • • • •

An hour later, they parked in front of the Home Depot on Seventy-fifth Street. A Walmart Supercenter sat across a vast commercial area along with a Costco, Marshall's, and several shoe stores. Plenty of parking available at this hour. Jack wondered how they all stayed in business.

"Everything's getting too big," he grumbled as he climbed out of the car. He'd always detested malls and anything larger than the corner mom and pop store of his childhood.

Automatic doors welcomed them into the store where a young Indian man in the ubiquitous orange Home Depot vest directed them to Paul Welton's office. The door was open, and a middle aged bald man sat at a cluttered desk in a small, sparsely furnished room.

"Paul Welton?" Jack held out his badge.

Concern flashed on Welton's face as he stood. "Yes?"

"I'm Detective Bailey, Bridgeport PD. This is my partner, Detective Sherkenbach."

Sherk showed his badge. "Mr. Welton, we're here to ask you a few questions about your nephew, Bruce."

Welton indicated two chairs across his desk. After the three men were seated, Jack said, "Mr. Welton— "

The man rose and closed the door. "Paul," he stuttered. "Call me Paul."

Jack ignored the request. "I'll get straight to the point. We know you've been informed of the cause of death of your nephew, and we need to know who his friends were, anyone he hung out with."

Welton's eyes darted between the two men. "Well, ah, I'm afraid I can't help much. Didn't know of any friends, just family, a couple cousins here and there, you know how it is."

"No, I don't." Jack gazed at him. "Suppose you tell me."

Welton cleared his throat. "Oh, well, when we'd get together for holidays, the cousins would all come. Don't know if they still hung out, you know, stayed in touch."

"Paul," Sherk said softly. "We talked to your mother, Louise, in Florida. She didn't seem to know Bruce was on the sex registry list."

Welton flinched. "Yeah, I mean, no, she doesn't know. It would kill her, her own flesh and blood doing that." He shook his head as if in apology.

Sherk took out his notebook and pen. "We won't address the family saga here. We would like to know, however, how you were able to arrange for Bruce's job."

Jack continued to gaze at Welton, who smoothed his shiny pate several times with the palm of his hand. He shrugged. "Okay, the HR guy in the regional office is an old friend. I came clean about Bruce and he arranged it so there wouldn't be anything on record."

Jack said, "That's a pretty big favor from your old friend."

"It certainly is," Sherk added. "Could get this old friend in considerable difficulty."

Welton's eyes glanced everywhere but on the detectives. Beads of sweat dotted his forehead. He pulled a wadded Kleenex from his shirt pocket and dried his face. "Look, guys, can this be off the record?"

"I'll give you a probably," Jack said. "Our job is to find your nephew's killer."

Welton nodded, visibly relieved. "Okay, my friend owed me one from years ago. I covered for him in ah, a situation. I figured we could bend the law a little, give Bruce a second chance to get it together."

Jack felt his blood pressure rising.

"I see" Sherk said. "The problem, Paul, is that— "

"Pedophiles don't get cured." Jack rose. "They're sick fucks who are a menace to society and should be permanently— "

"I think we're finished here." Sherk pushed in his chair. "We need you to write the names of Bruce's cousins you mentioned and anyone else you can think of with whom he was acquainted."

Welton's look of shock turned indignant. "I think you're out of line, Detective Bailey. You aren't allowed to talk to— "

"You listen to me, ass—" Jack leaned toward the man.

"Jack!" Sherk seized his partner's arm and pushed him to the door. "Wait outside."

Grumbling and mumbling curses, Jack shoved against the door, turned the knob, walked out, slammed the door shut. He stormed down several aisles, nearly knocking an elderly lady off her feet.

"Well, excuse you," she hissed as Jack kept tramping his way out the front doors.

He reached the cruiser and stood by the side door, panting. Deep breaths. Deep breaths. He held his temples with his hands.

"Oh god. What just happened?" he said aloud.

After unlocking the door, Jack slid into the driver's seat. Shaky, he slouched forward and rested his head on his hands atop the wheel. Closing his eyes, he continued to take deep breaths. Was his short fuse a foreboding sign of his PTSD creeping back? He'd had his share of that several years ago. Couldn't face calling a shrink again.

He heard the passenger door open. "Jack, what the hell happened in there?" Sherk climbed in. "I don't know whether to be concerned or angry."

"Be pissed, Sherk." Jack sat straight in his seat. "Tell me to get my shit together or get out."

"I thought you were doing better keeping your anger in check in the public eye." Sherk buckled his seat belt. "Where did that rage come from?"

"Always the shrink, aren't ya?" Jack shot back as he fired up the engine. "Sorry. Don't know what happened any more than you do. Thinking about these perverts, guess it reminds me of— "

"Of what they do to children like your daughter?"

Jack jerked his head toward Sherk. "Don't try—hell, Sherk. Here I am going down the toilet when you're the one with— "

"No one's free from life's adversities, Jack. They come at different times."

"I guess," Jack said and steered out of the parking lot onto Seventy-fifth Street east toward I-355. They passed a Lutheran church with a sign in front beckoning worshippers to visit their services. He read the sign aloud. "Betrayal Kissed a Guiltless Man."

He gave a half groan. "What the hell does that mean?"

Sherk sighed. "Yesterday was Palm Sunday."

"Yeah. So what?"

"I'm sure you remember that Judas betrayed Christ to the chief scribes who turned him over to Pontius Pilate."

"Guess it rings a bell, but the sign doesn't make sense."

Sherk looked out the window. "It does, but I'll explain it another time."

Just as well. Jack didn't give a damn. Why did he bring it up? They rode in silence until they crossed H-294. Jack thought about Paul Welton. "It's pretty certain Welton won't report me for police aggression or bullshit like that, not that I give a damn. We have him by the balls with his job scamming for his nephew. No help with the nephew's pals. Let's chuck him off the case list."

"I agree. In this instance, best to let sleeping dogs rest."

"Lay," Jack said.

"Pardon?"

"Lay. It's 'let sleeping dogs lay.'"

"Oh." Sherk scratched his chin. "In that case, wouldn't it be 'lie'?"

"You're killin' me, dude. Let's just drive."

Sherk chuckled. "You're a good diversion."

"Glad I'm good for something." Jack liked hearing his partner laugh. Even a little.

• • • • •

By the time they arrived at the station the afternoon was drawing to a welcome close. Jack was ready to head out. He'd take the list of Catholic school students home and work it tonight with a couple bottles of brew, Boone snoozing at his feet. He told Sherk his plan to leave early and suggested his partner do the same.

Sherk shuffled papers. "I've been thinking about your suggestion of asking Chub Nesbitt for time off rather than Miss Daisy. Think I'll do just that. Maybe tell her in a day or whenever."

Jack gathered printouts on his desk and put them in a file folder. "Good decision. See ya tomorrow." He began to walk off, then turned to Sherk. "I'm ah, not good at talking about stuff like this—what you're going through. No surprise at that. But give me a call any time ya wanna vent, cuss, drink, whatever." He cleared his throat.

"I know, Jack. But thanks for saying it." He smiled, looked at Jack's file. "How many boys are on the student list?"

"Forty. That narrows it down. Gonna ask Calvin to do a search on each one, but I'll get started tonight." He turned. "See ya tomorrow and good luck with Nesbitt."

Ten minutes later when Jack unlocked the front door to his duplex, Boone trotted over, sniffed, and looked up at him. "Hey, Buddy. Doin' okay?" The dog no longer barked and jumped up on Jack, but seemed happy and healthy.

Jack tossed his jacket on a chair and he and Boone headed for the kitchen. "Wanna go out?" Dumb question. The big hound ambled into the back yard, took a pee under a birch tree, and sniffed around several elderberry shrubs.

Leaving the door ajar for Boone, Jack opened the pantry door and took out a bottle of Guinness. In a perfect world, he'd drink the brew after half an hour of refrigeration for the correct temperature. But when were things ever perfect?

A stale, musty odor hung in the air from the old cardboard box in the corner. "Crap. Guess I should open that sooner or later."

After a dinner of frozen sausage pizza and another Guinness, Jack wasn't in the mood to tackle the file he'd brought home. He glanced at the box, thought he'd take a quick look and return it to his mother this week. Sitting on the kitchen chair, he shuffled himself over to the box, bent down, and opened it. The same stuffy, dank smell hit his nostrils.

Several yellowed newspapers lay on top, two in German, one announcing the Allied victory on May 8, 1945. Another's English headline read *Operation Elephant Victory*. Jack thought these were worth saving; maybe Tommy's kids would want them. Show their history teachers. Impress the hell outta them. Fat chance.

He rifled though more papers and pamphlets, including a booklet titled *War Department Basic Field Manual*. Leafing through its pages, he nearly missed a thin white envelope postmarked Munchen 7.46.4, addressed to Mr. John Bailey with his Bridgeport address. The handwriting was flowery, like calligraphy. Puzzled, Jack opened it and read the single page. He looked up slowly, staring at the wall. "Holy shit!"

Chapter 19

Boone whimpered and looked at Jack as if to ask what the problem was. The dog rose from the floor and put his snout on Jack's lap. He ruffled the big mutt's neck while grasping the letter. Aware of his pounding heart, Jack felt like he'd slipped into another world. Hadn't thought much about his old man for several years when Jack's shrink brought up a connection between his PTSD symptoms and his father's post war conduct. Hard to forget John Bailey's drinking, temper, not to mention yelling at his kids and worse.

But this? A woman? Guess he got himself a wartime affair. Jack's mother couldn't have known. Barely looked in the box, since she didn't know it had been stashed in the old coal bin in the basement.

"Gotta call Tommy," Jack told Boone. "Wonder if he saw it."

After inhaling a deep breath, he punched in his brother's number and turned on speaker mode.

"Hey, Jack, what's up?"

"That's what I'd like to know," Jack answered. "Ma said you pawed through that old box already, right?"

Silence. "Yeah."

"Find anything interesting? I mean, really interesting?"

Pause. "So, you found it," Tommy said.

"Sure did. Whadda ya make of it?"

"Pretty clear to me, Jack. The old man found a freulein over there—after killing all the Krauts he could." Tommy's laugh bitter.

"Hell, talk about shell shocked—that's me. I need a drink." Jack reached for a fifth of Jameson from the kitchen cabinet and poured a shot into a glass. "Do ya think Ma knows?"

"I doubt it. She may've seen the old newspapers on top and

figured more junk inside. She has things like Pa's discharge papers, and other important stuff."

"I dunno, Tommy. She's smarter than she looks." Jack knocked back his whiskey. "I'll look up the translation online, but I got the gist of it."

Tommy waited to speak. "You don't think we should tell her?"

"God, no. Wouldn't help any. Just make things worse."

"Can't argue with that. The mysterious Miss or Mrs. Schroeder should be kept in the vault."

Jack held the letter and read the signature. "Fur immer und ewig, Ari." I know I butchered the German, but must mean love or something."

"I looked it up. It means always and forever. Had other meanings too, but that's the general idea."

"Always and forever," Jack repeated. "Someone said that about our old man? Her real name's on the envelope. Ariana Schroeder."

"Does the detective in you wanna track her down?" Tommy gave a half chuckle.

"Yeah, let's hop the next plane to Germany and find her. Bound to be dead by now."

Jack poured another shot. "Man, I gotta think about this. Still unreal. Let's meet at the pub tomorrow after work and talk more."

"Sure thing. See ya at Shinnick's at five-thirty? And bring the letter."

"No shit. Auf wiedersehn, Tommy." Jack hung up and drained his glass.

During the night he dreamed of D-Day, gunfire, his mother speaking German.

• • • • •

Jack awoke before his alarm buzzed and immediately the letter popped into his mind. How could a wartime romance have happened with his old man? Guess he'd never know. He told himself to focus on today. Save the mystery letter until he met Tommy at the pub.

After arriving at the station, Jack headed for Gary Calvin's desk. Uniformed cops and other staff members wandered in, greeting and talking amongst themselves. Keyboards sang in discordant harmony. Calvin hunched over his computer, his curly red hair in need of a comb.

"Got a job for ya, Calvin." Jack approached the geek's desk. "Shouldn't take long."

Calvin looked up from his screen. "Got a busy day, Bailey." He sat up in his chair to reveal the writing on his green shirt. "This message fits you every day."

Jack read the words, *Sarcasm is just one other service I offer*. He groaned. "Change that to sarcasm is the *only* service I offer."

Calvin smirked. "Clever, Bailey." He eyed the file in Jack's hand. "What crap you have in there?"

Jack tossed his file on the cluttered desk. "The list of kids from the nun's school when that priest had allegations against him. Figure the killer's gotta be one of those kids who grew up to ice the good Sister. About forty boys to analyze, Calvin. A breeze."

Calvin scoffed. "Maybe I can work it in. I'll focus on the guys who live in the nearby suburbs, then branch out. Could be the perp lives outta town. More likely in the area though."

"Brilliant deduction, Cavin. Brilliant. I'll put in a good word with LePere for ya."

"Fuck off, Bailey." Calvin turned to his monitor.

Jack walked to his desk, snatched his empty mug, and trudged to the break room. He smelled strong coffee and cinnamon as he entered the area. Good. Donuts. He waited until two cops helped themselves to the pastry, then nabbed two glazed ones in a napkin. One of the cops eyed Jack's booty. "One for Sherk," he told the guy.

"Yeah, right," the cop sneered and walked away.

When Jack returned with coffee and donuts, Sherk walked in looking hollow-eyed. His smile seemed forced. "Morning, Jack."

"Brought you a donut. Good ones gone already. Buncha vultures swiped the cinnamon."

Sherk took the donut. "Thanks. I'll get coffee."

"I'll follow ya. We can sit in there. I wanna hear how your talk with Nesbitt went."

After they sat at a small table near the wall, Sherk drank his coffee. "Very well. Good advice of yours to see the captain. He was sympathetic and told me to take all the time I need."

"Figured that's how he'd react. Anything about LePere?"

"No. He just said to tell you where I'd be. That's it." Sherk chewed his donut. "I need to leave about nine this morning for the oncologist appointment. I'll pick up Erica on the way. We'll go to the U. Med Center."

"Shouldn't take more than twenty minutes. Good you live close to the place." Located several miles north of Bridgeport, the University of Illinois Chicago Medical Center boasted hospitals and clinics of various specialties. Jack's family spent many hours at the complex visiting his father and other relatives over the years. If you had to get sick, couldn't beat the med center.

After they finished their donuts, the men returned to their desks. Going over the case, they decided there wasn't much more they could do until Calvin finished his search of former students. Sherk tidied his desktop and told Jack he may be gone the rest of the afternoon depending how long his appointment lasted.

"Take your time, Sherk. Don't bother coming back." Jack planned to tie up loose ends on paper work and take off early. Unlike crime shows and detective novels, cops don't spend all their time working a case if it comes to a standstill. They work other crimes like burglaries and drug possession until a break occurs on their main case. They're not dashing here and there like they do on TV. Nothing that exciting.

Later in the morning Jack's cell rang. The caller ID read M Winters. Didn't recognize the name, but he pressed on speaker. "Detective Bailey."

"Hello, Detective. It's Molly Winters."

Jack drew a blank. Then remembered. "Yes, Sister Anne's niece." His heart skipped a beat. "How are you?"

"I'm good. Just wondering if you've made more progress on the case. Our family is still shaken up by what happened to Aunt Anne."

"Of course." Jack took a deep breath. "We're investigating all we can. We'll notify you when we know something definite." He was sick of the same bullshit response, but stuck with it.

"Oh, I see." She sounded disappointed. "I'm sorry I disturbed you, but—"

"No, not at all. In fact, maybe we could meet sometime when I have more information for you." Jack told himself to hurry and figure a plan to see her.

Her voice perked up. "Yes, that would be great. I'd like that."

"Good. Oak Lawn isn't that far—"

"Actually, I work part time in Brighton Park. Archer and Forty-third. About fifteen minutes from you."

Was she purposely making this easy? Hoped so. "Okay. Lemme check my schedule." Jack glanced at his calendar. "Would tomorrow late afternoon work?"

"Sounds good. Can I text you later about time and place?"

"Sure." He was tongue-tied. "Ah, see ya tomorrow." His spirits rose. Hadn't felt like this since— nope, don't visit the past.

The day hurried by, thanks to Jack's buoyant mood. He couldn't believe his luck. A date with Molly Winters falling into his lap. A mere week since meeting Bonnie at the pub. Two women after a long dry spell. When it rains, and all that.

• • • • •

At 5:30, the mood in Shinnick's pub was low-key when Jack walked in. He spotted Tommy at the bar chatting with Charlie.

"Both Baileys. How can I be so lucky?" the rotund bartender said as Jack joined them.

"You're livin' right," Tommy said.

"Join your brother in a Guinness?" Charlie dried his pudgy hands on a towel around his ample belly.

"Sure thing. Mayor been in?" Jack sat on a bar stool.

"Both Daleys. Just left." Charlie worked at the pub when both Chicago mayors frequented the place. He kept their memory alive with long-time patrons.

After the beer arrived, Jack and Tommy made their way to a booth along the wall in an adjoining room with a couple customers sitting at a table.

After settling in, Jack gulped his brew and took the letter from his pocket.

"Still in shock?" Tommy asked. His dark hair was grayer and shorter than Jack's, but they shared the same piercing blue eyes.

"Yeah, I guess. Can't picture the old man gettin' it on with anyone. War must've changed him."

Tommy suppressed a smile. "People don't see their parents that way, like they're human, same as us."

Jack took another swig. "If we wanted, we can try and track her down, but she's gotta be dead by now. Still curious though. Who was Ariana Schroeder?"

"Yeah. I wonder too, but why would we want to find out? Not like we'd go over to Germany and meet her or her relatives. What good would that do anyone?"

They talked about their father's war experience, what they'd been told. He never spoke of those times, but an uncle told Jack and his siblings the worst time for John Bailey was when his Army division liberated Dachau. The horrors reached beyond what the prisoners had endured, and Jack harbored a subtle message of probable crimes committed by the Allies. Jack and Tommy remembered a distant, but angry father, quick with the 'switch' as they called his belt, which found its way to their backsides for childhood offenses that escalated with the amount of whiskey he drank.

"Yeah, remember how Ma used to cover for him," Tommy said. *"Don't upset your father. He's had a hard day on the streets.* She'd say that even after he made sergeant."

Jack shrugged and looked at the letter, written in German. He'd looked online for the translation. "Curious about her saying both she and Pa were damaged, and maybe he'd recover. But she'd never heal from what was broken inside of her. Whadya think, Tom?"

Chapter 20

Tommy shrugged. "Damned if I know. Talk about a dear John letter."

Jack drained his glass, shifted himself from the booth, and stood. "Be right back with a couple more pints."

An hour later Jack and Tommy decided not to search for Ariana Schroeder. Jack would keep the letter and return the box to their mother, telling her that Tommy planned to save the newspapers for his children. Their other siblings could go through the box and take whatever they wished.

"We'll keep the letter between the two of us. No sense in anyone else in the family knowing about the freulein." Jack guzzled the last of his beer. "Still not sure about Ma. Something nags at me. Maybe she found the letter and wants to see if we'll mention it."

Tommy took his jacket from the seat beside him. "Who knows. I gave up trying to figure her and Pa out years ago. Let's put it to rest."

They waved to Charlie on their way out. The air was crisp and breezy as they headed through the parking lot to their cars and into the night.

• • • • •

The next morning when Jack arrived at the station, two cops stood at Gary Calvin's desk deep in conversation. "Hey Bailey," Calvin called and motioned Jack to come over.

"Got somethin' good?" Jack said.

"Just whatcha wanted." Calvin held up a file. "Should be clear, even for you."

Jack ignored him, took the report, and left Calvin to yak with the other guys.

Sitting at his desk, Jack thought about Molly Winters. At least he had something to look forward to after work. He opened the file and hoped for something interesting, but was interrupted by a voice he'd grown to detest.

"Bailey, what's the latest on your case?" Daisy LePere stood above him, one hand on her hip.

"Sarge, good to see you too." Jack closed the file. "We're pursuing all possible leads at this time and will keep you informed." He spoke in a monotone, reciting the typical cop answer.

LePere pursed her lips, started to say something, then stopped. "Have you looked into anybody, people or groups, both victims had in common?"

Jack bit his tongue. "Yes, Ma'am. Nothing yet." The broad watched too many cop shows.

"Where's Sherkenbach?" She held up her watch. "Late again it seems."

"Fer god's sake, Sarge, it's not even eight-thirty. Now if you'll excuse me, some of us have work to do."

LePere eyes bore into him. "Bailey, where do you get off talking to me like that? One of these days you'll get reported for insubordination."

He stood abruptly and stared at her. "I quake with fear."

"Fine. You asked for it." She turned and stomped away. Jack caught a sniff of her sickly rose perfume.

Was he losing it? At the moment he didn't give a damn if he ended up on the hot seat.

He finished reading the file and seized his empty mug when Sherk walked in. He looked no better than yesterday, gaunt and stoop-shouldered.

Jack wondered about Sherk's appointment yesterday. "Look, I won't ask ya about the doctor's — "

"It's all right." Sherk fiddled with a pencil. "We got lots of information, and the oncologist was cautiously optimistic. We heard all the statistics, got overwhelming. Erica's cancer is stage four, which isn't good." He cleared his throat. "The chemo treatment will be aggressive. Starts Friday morning. I won't have to drive her every time. Her mom will come and help."

"That's good, but you take all the time you want, and if that ol' —"

"It's okay, Jack. Believe it or not, I can stand up for myself." Sherk smiled.

"I know, but I still— "

"It's fine. Don't worry about me."

But Jack did worry. Couldn't help himself. Sherk was too nice and people walked all over him if he wasn't careful. Once again, he thought his partner would've done better as a college professor.

"Got the file of students from Calvin." Jack slurped his coffee. "Twelve boys from the nun's classes now live in the area. Includes outlying suburbs like Evanston. Five of those fit the profile according to our friendly consultant, Daryl Gray."

Sherk raised his brow. "Interesting. How should we approach this?"

"Can't question them outright, like 'you fit the profile of a serial killer. Where were you when the vics were murdered?' We'll start with a 'measured approach', to quote my old officer training teacher."

"Sounds like a wise assessment."

"Let's start with the two guys who live closest to the crime scenes." Jack handed Sherk a sheet of paper from the file. "Here's your guy, I'll do this one." He put another page on his desk and began his search.

Jack doubted this whole bullshit process would amount to anything but a waste of time. His heart wasn't in the case. Never was. How could he be determined to collar a guy who wanted to get rid of pedophiles? According to online research, these scumbags didn't, couldn't recover. The best they could hope for was taking meds and staying away from kids. Fat chance of that. Like an alcoholic they have to walk the line. At least if a drunk falls off the wagon he usually doesn't abuse children and ruin their lives. Didn't have to be a shrink to know that.

Jack's cell signaled a text, and he welcomed the interruption.

Didn't recognize the number, but it turned out to be from Molly. She suggested they meet at the White Lion, a casual restaurant on Archer and Thirty-sixth at 5:30.

He returned the text with *see you then*. Good choice. Take less than half an hour to get there. They'd have a drink and maybe dinner.

The afternoon progressed at the pace of an iceberg. Would the day ever end?

Jack and Sherk finished searching the men on their list, and came up with zilch. No sore thumbs stuck out.

"Let's track down these guys," Jack said. "Tell 'em about Sister Anne, ask about their school days, mention the priest." The killer should to be one of the twelve boys on the list.

Sherk thought for a second. "Yes, but the guys will think it strange we're investigating them thirty years after knowing the Sister. They were just kids."

"Yeah, but we focus on the allegations against Father McGarvey. Should be able to read their reactions if they were abused. We can spot liars a mile away."

"Guess I agree. Should we start with your guy, Len Abbott? Alphabetical order."

"Sure. He's closest. We'll wait till morning." Jack stood and rearranged the clutter on his desk. "I'm outta here. Gonna meet someone."

Sherk nodded. "Sounds intriguing, but 'twere to consider too curiously, to consider so.'" Nice try, Sherk. I ain't gonna ask what that means, but I bet it's the bard doin' the talkin'."

"Very good, Jack. True, the quote is from *Hamlet* when he's speaking to—"

"See ya tomorrow." Jack hurried away. Didn't need a literary lecture now.

● ● ● ● ●

Twenty-five minutes later, Jack pulled into the side parking lot of the White Lion. He climbed out of the car, walked past a white stone-carved lion near the front and entered the restaurant. The dimly lit room was partitioned into two dining areas. He glanced around and told the hostess he'd wait for someone who was joining him. He knew Molly would ask about her aunt's murder. Wish he knew something definite.

After several minutes, the door opened and Molly walked in. She wore a long black and white striped knit jacket over black pants. A red print scarf looped around her neck.

"Hey," Jack said. He breathed in a scent of lavender. God, she looked good. Hot even.

She smoothed her straight hair behind an ear. "Hi, Detective."

"Jack," he said. Time for a name change

Nodding, she said. "And Molly."

They followed the hostess into the second room where Jack asked for a booth in the far corner. He was glad to see only a smattering of customers in the place.

Touching the small of her back, he guided Molly into the red leather seat. He felt a shiver and wanted to wriggle in beside her, but knew better.

A tall young waiter stopped by and filled their water glasses. "Something more to drink?"

Eager for a pint, Jack looked at Molly. "What will you have?"

"I'll live a little and have a Shirley Temple." She smiled at the waiter.

Surprised, Jack said, "Oh." No law against not drinking. "I'll have a Guinness."

After talking about the weather and traffic, Molly asked, "Can you tell me anything more about the case?"

Jack gazed at her, taking in her jade green eyes and creamy skin. "It's against regulations to talk about an ongoing investigation." He took a gulp of water. "But I could go out on a limb since you're not a suspect or a relative of one."

She gave a Mona Lisa smile. "Well, you know in my job as a paralegal, confidentiality is key. Plus, as a good Catholic girl, or former one, I wouldn't break a confidence."

The waiter brought their drinks and asked if they'd like to order something to eat. Jack shook his head. "Maybe later."

Molly stirred her rosy cocktail with a swizzle stick and held up her glass. "Here's to confidentiality."

Jack clinked his glass with hers. "Always."

She eased the maraschino cherry off the stick with her teeth, chewed sensuously and swallowed. God, the chemistry was palpable. He could take her right here on the damn table. Did she feel the same?

"Decided on dinner yet?" The waiter again. What a pest.

"I'll let you know." Jack gritted his teeth as the guy walked off.

Molly laughed. "I could eat something. How 'bout you?"

"Sure." Jack handed her a menu and opened his. Maybe this evening would work out after all.

Chapter 21

An hour later they'd finished dinner and debated ordering dessert.

"Their cheesecake is delicious, Jack, but I'm pretty full. How about coffee?"

"Works for me." He signaled the waiter, who ambled over and took their orders.

Molly straightened her scarf. "I don't want to pry, but how are you doing these days? I'd heard about what happened with your family in Ireland all those years ago. I hope you've—"

"Yeah, it's been twelve years now." Jack flinched. "I'll never get over it, but time helps cover the black hole." He wasn't used to speaking about his wife and child to anyone except family when they mentioned the subject. Molly seemed empathetic and he was comfortable with her concern.

"I suppose it helped you to move to Texas for a few years, but your mom must've missed you."

The waiter brought their coffee and two chocolate mints. "Thanks." Molly unwrapped her candy, held it to her nose, and breathed in its savory flavor.

"Yeah, Ma wanted me back here, and I got sick of the heat." Jack gulped his coffee. "After six years, I was ready to face the reminders again, thanks to a good shrink." He surprised himself at his candor, so unlike his usual closed-door policy.

"That's good, Jack. I'm all for therapy. God knows, I've had plenty myself."

"Oh? You seem pretty together to me, but— "

Molly laughed. "Thanks, but you don't know the real me. Before and after my divorce I got counseling, but some things aren't meant to be. Not to mention my weekly trips to AA."

"I see." Jack wished for a shot of Jameson to pour in his coffee. "Well, we're quite a pair, ain't we?"

"For sure." She sipped her coffee. "Had a relapse when I heard about Aunt Anne. I recall offering you a drink. I keep the wine on hand for friends, but I'm back on the wagon now."

Molly talked about her two children, a daughter in college, son a high school senior, and the divorce five years ago. She dated off and on, but nothing serious.

"I like to keep things casual," she said. "Not sure about ever marrying again."

Jack was relieved to hear that. "Yeah. I haven't been out much. Not interested. Sorry, no offense, I just meant— "

"It's okay. I know what you mean." Molly drained her cup and glanced at her watch. "About that time."

"Yeah, past my bedtime." He signaled the waiter, who arrived with the tab. Jack took out his wallet, extracted several bills, and handed them to the guy.

Molly wriggled out of the booth. "Thank you, Jack. Next time it'll be my treat."

"I'll remember that." Jack hoped there would be a next time. So she's divorced, has baggage with two kids, is an alcoholic. Hell, nobody's perfect.

• • • • •

The next morning when Jack arrived at his desk, he spotted the note by his phone. He unfolded it and read *See Me*, signed by Chub Nesbitt. True to her word, that bitch LePere reported him to the captain.

On his way out of the bull pen, Jack ran into Sherk. "Gonna see the cap," Jack said. "If I don't return in half an hour, send backup."

Sherk chortled. "He'll go easy on you, Jack."

"Not worried about Chub. It's what I might do to LePere."

Jack walked down the hall and rapped on Captain Nesbitt's door.

"Yeah," came a gravely voice, and Jack stepped inside. Nesbitt sat at his huge desk in front of a row of windows. The office was vast, painted bright yellow, shelves neatly arranged with manuals, books, and pottery pieces. Several framed certificates and commendations punctuated the walls, along with pictures of snow-capped mountains and castles Nesbitt photographed on an Austrian trip a couple years ago.

His dark square face broke into a grin. "Jack. Good to see you. How's Tommy doing these days?"

"Good. Just saw him at Shinnick's couple nights ago."

Nesbitt wiped his shiny brow with his hand. He wore an expensive looking gray suit and red tie. His smile faded. "Look, Jack, I'm getting more complaints from LePere. You and I talked about this last year." He sighed. "I know she's a pain in the ass, but you gotta try harder to get along. Quit pushing her buttons."

"I know, Cap. No excuses here."

"You doin' okay, you know, personally? Life in general? And don't bullshit a bullshitter."

"Never could kid you." Jack half smiled. "I dunno. Maybe things are slipping." God, he hated conversations like this.

"Well, if that's the case, you know what to do. Get help. You did it before. I gotta run a smooth ship here, and I'm gettin' the squeeze from the brass about the nun's case. Not supposed to happen in Bridgeport." Nesbitt took a gulp from his large mug. "You know as well as I do, this is still a small town even though most won't admit it. Certain people run the place, not as bad as Daley's time, but that small town mentality's here to stay."

Jack nodded. "I know, Cap. I'll handle it. Try with LePere. Keep my mouth shut."

"Yes, Jack." Nesbitt stood. "Always said, you can be an ass, but you're a damn good cop. Now get the hell outta here and close that case."

Jack got up from his chair. "Thanks, Cap." He opened the door and walked out.

Resisting the temptation to burst into LePere's office to tell her off,

Jack stomped to his desk. He needed to get his shit together and focus on the frickin' case.

• • • • •

Thirty minutes later, Jack and Sherk made their way to the parking lot for their drive to interview Len Abbott, a former student of Sister Anne's. The guy lived in West Lawn, southwest of Bridgeport, and worked at a nearby software company.

The sun chased dark gray clouds away, along with predictions of rain. Sherk looked at the sky. "April is the cruellest month, breeding lilacs from— "

"Enough of the Shakespeare, too— "

"T. S. Eliot, Jack. From *The Waste Land*. It's often misquoted— "

"Yeah, yeah," Jack grumbled. He should let Sherk wax poetic, but he wasn't in the mood.

They climbed into an unmarked and rode along Thirty-first Street toward I-55. Jack told his partner about meeting with Nesbitt. Sherk didn't comment. Was he thinking about Erica's first chemo tomorrow? Why did good people get cancer? Wonder how many pedophiles get it. Poor Sherk. Guess it's human nature to imagine the worst case scenario when faced with a cancer diagnosis. Primarily when the odds might be against recovery, but what did Jack know?

Five minutes from Abbott's workplace, dispatch called, the operator's voice filling the car. "Body of a white male at 1297 Kedvale Drive, Skokie. Outside our precinct, but one of their cops knows about the Bible thumper. Figures it's yours, Bailey. Bible verse with the body."

"Yer shittin' me, man." Jack pounded the steering wheel with his fist. "Yeah, on our way. Should be there in forty-five, hour tops."

"My god, three murders," Sherk said. "An official serial killer on our hands."

Jack checked the rear view, squealing the brakes as he waited for a van to pass so he could make a U-turn in the middle of Pulaski Road. He sped north until he hit I-55 and exited east. "Think Fifty'll be okay? Quicker than Ninety if traffic's light."

"Should be good this time of day," Sherk answered. "Then we can catch Ninety-four into Skokie." He'd already entered the address in the GPS.

Jack put his sunglasses on. "What's it been? Nine, ten days since Welton?" He felt the walls closing in.

"Eleven days," Sherk said.

Crap. Nesbitt'll have my ass for sure. "Gotta get this prick." He heard the ticking clock.

Chapter 22

They didn't say much as Jack raced east on the freeway. He caught up close behind a couple semis slowing traffic, their immense frames side by side. Couldn't see a damn thing, and the asshole in the third lane drove his Chevy sedan like it was Sunday afternoon in the country.

The idiot truck drivers wouldn't hear Jack honk, so he laid on the horn behind the slowpoke. The guy looked in the rear view, raised his shoulders as if he wondered what Jack wanted.

He beeped again. "Come on, moron, move that heap before I ram your ass."

"Take it easy, Jack. There's an exit coming up, you can get on the shoulder."

"Yeah, yeah." Didn't need a back seat driver. Wished he worked alone at times like this.

The straggler accelerated until he was a car length in front of the truck, but by that time Jack took the right exit lane until he passed the guy, leaving him and the trucks in the dust.

"I wouldn't be surprised if we're stopped for speeding." Sherk cleared his throat. "Want to run the siren?"

"Nah, just quit your nagging."

Like most detectives, Jack avoided flashing lights and sirens unless it was a chase or crime in progress. Public safety was first priority, but compromised by high speeds.

"Am curious as hell about this vic," Jack said as he exited north onto Highway 50. "First two couldn't be more different, an old nun and a young guy. Possible abuse connection though."

"I have no idea either. Guess we put Sister's former students' interviews on hold for now."

"Too bad we didn't get to see Abbott. Damn, if dispatch called twenty minutes later we would've made the interview. Need to postpone."

When they reached the interchange with I-90 toward Park Ridge, Jack felt a tug in his gut at the familiar highway close to Karen's parents' home. They continued past signs for Cicero and several miles later, Oak Park.

"Did you know Hemingway was born in Oak Park?" Sherk gazed out the window at the drab gray square warehouses and unadorned office buildings.

"Of course I knew that. Grew up here, remember? You're not the only cultured guy around." Jack slowed down for yellow construction signs. "Tony Accardo hung out here too."

"In Oak Park?" Sherk asked.

"No, in Sicily."

"Sarcasm is the lowest form of humor, Jack."

"Says you." Gunning the engine after the lanes cleared, they reached Skokie Boulevard ten minutes later. Jack slowed down through residential neighborhoods reflecting an older middle class area. Small brick houses, mostly one story ranches, sat back from green ash-shaded streets. Several lawns needed landscaping, but a decent neighborhood.

"We're there," Sherk said as Jack turned right, following GPS directions.

Turning onto Kedvale, he spotted a cruiser and parked behind it.

They climbed out of the car and headed toward a postage stamp-sized one story tan house with black trim. The yard displayed no decorative touches; two oak trees stood on either side of the walkway. Low bushes in various stages of deterioration flanked a small concrete porch.

The front door opened before Jack rang the bell, and a young Latino patrol cop greeted them. "You must be Bailey." The guy held out his hand. "Toby Perez here."

Jack gave a half nod. "My partner, Karl Sherkenbach. Fill us in."

Perez led the men through a small living room with dingy light green furniture into a short hallway with three closed doors. He opened the last door. "Better hold your noses."

The room stunk like an outhouse. Jack breathed through his mouth "Shit, how long has he been here?"

"Dunno," said Perez. "Maybe he had the runs before he croaked."

Jack grunted. "Yeah, these murder scenes, always a crapshoot."

Sherk groaned. The three men stood beside a double bed and gazed down at the body of a pudgy middle-aged man lying on his back. A fringe of graying brown hair circled a shiny head. He wore a drab gray sweatshirt with a Cubs logo and loose gray sweatpants, feet bare. Brown mottled stains seeped through the pants onto the tan bedspread. Jack had seen worse. Not sure about the smell.

"Don't know details yet," Perez said. "A friend called 911 when he couldn't get in the house. The vic was supposed to meet a few buddies for breakfast at Perkins, but didn't show. The friend said the vic was always on time, and when he didn't answer their phone calls, the friend came over."

"Did he try and enter the house?" Sherk asked.

"No, but he heard the dog barking from inside, so he called the cops."

"Where's the friend now?" Jack bent down to examine the body's face and neck.

"He's waiting in his car with the cop who came with me. He'll stick around to answer your questions. The dog's at the next door neighbor's."

"What details on the deceased do you have thus far?" Sherk's typical lofty vocabulary.

Perez flipped his notebook open. "Name's Grant Adams, retired, around sixty. Been divorced for years, wife lives in Rockford."

Jack ambled to the other side of the bed. "Where's the Bible verse?"

Perez hesitated. "It's with my buddy in the car. Put it in an evidence bag." He noted Jack's sour expression. "Oh, don't worry, he used gloves."

Sherk spoke softly. "It shouldn't have been moved."

Jack shook his head. "Gotta lot to learn, Perez. Show me where it was without touching anything."

Perez leaned over the body and lowered his index finger to the edge of the body's right wrist. Same place as the other two vics.

"Okay," Jack said. "The ME on the way?"

"Any minute now." Perez coughed. "Should I go get the friend in here now?"

"Yes, thank you," Sherk answered. "We'll wait in the kitchen."

Perez left the bedroom, and after glancing at the corpse and surrounding area, Jack led the way through the dim hallway into a worn-out looking dining and kitchen space. They sat at a small blond laminate table straight out of the 1950's.

Jack took in the harvest gold refrigerator and oven. "God, do ya think Ozzie and Harriet are gonna come through the door any minute?"

"Ozzie who?"

"Never mind. Just heard the front door."

Three men walked into the kitchen. Perez said, "Detectives, this is Morty Brown, friend of the deceased. We'll be outside till you're done talking." The other cop held out a plastic bag containing a folded paper.

"Thanks," Sherk stood. "I'm Detective Sherkenbach, this is my partner, Detective Bailey." Sherk put the bag in a pocket inside his jacket. "Next time, leave all evidence in place."

After Perez and the cop left the room, Sherk indicated a chair for Brown.

"Okay," Brown said as he took a seat. He looked like he was in his late sixties, maybe seventies. His navy windbreaker overlapped a protruding belly. Rubbing his close-cropped white hair, he said, "I'm still in shock. Can't get over it. Grant was so healthy."

Not anymore, Jack thought. "How long were you friends with—" he looked at his notes. "Grant Adams?"

Brown rose and walked to the sink. "I need water. You guys?" He opened a cabinet and retrieved a glass.

"No thank you," Sherk said.

"I've known Grant for ah, maybe twenty-five years. Met in the late eighties. Our kids were in Little League, Grant coached. A few of us dads would get together. Then he talked me into coaching— "

"Where did Grant work?" Jack didn't need a life story, but his brain registered a red flag when Brown mentioned the coaching bit.

"Carver Central High in Des Plaines, lived there till he retired. Taught history and coached baseball. Did Little League too."

Brown talked for another ten minutes, elevating Grant Adams to sainthood, how highly regarded he was by co-workers, parents, students, and Little League players. Everyone seemed to worship the guy except his wife. She moved to Rockford after the divorce.

"Why did they divorce?" Jack asked.

Brown cleared his throat. "Ah, well, I don't know." He gave a half chuckle. "Guess they had some differences, you know how that goes."

"No, I don't." Jack gazed at the man. "But I'd like to."

Brown shrugged. "Well, I really don't— "

"Look, ah Morty, is it? You need to come clean with me. The guy's dead. He ain't comin' back. The more we know about everything in his life, the sooner we'll find the killer."

Looking flustered, Brown gulped his water. "Okay, there was some talk—just rumor, that Grant may have been ah, inappropriate with some kids. Seems Sara, his wife believed it, she took their kids and left."

Showing no visible reaction, Jack's instinct was confirmed. An older pervert this time.

"So nothing was ever substantiated about the rumors?" Sherk asked.

"No, nothing. I never believed it. Not Grant. Would never mess around, certainly not with boys."

"Of course," Jack said. "People believed Clinton too."

"Look, Detective, I knew Grant for— "

"I know, I know." Jack held up his hands in mock defeat. "Think we're done. We may wanna talk again."

The three men pushed back their chairs and stood. "Here's my card," Sherk said. "Call if you think of anything, even if it seems unimportant."

Brown took the card. "Okay, will do." He glanced at Jack, an uncertain expression on his face. "Sure hope you catch who did this. Grant was such a good friend, a terrific guy."

Jack wanted to roll his eyes, but refrained. He led Brown through the living room past the two cops and opened the front door.

Brown stopped and looked at Sherk. "Oh god, who's going to tell Sara and the kids?"

"We'll notify the Rockford police, and they'll send a couple officers and a chaplain if they employ one." Sherk touched the man's upper arm.

Brown furrowed his brow and walked out the door, closing it behind him.

Sherk and Jack joined Perez and the other officer in the living room.

Perez said, "So, you guys gonna take over the case or what's next?"

"Probably. Need to check with the supervisor at the Skokie PD." Jack wanted the cops to disappear. "You can check in and see if you need to hang around. We'll wait for the ME."

"Gotcha," Perez said as he turned away and called on his cell.

Jack motioned Sherk toward the kitchen. As they sat at the table, Jack said, "Let's look at the verse."

"Yes, I'm curious as well." Sherk reached inside his jacket and took the bag out. He dug in his side pocket for his latex gloves, and pulled them onto his hands.

"Looks like the same type of paper as the others," Jack said.

"Yes, and the blue printing evidently the same." Sherk unfolded the note and read, "Then when lust hath conceived, it bringeth forth sin, and sin, when it is finished, bringeth forth death. James 1:15."

Jack scratched his temple. "Someone sure broughteth forth death on this guy. What's your translation?"

"Pretty much literal—that temptation or desire is acted upon, sin is the result, and in the long run, brings death. So, it's the same theme as the other verses."

Perez stuck his head in the kitchen. "ME and forensic guys are here. Me and my partner are cleared to head out. Boss on his way too." He hesitated. Gazed at Jack. "Anyone ever say you look like Liam Neeson?"

"Once or twice." Jack stood and asked Sherk, "Ready to turn the verse over to the CSI guys?"

Sherk folded the note and placed it in the bag. "Yes, it's ready."

The ME and CSI team of two men wearing paper booties, hurried into the living room where Jack introduced himself and Sherk.

"Dude on ice is in here." Jack led the men into the bedroom. The stench seemed more powerful than before. The ME, a tall, gangly balding man, wore the standard white lab coat and proceeded to open his bag and don his blue paper cap and gloves. The CSI guys busied themselves with separate tasks, one clicking away on his state-of-the-art camera, the other kneeling on the floor examining the beige carpet.

"We'll leave you to it," Sherk said. The ME nodded at him and bent over the body.

Jack and Sherk made their way to the kitchen. "Chatty group, ain't they?"

"I noticed. Do you want to call Skokie PD to coordinate, or wait for the boss, whoever he may be?"

"I'll call. See what's going on." Jack found the number and punched it in.

● ● ● ● ●

Two hours later, Grant Adams's house was cleared of all people, dead or alive, and Jack and Sherk rode off heading south toward Bridgeport. The ME had judged time of death to be somewhere between midnight Wednesday to around five this morning. After learning Bruce Welton's cause of death, the ME found a puncture mark on the corpse's left side of his neck, same as Welton's. Somulose was most likely used, but the exact substance would not be known until lab results were obtained.

Sergeant Joe Rossi had arrived at the Adams house shortly after the ME. His tough appearance and burly manner fit his Italian name. He reminded Jack of an aging Brando.

"You guys keep us in the loop at all times," the sergeant had said. "We don't have the crime here in Skokie that you do, but we got a couple good detectives in the department."

Exiting onto south 94, Jack said, "Can you believe that arrogant prick Rossi? All the guy needed was a cigar hanging out the corner of his mouth."

Sherk smiled. "I'm glad you defended Bridgeport's crime rate. The man does have an attitude."

Jack protruded his jaw, spoke as if he had a mouthful of cotton. "Yeah, revenge is a dish best served cold." He smoothed his hair.

Sherk laughed. "Not bad, Vito. Not bad at all."

"Think the murder will hit the evening news or morning papers?" Jack's voice back to normal.

"I'm sure of it. As the good sergeant said, a crime in Skokie is a pivotal event."

They rode in silence as traffic thickened and slowed them down. Too many Sunday drivers on the road. Seemed no one kept up with the flow anymore. Jack weaved in and out between trucks and cars alike.

"I just checked, and Grant Adams doesn't show up on the sex registry." Sherk took his glasses off and cleaned them with a micro cloth. "I'll ask Gary Calvin to do a more thorough search."

"Damn, figured we wouldn't be lucky enough to find a hit online. I knew the guy was a perv the minute his friend mentioned Little League. Sick bastard."

"Yes, it all fits, unfortunately," Sherk said. "Hopefully the killer's bound to slip up before long, according to the profiler. As they gain confidence, they become careless."

"Yeah. Problem now is facing Nesbitt when we get back."

"Not to mention Ms. LePere." Sherk sighed.

"I don't give a damn about her. It's the cap who'll have my ass, maybe sooner than we think. The damn clock's ticking louder than ever."

Chapter 23

Donald Sowder pulled out of Goldpine Home's parking lot and drove toward his crappy apartment near Midway Airport. On the way, he stopped at a Shell station to fill up his gray Toyota clunker. He once saw a bumper sticker several years ago that said: *My other car is a piece of shit too.* He'd been tempted, but didn't want to attract even a modicum of attention.

Why was that fat girl at the next pump staring at him? He wanted to stare back, but told himself to focus on grabbing his receipt and getting the hell out of there. Can't let anyone remember him for any reason. Couldn't risk someone identifying him in a lineup.

He reached his apartment building, a square, three story concrete structure, and pulled in the back, facing Fifty-fifth Street. He'd found the place here in Garfield Ridge, a community near Midway where he worked. His mother had given him used furniture and tried to foist several framed landscape prints on him. *The place needs to look lived in, Donny, it should show who you are.* How ironic was that? Yeah, in that case, he needed photos of kids in Belleview or Menninger.

Donald willed his brain to stay put. Quit flying around like a moth trapped in a lampshade. After unlocking the door, he hung up his jacket and plodded to the kitchen. Too early to drink, but what the hell. He grabbed a can of Bud from the fridge, poured it into a glass tumbler, and flopped into a worn blue corduroy chair in the living room. He turned on the TV and watched *Jeopardy.*

"Ah, ah, who was Longfellow?" he yelled at the TV. "Thanks, Ma." "The Village Blacksmith", one of his mother's favorite poems. *Under the spreading chestnut tree....* Yada yada yada. Poor old Ma. Stuck in a home. Hardly knows her own son, much less who wrote what poem. But he'd heard Alzheimer's patients remembered songs from childhood. Who the hell knew.

His mother. She did what she could, he guessed. Should've stood up to his dad more. He wanted to blame her for drumming the church into him. For telling him about the new priest. Father McGarvey. Father Daniel McGarvey. Looking back, the priest knew Donald was an easy mark. Like a predatory animal, Father Dan had instincts. Sniff out weakness and go for the kill. Oh, it started gradually. Grooming they call it. Grooming.

Chuckling bitterly, Donald thought there should be a handbook for priests…. 'Altar Boy Abuse 101'. Little Donny had been ripe for the taking. Skinny kid with inch-thick glasses, a bully magnet. Never told his mother when the kids would taunt, *Donny Sowder's mama's a sow, Mrs. Sowder the sow*. She babied him too much, at least that's what his old man said. *Gotta cut the apron strings some time. You're making a sissy outta him.*

Donald convinced himself to focus on the TV. Switched to CNN, heard about some follow-up rantings about a kid, Trayvon somebody who got shot in Florida. What else was new? More talk about gas prices, $3.39 for regular. Can't even afford to drive around this miserable city. At least his clunker didn't need premium, as if he'd ever afford a luxury car.

Time for an early dinner so he could draw the final plans for his next project. Had the scumball picked out, cased his house and neighborhood. Should be easy access. He felt high thinking about it. Wasn't nervous, scared like the first time with Sister Anne. Practice makes perfect, and all that.

After a supper of frozen hamburger pizza and another Bud, Donald went into his workshop, as he called the second bedroom. He sat at a long table with two computers, a printer in between. Book shelves with neatly stacked files and magazines covered half of one wall. A twin bed with a blue plaid comforter sat against another wall. *In case you have overnight company, or I come cook a late dinner.* Thank God his mother hadn't spent the night, nor would she ever. His father and sister didn't bother with him, so the bed would never be used.

Not by a girlfriend. No luck there. Wonder why.

After opening a manila file beside his monitor, he read several pages. He wrote incriminating notes in longhand which he could easily destroy, notes that cited names and addresses of evil-doers. He could cover his ass on his computer for research like which poisons worked best. Even googling 'how to commit murder' couldn't prove anything.

Twenty minutes later, stretching back in his chair, Donald took off his glasses and set them on the desk. He rubbed his eyes, decided to call it a night, and sauntered to the bedroom. Damn, he shouldn't have had that second Bud.

His thoughts fluttered their way to the Closed Door. No, can't go there. The door must remain shut and locked. He could see the door now. The door to the sacristy. Where the altar boys went.

Chapter 24

Jack plowed through heavy traffic, and arrived at the station by mid afternoon. Thinking of facing Chub Nesbitt, Jack decided to bite the bullet and head for the man's office. The captain would be ready to explode, but better get it over with. Sherk nodded his agreement.

As they made their way to Nesbitt's office, Velda Vatava strolled down the hallway, arms laden with files and pamphlets. "Bailey, decided to grace us with your presence," she sang.

"Not that you deserve it." He and Sherk were at Nesbitt's door.

"If you're looking for the captain, he's out for the afternoon. But maybe I can help you."

"I doubt that, thanks anyway." Jack stopped. "Know when he'll be back?"

"No. He doesn't tell me everything." Velda shifted the papers in her hands. "But your favorite lady boss, You-Know-Who, is on the premises."

"In that case, it's time to raid my stash." Jack was ready for a shot of Jameson.

"Think I'll join you," Velda said as Jack led the way to the bull pen. He opened the door and ran into Daisy LePere, the odor of rose perfume assaulting his nostrils.

"Bailey, Sherkenbach, my office, now."

Jack gave a mock salute. "Yes Sir, uh, Ma'am."

She glared at him and elbowed her way past them into the hall, brushing against Velda's arm. "Excuse us, Ms. Vatava, we have work to do. Carry on."

"Of course, Ma'am. Always carry on. It's all I do."

When they reached LePere's office, she unlocked her door and indicated two chairs across from her desk. "Sit," she barked.

"Woof, woof," Jack said as he and Sherk followed her command.

"Watch it, Bailey." She sat behind her pristine desk. "You're skating on thin ice."

Jack convinced himself to shut up. He'd promised Nesbitt, and didn't want to push his luck with the cap.

LePere smoothed her navy jacket lapels. "Well, now that you have a bona fide serial killer on your hands, what can you tell me?"

Sherk relayed everything he and Jack knew about Grant Adams, and their plans to pursue leads.

"What does the Bible verse say?" LePere asked.

Jack fished his notebook from his pocket and flipped it open. "Then when lust hath conceived, it bringeth forth sin, and— "

"Okay, I get the drift."

"Don't you wanna know where it's from? James one— "

"I said, okay, Bailey. I'm not a theologian."

You can say that again, Jack thought. "No comment, Ma'am." He tightened his lips together . "If that's all, me and Sherk'll get busy."

LePere sneered. "I'll say when we're done here. Be sure and keep that Skokie sergeant in the loop. Coordinating with another department, always a pain in the ass, but it is what it is." She stood.

"Okay, we're done. Sherkenbach, be on time tomorrow. I'll expect a full report in the afternoon."

Sherk cleared his throat. "Tomorrow I have— "

"No problem, Sarge, uh, Ma'am. We'll get to it." Jack practically dragged Sherk from the old bag's office and closed the door. "Don't say anything about your appointment with Erica tomorrow. You told the cap. Good enough."

Sherk looked worried as they headed to their desks. "I guess, but she should know— "

"She'll find out soon. Quit worrying. You're covered."

• • • • •

That evening Jack sat in his recliner guzzling beer and watching the news. Boone slept at Jack's feet, snoring and twitching now and then. Some guy on CNN yakked about China and Russia endorsing a cease fire by this creep, Assad, who says he'll withdraw his troops from Syria's cities by April 10. What a joke. And there will soon be peace throughout the Middle East.

Jack reached for the remote to change channels when his phone buzzed. Irritated at the interruption, he read the caller ID: Stewart Buckley. Crap, what did his former father-in-law want?

Muting the TV, Jack punched on the phone. "Stewart, what do you need?"

The man chuckled. "Hi, Jack. Right to the point, as usual. How are you getting along these days?"

"Good." Pause. "Any reason I shouldn't be?"

Chuckling again. "No, no. Just asking. I hope I'm not disturbing your evening."

God, these rich lawyers all sounded the same. "No, just hanging with Boone. We're doing nothing."

"Okay. I'll get to the point." Finally, Jack thought.

Buckley cleared his throat. "I'd like to meet with you sometime soon. Nothing's wrong, but we'll need privacy. If you don't mind, we could meet at the club. That's closer to you than my house."

"Gotta tell ya, Stewart, this sounds a little — "

"Mysterious? Sorry, Jack. Don't mean to be. It's important to you, but not in a negative way. I'll leave it at that."

"Okay, when did you have in mind?"

"If you're free this Saturday, let's meet for lunch or dinner, whatever's best."

Jack thought a few seconds. As usual, he had no plans for the weekend. Could always work on the new murder, as well as trying to see Molly again. His curiosity overruled. "Lunch would be good." That way he could see Molly in the evening if he had the courage to call her.

He and Buckley agreed on a 1:00 meeting at Park Ridge Country

Club, where the Buckleys had been members for years. Wonder what the man wants. Said there wasn't a problem. If not, what could it be?

"Calls for another beer," Jack said to Boone, who looked up, sleepy-eyed and wagged his long yellow tail.

Returning to his chair with another Guinness, he noticed the same guy on TV yakking and turned the damn thing off. He thought about Molly, her green eyes, lavender scent, perfect butt. Maybe he'd muster up the ambition to call her. Then again—

• • • • •

The next morning, rain spattered Jack's windshield as he drove to the station. A biting north wind scattered leaves over lawns and sidewalks and bent branches of young trees. He could hear his mother recite *The north wind doth blow, and we shall have snow. What will the robin do then, poor thing*? She chanted the entire poem whenever the wind blew. Is this part of the aging process? His mother's words infringing on his thoughts.

He spotted Chub Nesbitt's car turning into the parking lot, and circled around the block to avoid him. Didn't feel like facing the music yet. Needed coffee first.

When Jack entered the bull pen, the place was half empty. Gary Calvin stood at his desk. "Hey, Bailey, check out my new shirt."

Jack groaned. "If I have to, but you owe me." He didn't mention he needed to talk to the guy anyway as he approached the desk.

Calvin resembled Bozo, with his unkempt carrot mop and toothy grin. He stuck his chest out like a peacock. "Gotta admit, this shirt was custom made just for me."

Jack gazed at the rusty colored shirt with white print. He read aloud to humor Calvin. "So if a redhead goes crazy, is it called ginger snaps?"

"Not bad, eh, Bailey?" The geek seemed more keyed up than usual.

"A real knee-slapper. You can sit now. Got some work for ya." Jack pulled up a nearby chair and flopped down beside Calvin.

"One step ahead of you. The whole place is buzzing about the Bridgeport serial killer." Calvin turned to his monitor and began typing.

Jack looked around. "Stop exaggerating. No buzzing. Didn't make the evening papers. Haven't checked this morning."

"Don't bother. Made the front page of the *Leader* and third in the *Tribune*." Calvin slid to one side of the screen. "Here, take a look."

Jack leaned in and squinted. "They do things different in the Skokie press. Hate to see my name in print. Why did those idiots need to quote me and that Vito wannabe of a sergeant of theirs? Damn, now every freak'll be calling here."

Calvin guffawed. "Calm down, Bailey. No one would dare bother you. Now let's see. Got some stuff on the vic. Grant Adams, age sixty, taught history at Carver—you know all that. I dug up some comments, not allegations, just rumors about the guy." He continued to move and press the mouse to find a link.

"Good," Jack said. "What I wanted."

Calvin pointed to a short article on the screen. "Here. I'll print it for ya, but it raises the ugly head of doubt or whatever about this character." He punched the printer button and handed the copy to Jack.

"Keep lookin', see what else you come up with." Jack stood.

"What else? This ain't chopped liver." Calvin brushed his floppy mane from his forehead. "Some people have no gratitude." He laughed at his own comment as if it were hilarious.

"Check ya later." Jack turned and walked toward his desk. A couple cops sidetracked him with questions about the Skokie murder. Getting plenty of unwanted attention on this one. He reached for his mug and headed toward the break room, where he was bombarded with more interrogations.

"Okay, okay, guys, I ain't a damn celebrity, keep ya posted." Jack poured his coffee and looked at a young patrol cop. "All I'm missing is a bald head and a lollipop."

"Huh? Whadda ya mean?" the brat asked. Several guys cackled.

"Ask your mother." Jack waved them off and left the room.

He hoped no one would bother him as he took a seat at his desk and began reading the printouts from Calvin. The geek had done his job. Nothing noteworthy popped up on Grant Adams's phone records, finances seemed to be in order, normal portfolio for someone his age, still owed a few grand on his mortgage, unremarkable credit card debt. Looked like Mr. Average all American retired geezer.

Gulping his coffee, Jack came across a short hit from an obscure source that piqued his interest. "Hmm," he said aloud. "What have we here?"

Chapter 25

Before he read ten words, Jack smelled the sickly odor of roses and knew he was in for an assault from the queen bitch.

"Where's Sherkenbach?" LePere sidled up to his desk, hands on hips.

"Good morning, Sarge." Jack faked a smile. "How are you today?"

"Knock it off, Bailey. Where is he?" She glanced at her shiny gold watch. "It's mid morning."

Jack shrugged. "Sorry. Can't help ya. Now if you'll excuse me I have a case to work on."

LePere stiffened and put her hand on a bare space on the desk. She clicked her red manicured claws on the wooden veneer as several gold bangles slid down her wrist. Jack could feel her nails indenting his skin. "Bailey, the captain assured me you would turn over a new attitude. Haven't seen it so far."

Before Jack could utter a response, she turned and pranced toward the door, silk pants swishing in the air.

He tightened his jaw and returned to his paper. Where was he? Oh yeah, a blurb titled *Allegations Against Coach Unfounded* dated September 9, 2007. According to the piece, several parents claimed Grant Adams, a Little League coach in Des Plaines, possessed child pornography in August, 1992. Authorities were notified, but could find no evidence to support the accusations.

Jack drained his cup. The article was good enough for him. No need for further investigation, same killer, the connection obvious. God, like that Sandusky bastard. What the fuck's with these old geezers? Hell, anyone. No answer, never was, never will be.

Nothing much to do until Sherk came back from his wife's chemo treatment. Pushing his chair back, Jack moseyed his way to the break room for coffee. He'd call Skokie PD, see about autopsy and lab results. Then revisit the list of Sister Anne's former students. He and Sherk could drive back to see Len Abbott in West Lawn if they had time. If not, wait till Monday.

When noon rolled around, Jack's stomach rumbled in protest. Antsy to leave his mound of paperwork for fresh air, he decided to grab takeout at Jackalope across the street, and eat in solitude at his desk. A swig of Jameson from his desk drawer would enhance his dining experience.

When Jack stepped outside the front entrance of the station, the wind's sharp teeth nipped at his face. The earlier rain had faded into an Irish mist, an unofficial weather term used by his mother. Ducking his head, he hurried across Halsted to the psychedelic colored windows of the coffee shop and peeked in the door. He spotted Nesbitt's bulky frame sitting across the room with another sizeable older man. Jack jerked around and hurried away before the captain turned. Didn't want to face explaining a third murder to the cap at lunch time.

"Hell, can't even grab a burger," Jack groused to himself. He headed down the block to Willy's, a greasy spoon that featured thick burgers, ordered one with fries, and returned to the station.

He devoured the burger and fries, educated with a couple splashes of Jameson he added to his leftover coffee.

Velda Vatava stopped by. "Umm, smelled your lunch, Bailey. Any more to share with your favorite colleague?"

"He's not here yet, Velda." Jack bunched up his napkin. "Sure was good though."

Velda peered into his mug and sniffed. "Yeah, and your coffee must be the perfect addition to your lunch."

"You know me too well, Vatava. Now if you'll excuse me, I got a case to work."

"A real serial killer so I hear. Way to go, Bailey." She laughed and walked away.

Jack glowered and pretended to study his computer screen.

Ten minutes later Sherk plodded his way to his desk and sat down.

Jack looked up. "Rough time?"

Sliding his glasses off his nose, Sherk sighed. "Yeah. Never been around hospitals much. Or people with life-threatening illness. Erica's resting at home now. Feels fine. Doc says the first round of chemo usually doesn't produce side effects. It's a cumulative process."

"Should've stayed home, dude. Not much to do that can't wait till Monday." Jack drained the last of his drink.

"No, I need the distraction that work offers. Did anyone miss me this morning?"

"Yeah, the ol' bag asked. Said I couldn't help. At least Cap didn't call me in. Saw him in Jackalope before he saw me. Got the hell out and went to Willy's for lunch."

Sherk held his glasses up and polished them with his usual micro cloth. "Anything more on our Skokie victim?"

Jack relayed Gary Calvin's information. They'd wait for the autopsy and lab reports from Skokie to verify the forensic evidence matched the previous two victims. "Still have a hunch the key is Sister Anne. Hoping to luck out with one of the five students on our list. Revisit that Len Abbott guy we missed seeing yesterday."

Sherk glanced at his watch. "Think there's still time this afternoon?"

"Nah, too much traffic. He'd be getting off work. Let's wait till Monday." Knew they should work the case now, but Jack felt the walls closing in. Ready to get the hell out.

Sherk clicked his ballpoint pen back and forth. "You know our trip to Germany Erica and I planned for this summer? Got our flight reservations already. We'll ask the doc, but I don't see how she can make it now that— "

Jack raised his eyebrows. "You never know. She could feel better by then. In remission."

"Highly doubtful she'd be to that point in less than three months.

We're booked at the end of June. That way the kids are out of school. Stay with their grandparents."

Jack wished he could think of profound, intelligent words to say, but nothing came to him. "Something'll work out, Sherk. Maybe a relative can take the tickets."

"In the meantime, 'hope is the thing with feathers' — "

"Gonna go out on a limb here, but that doesn't sound like Shakespeare to me."

Sherk smiled. "Emily Dickinson. Would you like to hear the entire poem?"

"No offense, but I have an appointment." Jack stood and stuffed papers into a folder. "Some other time."

"Leaving for the day, Jack? Have a good weekend."

"You too. Don't stay too long. Best to Erica." He turned and hurried out of the bull pen and exited the building, hoping to avoid Nesbitt.

• • • • •

Two hours later, Jack dropped onto his sofa. He thought about the coach's murder. A serial killer in Bridgeport? Gotta get on it. When the phone buzzed, he read the caller ID, debated not answering, then gave in. "Yeah, Ma. What's up?"

"Nothing is up, Jacky. Can't a mother call her son once in awhile to see if he's still amongst the living?"

"Ma, it's been a long week. Not in the mood for a guilt trip."

"All right, all right. Just wondering if you've gone through that box of your father's." Did her voice seem shriller than usual?

Jack shifted in the chair. "Yeah, went through it. Not much I want. I'll drop it off so the rest can look through it. The grandkids might like the newspapers and other stuff. Historical interest, and all that." A painful reminder he had no children to inherit anything.

"Okay. I think Jenny's waiting to look at it, so when can you bring it over?"

Jack sighed. He doubted his sister cared about the box, but Andy, his brother in Arlington Heights, might be interested. He wondered again if his mother knew about the letter from the mystery German woman. "I dunno, Ma. Maybe this weekend if you're in that big a hurry."

He could visualize his mother rolling her eyes, smoothing her henna curls. "Well, pardon me, Jacky. You'd think I lived a hundred miles from you. You're all of seven minutes away from your poor old mither."

"Ha, your Irish is showing Ma. You're not poor. You're not old. No violins tonight. I'll try and come by this weekend. Maybe during Mass."

"Not funny. Wouldn't kill you to start going again. Just last week Father — "

"Ma, I gotta go. See ya soon." He hung up.

After polishing off his beer, he reached for the remote. Needed to distract himself from thoughts of Stewart Buckley. Why did he arrange tomorrow's meeting? Why the privacy? He dreaded passing through the doors of the Park Ridge Country Club. Memories of happier times with Karen and Elizabeth swimming, dining.

Should he call Molly? It might work out. Then again, easier to stream a movie.

Chapter 26

Jack tossed and turned throughout the night, dreaming of blinding eruptions, raging orange colors, Sherk dashing through a forest, Karen driving down a street. As dawn crept through the window shades, he untangled his legs from bunched-up sheets and staggered into the bathroom. He turned on the cold water, splashed his face. Bleary eyes gazed in the mirror. Two black pools sunken into a lopsided head stared back at him. Thoughts of doom hid in the recess of his mind.

Several hours later, he drove north on I-90 headed for Park Ridge. Clouds rolled over a gray sky, no rain yet. Wondering what to wear, Jack decided on a white polo shirt and khakis. Figured he'd blend in with the geezers having lunch after their nine o'clock tee time.

He turned onto Highway 43 heading northwest until North Prospect took him to the country club's entrance. Stopping at the red brick guard gate, Jack identified himself to the chubby uniformed guy who leaned out the window. "Yes, Mr. Bailey, go right ahead. Enjoy your lunch with Mr. Buckley."

Money talks, Jack thought, and continued along the winding pavement lined with ash trees and lush hedges. Purple and white crocus dotted the lawns as the clubhouse came into view. The imposing red brick structure displayed squared white pillars and arched window trim and soffits. Black wrought iron benches and manicured shrubs surrounded the atrium.

Thinking he should replace his old Beemer one of these years, he handed his keys to the valet guy. Jack ascended the stairs and was greeted at the door by a skinny balding man. Jack was surprised the club still employed a doorman, but what did he know. Seemed archaic. He hadn't been here since the nineties with Karen.

Stewart Buckley was sitting in a tweed easy chair in the lobby. He stood and strode to the entrance. "Jack, good to see you." He held out his hand, his John Kennedy smile showcasing polished teeth.

"Hey, Stu." Jack shook the man's hand, taking in his pale blue dress shirt and gray trousers. Doubtful he played eighteen holes this morning.

"Let's have lunch and then we can talk," Buckley said as he led the way to the dining room. The maître d' stood stiffly until he glanced at them. "Yes, Mr. Buckley, right this way."

What a suck up.

The dining room overlooked green gardens, a small pond, and two adorned fountains. Open, bright and airy with high ceilings, the room featured cream colored tablecloths with chairs upholstered in ivory and brown designs. Most diners were older white men, some seated with women in casual business attire. Several greeted Buckley as he threaded his way across the room. A subtle trace of grilled steak flowed through the air. Naturally, they rated a table for two next to the wall of floor-to-ceiling windows displaying the view.

A young waiter appeared, menus in hand. He poured their water, and took drink orders. "Jameson okay for you, Jack?" Buckley asked.

"Fine."

"You may remember the salmon dish. Still serve it with cranberry glaze." Buckley opened his menu as if he didn't have the whole thing memorized. "I'm leaning toward a steak myself."

Jack wished he were anywhere but here. Why didn't he suggest another place?

"I'm not that hungry." God, he sounded like a wuss. He looked at the lunch options.

Stewart asked, "You're feeling all right, aren't you?"

"Yeah, fine. I agree. The salmon looks good." A couple glasses of pinot grigio would sweeten the pot.

"Great. You know they make an excellent Lake Superior whitefish too."

Jack spotted the entree on the menu. What is Milanese style? Like reading a foreign language trying to decipher all the ingredients surrounding the fish. "I'll go with the salmon."

Buckley ordered the ribeye steak rare with braised fennel and shallots. Before their dinners came, several white-haired men stopped by the table to say hello. The last man had the craggy, handsome features of a British diplomat. "Stewart, good to see you. How are Beth and the grandkids?"

"All fine, Robert. Meet Jack Bailey. Jack, Robert Weaver."

Jack started to rise. "Don't get up, Jack," Weaver said, staring at him. The men shook hands. "You're probably tired of people saying you're a dead ringer for, uh, can't think of his name. An actor I think."

Jack cringed, gave a half smile. "Liam Neeson?"

"Yes, that's it. You're obviously Irish too."

The men chortled, and Weaver took his leave.

Their dinners were served in good order, the waiter polite but not intrusive. Perfectly trained, Jack thought. He glanced at Buckley as the man took his knife and sawed into his slab of meat, red juice oozing onto the plate. Never could hack rare beef.

While they ate and drank, the men conversed about their families, the weather, Jack's job, anything except Karen and Elizabeth.

"Any interesting cases these days?" Buckley drained his glass of Bordeaux.

"None that I can talk about." Jack dabbed his mouth with his cloth napkin.

Buckley grinned. "Same answer as always. I heard about the nun's murder in Bridgeport."

Jack nodded, but said nothing.

"Thought we'd have coffee in the lounge if that's all right." The man phrased his commands to sound like suggestions for approval. "Cigar or not?"

"I'll pass today, Stu." Jack was tempted, but needed no distractions, like dropping an ash, burning a hole in his pants leg. He still had no idea what the meeting was about.

After they finished their meals, Buckley rose from his chair.

"Thanks, Stu. That was delicious." Jack placed his napkin by his plate.

Buckley greeted several codgers and their wives as he led Jack out of the dining room and down a wide hallway with white crown molding and tan wallpaper. They entered a small lobby area where an elderly man sat at a large maple desk. He stared out of pale watery eyes, his face mapped with wrinkles. God, this guy had to be between ninety and embalmed. Jack could've sworn the man's bones creaked when he began to rise.

"Don't get up, George." Buckley smiled. "I assume Room Two is available."

"Oh yes, Mr. Buckley. All ready for you." George gave Jack a smile that didn't reach his eyes. "Coffee or the usual?"

Buckley looked at Jack, who said, "Coffee's fine." He resisted the temptation of another Jameson.

"Black coffee and the usual, thanks, George." Buckley led Jack to a semi circle of closed doors. He caught a scent of cigar smoke as Buckley opened a door at the end. The smoke smelled damn good. Jack craved a Marlboro. A couple rooms were designated as cigar lounges, equipped with requisite ventilation systems.

Buckley indicated a chair for Jack and took a seat opposite. The room, the quintessential reflection of old money, boasted two burgundy leather arm chairs and matching sofa. An enormous mahogany coffee table held vases of fresh red and white roses. Unlike LePere's perfume, the fragrance was pleasant.

"I know you're wondering what this is all about, Jack, so I'll get to the point." Buckley crossed his legs and leaned back. "It has to do with my estate, to put it bluntly."

Jack stared at the man. "Okay." He drew out the word.

"I know it's painful to talk about Karen. Is for me as well." He cleared his throat. "But I'm not getting any younger, and since her death, I've revised my estate directives."

Aware of his heart hammering in his chest, Jack stared at Buckley, wondering why he was hearing this.

"Oh, it took awhile. Didn't want to think about it, but— "

A tapping at the door. "Come in," Buckley said.

A young, brown-haired lady with a tray of drinks walked in. "Here you are, Mr. Buckley." She smiled as she placed the tray on the coffee table. "Do you need anything more?"

"Thank you, Erin. That'll be all." When she left the room, Buckley reached for his glass of Dry Sack sherry, his after dinner drink of choice for years. "Help yourself, Jack."

He still felt shocked at the conversation, and automatically took the cup and saucer. Why the hell hadn't he ordered a whiskey?

"I'm going to be honest with you, Jack. My will is pretty standard. Assets divided equally between descendants after both parents' deaths. Mine's no different, right down the bloodline. I don't need to tell you after Karen and Elizabeth died, it damn near killed me. Beth couldn't get out of bed for months."

Jack gulped his coffee. "I know, Stu."

Buckley took a drink. "As of now, of course, everything goes to Laura and her children. Two problems with that, Jack." The man shifted in his chair as if trying to get comfortable. "One is I don't trust her husband not to take control. Frankly, Dan's an asshole, but I don't say anything. Need to keep the peace. The other thing is this."

Jack drank more coffee. Tasted like tar.

Buckley looked to the side. "You no doubt know that Karen was the happiest in her life when she met you. She'd had problems with ah, finding herself or whatever they called it back then. Anyway, her years with you and Elizabeth were the greatest a parent could hope for."

Jack looked at the floor. Felt like squirming. Didn't know what to say.

"Anyway, I'll always be grateful to you, Jack. Don't want to get all maudlin here, but that's the way it is. She said more than once, *Daddy, if anything ever happens to me, I want you to promise you'll take care of Jack.*"

Jack wasn't shocked. Karen told him that as well. He'd gotten defensive saying he wasn't that poor, he didn't need taking care of.

"I made that promise. And I'm keeping it today. I've talked with my estate attorney, and with Beth. Yes, we lawyers have lawyers too.

I'm hoping you'll accept our gift to you." He pulled out an envelope from his pants pocket. "This lists the amount to be given to you in trust over the next several years. We worked around the current gift tax issues, which will change next year."

"Whoa, you're going too fast. Are you saying this is Karen's inheritance?"

"No, Jack. Not entirely, but it's enough for you to be quite comfortable. If managed well, you may never need to work again." He held out the envelope.

The words stunned Jack. A life-changing moment. One of those times, nothing is ever the same. Life after this moment will be different. Like it was after his wife and child died. Did he just hear *you may never need to work again*?

Jack shook his head as if he were ridding it of cobwebs. "Jesus, Stu. I'm speechless."

Buckley smiled. "I suppose it is a bit of a shock." An understatement spoken like a true Brit.

Jack stared at the envelope. Buckley said, "Go ahead, take it.... won't bite."

He haltingly took the envelope, gazed at it, then at Buckley, who nodded.

Damn hands were shaky, but he managed to open the flap and take out two sheets of paper. He unfolded them, stared, transfixed.

He looked at Buckley. "Holy shit, Stu."

Chapter 27

Again, he tried to shake his head into reality. Couldn't get a grasp on the figure he thought he read. Never seen so many zeroes. He couldn't process his thoughts. What's the catch? Too good to be true. What does Buckley want from him?

"You look dazed, Jack," Buckley chuckled.

Jack shifted in his chair. "Not every day I get offered over a million bucks. It'll take awhile to sink in." He stared at a gilded framed print above Buckley's head. A yellow bouquet of sunflowers. Looked like Van Gogh's famous painting. Karen had liked it.

"I need to mention that the amount will be allotted over the span of several years to get around the gift tax loopholes My financial advisor and I feel that with careful management, this could last you to the end the of your life."

Jack coughed. "Yeah, no kidding." The walls seemed to shift. Like an out of body experience. If he accepted Buckley's offer, his life would change drastically. He could quit his job. Do whatever he wanted. Give Ma a trip to Ireland.

Vaguely aware of Buckley speaking in the background, Jack blinked himself into the present. "What's that?"

Buckley drained his glass. "I thought Andy would be a good choice to manage your portfolio." Jack's brother was a CPA with a firm in Arlington Heights, a suburb forty-five miles northwest of Bridgeport. Known as the family bookworm, Andy managed their mother's finances and advised anyone else in the family who asked about money matters.

"Uh, yeah." Jack rubbed his forehead. "I'll tell ya, Stu, this hasn't sunk in. I need time. Time to think." He stood. "Can I get back to you in a few days?"

Buckley raised his eyebrows. "Sure, Jack. Lots to think about. We'll need to meet at my bank for the transfer. Next week some time?"

Jack needed air. "Yeah, sure." He stepped into the hallway. Buckley followed him, and they walked through lobbies and past furniture and people. Jack barely noticed Buckley saying goodbye to several friends on their way. When they reached the front door, Jack breathed in the cool, inviting air.

Two valet guys greeted them at the bottom of the steps. One took Jack's stub, and both were off to retrieve the cars.

Shaking hands, Jack said, "I'm still at a loss for words, Stu. I'll keep in touch."

Buckley patted Jack's shoulder. "You know, Jack, it's about honoring Karen. Doing what she wanted."

Jack nodded and climbed in his old Beemer, a poor cousin to Buckley's new Rolls. The thought struck him that he could buy a Rolls too, not that he ever would. And what about his family's reaction?

• • • • •

That evening, Guinness in hand, Boone stretched out on the floor, Jack remembered nothing about the drive back from the country club to his duplex. Thoughts of Buckley's offer and Karen leeched onto his brain. Wouldn't let go. Having that windfall was like winning the lottery. Tempting. Was there a catch? Didn't seem like it. Buckley said nothing about Jack's owing him in any way. No selling his soul to the devil. Most people would be turning cartwheels. Not him. Too cautious, suspicious. He gave up trying to watch TV or reading. Told himself to think about the case. Interview the Sister's former student on Monday. Needed to get Nesbitt off his back. He finally popped a couple Ambien and hit the sack.

• • • • •

The next afternoon Jack drove to his mother's house to drop off the box. He hid the mystery letter from the German lady inside his nightstand. Still not sure if Ma had seen it. Wouldn't she croak if she knew about Buckley's offer? He'd thought about nothing else since he woke up this morning. Told himself to weigh the pros and cons, but couldn't come up with any cons. The Buckleys had left him alone since Karen's death, except for Beth's annual trek to the cemetery. Jack felt certain he wouldn't be obligated in any way, that this was a gift for him to use as he wished. Of course, he'd get Andy to handle the portfolio. He knew about investments, the market. Hell, Jack hadn't needed to worry about high finance.

After parking in front of Maureen Bailey's house, he climbed out and retrieved the box from the back seat. The two ash trees on the side lawn weren't leafed out yet, but getting there. Red tulips peeked through the ground beside white daffodils, promising blooms dancing in sequence by the white picket porch railings. Ma had a green thumb, always had.

Jack rapped on the door, opened it, and walked in. The scent of apple pie permeated the air.

"Someone's in trouble if she didn't save me a piece of pie," he called.

"Jacky, what a surprise," Maureen gushed as she scurried into the entry way. "Oh, you have the box. Good. Just set it in here and Jenny or Andy can take it next."

"And then there's Mike." Jack put the box inside the coat closet.

"Oh, pooh, as if he'd be interested." Mike, Jack's youngest brother, was single, lived in Denver, hadn't settled down, was still 'finding himself'. "Who knows what shenanigans he's been up to, and I don't want to know." He was Maureen's only child she seldom mentioned, except to say, *oh well, we all have our cross to bear, or some of us do anyway*.

"By the way, have you found out who murdered that poor nun yet?"

"Ma, you know I can't talk about an ongoing case."

"Well, you'd think—your own mother. You know I wouldn't

breathe a word — "

"Got some pie for me, Ma?" Jack walked toward the kitchen.

"You're lucky there's still a piece left. Jenny was over for lunch. You know it wouldn't hurt you to — "

"I know, I know." He reached for a plate and fork, scooping the last of the pie out of the pan. "Got any ice cream?"

"Of course I do. Think I'd serve apple pie without vanilla ice cream?" She shook her curls and took a carton from the freezer. "Here, use the scoop."

"Now all I need is a cup of strong coffee."

"Would his highness care if it's heated up, or do I have to brew a new pot?"

"I'll let ya get by with nuking it this time, Ma, as long as you splash some Jameson or Beam in it. Forget the brown sugar and cream."

"Lord, what I put up with," Maureen lamented as she poured leftover coffee into a mug. You and your father. Cut from the same cloth."

"You have amnesia. I can hold my booze. Pa couldn't."

"Don't be smart, Jacky. Your father didn't have an easy life. The war and all." Maureen took the mug from the microwave and set it on the table. "Here. You don't need whiskey on a Sunday afternoon."

"What happened to the Maureen O'Leary who used to make Irish coffee for breakfast?"

"Not true and you know it." She sat across from Jack. "So, did you find anything interesting in the box?"

"You already asked me. I'm beginning to wonder about your memory." Jack took a generous bite of pie. "Umm. Haven't lost your touch for desserts."

"Hmmph. Well, what about the box?"

Jack sighed. "Nothing I want. Kinda interested in seeing the old newspapers, but they should go to the grandkids." Was his mother staring at him? Maybe she knows about the letter after all.

"Okay. Just thought you'd be more interested. Your father went through a lot during the war."

"Yeah, you said that already. Lots of men were in the war. Didn't make Pa a saint."

"What does that mean? He drank to cover up the pain."

Jack took a gulp of coffee. "Come on, Ma. You always made excuses for him. Like he was the one guy who had it tough. Not everyone took it out on his family." He knew he was walking on eggshells, but he was tired of her denial.

"Jacky, I'm not going to talk about that. You kids had a good upbringing and—"

"Okay, okay." He scooped up the last of the pie and melted ice cream. "Gotta get going. Work to do."

"Eat and run. That's all you do." Maureen stood and took the empty plate to the sink. "At least finish your coffee."

"Yeah, yeah." He drained his mug and put it on the counter. "See ya soon, Ma. Thanks for the pie."

"I'll let you know the next time I make my Guinness chocolate cheesecake. One way to get you to come over and see your poor mither." She hustled him out of the kitchen.

"Hm, haven't had that for awhile. I'll eat that even though it's a waste of good beer. Maybe next weekend?"

"Get on with you. Thanks for gracing me with your presence, Jacky." She closed the door behind him, then opened it. "And find that killer. A body can't feel safe—"

"Bye, Ma."

Later that evening he mustered up his courage and called Molly.

"Hey, Jack. How are you?" Her voice sounded cheerful.

"Doin' fine. You?"

"I'm good."

"Just wondering if you'd like to get together sometime. Next week maybe?" Why was his heart thumping?

"Oh, sorry. Not a good week." She cleared her throat. "Got a big case, lots of overtime. We're slaves to the lawyers, you know. But thanks anyway."

What? Thanks anyway? What the did that mean? "Okay, maybe when things lighten up?"

She cleared her throat. "Oh, sure, Jack. I'll let you know." Pause. "Well, good to talk. Thanks for calling."

"Sure." He winced. "Anytime." He clicked off. What the hell? Had he misread the signals the other night? Wouldn't be the first time. Hell, he knew a brush-off when he heard it. Who cares. He'd had it with women. Screw 'em all.

Jack thought for a couple minutes, jaw tight. He told himself to calm down. Studied Boone lying at his feet. "At least you tolerate me." He reached for his phone and tapped in Stewart Buckley's number.

"Jack. Good to hear from you."

"I've thought a lot about your offer. Must admit, it threw me for a loop. Lasted the whole weekend. Still doesn't seem real." Jack inhaled deeply. "You know me, Stu. I'm not one to take charity. I know that's not what you're doing. I'm fine on my salary. Just me to worry about."

"Of course, Jack. I know you're a man of integrity."

Jack gripped the phone. "Like you said, this is for Karen. To honor her. I was thinking about the scholarship fund you set up in her name. I could add to that." He paused. Did he say that for Buckley's benefit or his own? "Anyway, I've decided to accept your generosity. Many thanks, of course."

"That's great, Jack. Wonderful news. I was a little worried your pride might stand in the way."

"I may be proud, but I'm not stupid. Only a fool would turn you down, but I needed to think it over. Take some time."

"I understand. Let's set up a meeting next week. We'll go to my bank for the transfer and other paperwork."

"Sounds good. Mid to late week works for me. I'll wait for your call."

"I'll see you soon. Glad we're on board."

After they hung up, Jack felt relieved. Decision done. His imagination took over. He could tell LePere to go to hell and shove his frickin' job. Send Maureen to Ireland with Jenny or Tommy. Hell, the whole family. Not him though. He'd never go back there. Never.

Chapter 28

Monday morning dawned bright with a warm breeze fluttering through trees, heralding its welcome spring to Chicago. Karen had loved spring with the emerging tulips, daffodils, and all things green. Jack's step was lighter as he strolled into the station. Whose wouldn't be with a high of someone winning the lottery. Can't let himself get too excited. Keep a cool head. Be cautious. Too-good-to-be-true thoughts seeped into the corners of his mind.

Jack no sooner walked through the door of the station than he ran into Chub Nesbitt.

"Bailey," the big man boomed. "Been hiding from me?"

"Not good enough apparently." He and Nesbitt continued down the hall. "You weren't around last week when I looked for ya. Let's have a chat."

"What I've been afraid of."

Nesbitt chortled. "Seen the morning papers?" He unlocked his door and closed it after they stepped inside. "Have a seat."

Nesbitt walked around his large desk and sat. "News of our serial killer made the *Tribune* this morning. The *Leader* too. Says the Skokie killer may be linked to the nun and Welton murders."

"What?" Jack's jaw dropped. "Who the hell leaked that? They mention the Bible verses?"

Nesbitt rubbed his shiny temples. "No, just the latest vic may have been involved in inappropriate crap with Little League boys."

"Shit," Jack said. "Some idiot in Skokie must've leaked the information."

"Yeah, well I don't have to tell you, Bailey. Get on it. What's your next move?"

"Me and Sherk are gonna start interviewing Sister Anne's former students when this McGarvey priest was at her church during his time. Allegations against him were never proven, but that means nothing. Look at all the priest cover-ups in the last ten years."

"Think that's the key? McGarvey messed with a kid that started his path to serial killing?"

"Sure of it. My gut's usually right. We're on it pronto."

"Good." Nesbitt stood. "And watch it with LePere."

"Right, Cap. Keep ya posted." Jack stood and hurried out the door.

Walking into the bull pen, he spotted Sherk at his desk staring at his computer screen.

"You're here early," Jack said. "How's Erica feeling?"

"So far so good. Her mom wants to come help out, but Erica doesn't like the idea." Sherk took a drink of coffee. "Yes, I'm early. Thought I'd surprise Ms. LePere, but haven't seen her yet."

"Did she come by Friday afternoon busting your balls about going AWOL in the morning?"

"Not a word. Nesbitt must've clued her in."

Jack picked up his mug from a pile of folders. "See the papers this morning?"

Sherk sighed. "Afraid so. It seems the Skokie PD is focusing on their own importance in the case, making us the less intelligent guys who need their help."

Jack murmured in agreement and headed for the break room. He dodged questions from Velda Vatava and several cops about the newspaper columns. Leaving this frickin' job grew more and more tempting.

Coffee in hand, he returned to his desk and booted up the computer. "Let's head out and talk to that Len Abbott guy. Maybe we won't get sidetracked by another murder this time."

"Right," Sherk said. "Think we should show him the list of the other boys who were Sister Anne's students? We may be able to read something in his face. Not sure what though."

"Yeah. I'm sure McGarvey messed with more than one kid. Sick bastard."

"We're operating on pure assumption at this point, Jack. Let's not get ahead of ourselves."

"Sherk, you can be a real pain in the butt."

"I know. I'll be ready in ten minutes. Should get us there by nine o'clock when the company opens."

• • • • •

Jack and Sherk drove down Pulaski Road until they were a couple blocks from Abbott's software company.

"Look at that." Jack pointed toward a huge cigar store Indian standing atop two white pillars on a one story building on the corner of Sixty-third Street. "Still standing after all these years."

"Quite amazing in this politically correct day and age," Sherk said. "How long has it been there?"

"At least forty years. Used to be a cigar company. No surprise there." They passed the enormous landmark, the Geronimo-like image holding one hand high in the air. A sign across its chest read *Eye Can See Now*.

"Wow," Sherk exclaimed. "He's wearing glasses. Must be advertising the Midwest Eye Clinic below."

"Hard to get anything past you."

"I'm truly amazed there haven't been protests from Native Americans. It could easily be construed — "

"Give it a rest, Sherk. We're about at Abbott's place. Wonder if Costello's there."

"Who?"

"Never mind." Wasn't about to start a 'who's on first' conversation.

Jack pulled into a parking lot beside a two story unadorned gray building with a sign above its door reading PrimeWare. "Sounds like a store for boxer shorts," he said as they walked in the front door.

"They'd need to correct the spelling of 'ware' in that case."

Was Sherk serious? No patience to find out.

A young, attractive woman with long red hair sat at a desk in the sparsely decorated entry area. She looked up from her keyboard "May I help you?" Her manicured nails were black, matching her lipstick.

"We're here to see Len Abbott," Sherk said.

Her teeth contrasted sharply with the dark lip color. "Do you have an appointment?"

Sherk took his badge from his pocket. "I'm Detective Sherkenbach, Bridgeport PD. This is my partner Detective Bailey." Both men held out their ID's.

Noting the look of concern on the girl's face, Jack said, "He's not in any trouble, Ma'am. We're gathering information, and we have a few questions for Mr. Abbott. Won't take more than a few minutes."

She reached for her phone and punched a button. "Len, someone's here to see you. Can you come to the desk?" After hanging up, she said, "He'll be right out. Would you like to sit?"

"Thank you, Ma'am." Sherk smiled as he and Jack walked to the other side and sat in black vinyl armchairs.

Within two minutes, the door across from them opened and a short, skinny wisp of a man walked through. A strong wind could blow him away. He glanced at the receptionist, then at Jack and Sherk, who stood. Len Abbott looked like the poster kid who got sand kicked in his face at the beach.

"Len Abbott?" Sherk asked.

"Yes?" The man wore a rumpled yellow short-sleeved dress shirt, baggy khakis. His thin black hair receded from his forehead, plastic framed glasses and a stubble beard covered most of his small round face.

After introductions, Abbott led the way into a large room with a dozen cubicles arranged throughout, where young men in shirts and jeans pinged away on their keyboards. Abbott made his way to a closed door which he opened, revealing a small conference room with a table and six chairs.

"We can use this." Abbott's voice was soft, tentative, womanish. "Sit anywhere."

He took a seat at one end, Jack and Sherk sat on either side.

"So, Len," Jack half smiled. "Or do you prefer Bud?"

Abbott stared at Jack. "Huh?"

"Sorry. I'm sure you heard that all your life. Stuff like, 'where's Lou?' and 'who's on first?'

Finally, the lightbulb. "Oh, you mean Costello. Yeah, not so much any more." Abbott seemed to relax.

"Tell me, what does PrimeWare do," Sherk asked. "Primarily."

"Oh, the company enhances, maintains, and provides support for a software payroll system."

"And what's your job here?" Jack wanted the guy to keep feeling at ease.

"Well, as a programmer, I update the code with new features, changes in laws, bugs, and customer support. The program was originally designed to run batch, then we reprogrammed it to run online, and now we anticipate using the cloud— "

"Hey, you're talkin' Greek, man." Jack leaned back. "What kinda degree do you have to do all that?"

Abbott shrugged, his cheeks flushed. "Oh, I enrolled at Dawson Tech for a couple years and worked at— "

"That's good." Jack had enough small talk. Not that he understood a word of it. "We're here to gather information on a case we're working on." Jack noticed the pocket protector on Abbott's shirt. Hadn't seen one of those in awhile.

"Oh?" Abbott's eyes widened. "I don't see how— "

"Don't worry, just a few questions and we'll be done," Sherk said. Abbott looked back and forth at the detectives like he was watching a tennis match.

Jack jumped in. "Did you know Father Daniel McGarvey from Nativity of Our Lord Church?" Catch the little punk off guard.

"Uh, what?" Abbott's pupils expanded. "Oh, I'm not sure. Uh— "

"This would've been back in the seventies. In grade school," Sherk said.

"Oh." Abbott's face looked as if he'd solved a math problem. "Is this about that nun's murder a couple weeks ago?"

The guy was a quick study. "Yeah, it is." Jack leaned in. "Sister Anne Celeste. You had her in what, fifth grade?"

"Uh, yeah. About fifth grade I think." Sweat lit up his balding hairline. "Are you asking everyone who had her for a teacher?"

"No," Jack said. Did Abbott think he was a suspect? "Just her students during the time Father Daniel McGarvey was there."

"What did you think of Father Daniel?" Sherk asked, removing his glasses.

"Oh, uh, I don't actually remember. That was years ago." He swiped his brow with his hand. "Too many years to recall." He shrugged. Looked at his hands.

"Some allegations against him," Jack said. "That jog your memory?"

The corners of Abbott's mouth twitched. "Uh. No, afraid not." He started to rise. "Sorry I can't help you. I need to get back. In the middle of a— "

"Yeah, a program to enhance and maintain something," Jack said.

Sherk took a piece of paper from his notebook and handed it to Abbott. "Could you take a look at these names and tell me if you knew any of them?"

Abbott took his time reading the list. "Uh, a couple sound familiar, but I can't be sure."

He paused and pointed his finger on the paper. "These two were in my class."

Sherk took the paper. Thank you, Mr. Abbott. That'll be all for now." He reached in his pocket. "Here's my card. Call if you think of anything else."

"One more thing." Jack pushed back his chair and stood. "Did Sister Anne ever rap your knuckles with her ruler when you didn't write your letter A's correctly?"

Abbott looked deadpan. "That didn't happen much."

So much for the guy's sense of humor. They said their good-byes, and Abbott headed back to his computer and cloud nine or whatever. The receptionist was busy examining her nails as Sherk thanked her and led the way out the door.

Driving back on Pulaski Road, Jack said, "Classic case of a guy lying through his teeth. Can't prove anything, but I bet my left nut he was messed with by the McGarvey prick."

Sherk sighed. "I'm afraid so. Even if he wasn't abused, he certainly knew about the allegations."

"I think we're zeroing in, Sherk. I'm sure the killer was a vic of the priest's. Doesn't sound like Sister Anne did anything except turn a blind eye. Since the priest's pushing daisies, the nun was the target. Then the perp goes after other pedophiles he's heard about or seen on the registry."

"Yes, to rid the world of them. We need to stop him before—" Sherk's voice trailed off.

• • • • •

Thirty minutes later they sat at their desks updating paperwork. Sherk's phone buzzed.

"Yes." Pause. "I see. Thanks. We'll keep you posted." He hung up. "That was the Skokie detective about the autopsy report on our coach Grant Adams. Cause of death is the same type of somulose used on Bruce Welton. Injected into the same place, upper throat. Same amount, 120 cubic centimeters."

"No surprise. The perp probably knew about the coach or heard the rumors. Vigilante justice." Jack stretched back in his chair. "By the way, who did Len Abbott know from the list of students he looked at?"

"He knew the last two names." Sherk reached for his notebook. "Let's see here. Mark Percy and Donald Sowder."

Chapter 29

Eight miles away from the Bridgeport PD, Donald Sowder, bored as hell with the morning's national news, switched channels to a local station. Chomping his toast, he missed part of the crime story the slick-haired anchor spoke about. All Donald heard was an unidentified man found dead, cause of death unknown. Nothing earthshaking about that. Just another murder in the big city.

He hadn't been sleeping well lately. He popped Unisom most nights, but they didn't help much. He shouldn't have gone off his meds without telling his long-ago shrink.

Last night he woke in a sweat. Why? Oh yeah, that damn door again in his nightmare. This time it opened several inches, hinges creaked, a large hand beckoned.

Come in Donny, come learn your lesson.

Had he dreamed that voice?

Covering his head with the blanket, he whispered *No, Father, No, Father* over and over.

After Donald finished breakfast, he rinsed the plate and cup in the sink. Cleaned his glasses for the second time, always with a micro cloth. He brushed his teeth, came close to glancing in the mirror, but averted his eyes. Why can't you look in the mirror, he asked himself time and again. Couldn't think when that reaction began. Maybe last year?

Before he unlocked the front door, he pulled the living room curtain aside and peered out. No strange vehicles lurking about. Partly sunny, a few cotton ball clouds, grass turning green. Should be a smooth drive to Midway.

Blind Eye

• • • • •

By 5:00, Donald was anxious to ditch work and head home. He stopped at his favorite 7-Eleven on West Archer to grab dinner and replenish his supply of beer. He bought a six-pack of Old Style and a hot meatball sandwich. After a guy at work had sworn the place sold great food, Donald reluctantly tried it out. Had to admit, the pizza and sandwiches were top drawer in his opinion, although most nights he ate frozen dinners on his sofa while he watched TV.

After entering his apartment building, Donald stopped in the vestibule for his mail. The usual junk and his newspaper were crammed into the box. He rode the elevator to the third floor, unlocked his door, tossed the mail onto an end table, and hurried into the kitchen. Didn't want his sandwich to get cold, so he unwrapped it, opened a can of Old Style and put the remaining six-pack in the fridge.

He settled into his shabby armchair and turned on the TV. Biting into his sandwich, he watched a young brunette jabbering about the spring-like Chicago weather. He took a swig of beer and glanced at the mail on the table next to him. A brochure of an airline special to Costa Rica promised a romantic get-away if one booked a flight before the end of April.

Donald scoffed. He never thought about travel. Why bother? Who'd go on a trip with him? He glanced at the pamphlet's cover photo, a small boy and girl splashing in white, frothy waves on a sandy beach. What a crock. Who's that happy? He tossed the flyer back on the table beside his book of Edgar Allan Poe short stories.

Draining his beer, Donald thought of his childhood before 'the happening' as he euphemistically called it. When life was carefree. The place he'd go to in his mind when darkness overtook him. The summer his family spent a week at the Wisconsin Dells with Uncle Phil and his kids. Phil was the best role model in the world for eight-year-old Donald. Took him boating, fishing, hiking. He'd tell Donald what a smart kid he was. More than his father ever did. The good times ended a year later when Phil was killed in a car accident. Part of Donald died with him.

Words from the newscaster jolted him back to the present. What was that about a murder in Skokie? The same newsfeed he heard this morning? "According to Sergeant Joe Rossi, the victim may be connected to two other area murders last month, including Sister Anne Celeste of Bridgeport."

What? An invisible force seemed to knock Donald over. His heart throbbed, he couldn't breathe. Hot coals seared through his body. The next words came from a distant sphere.

"The two departments are working together to determine motive. When asked for details, Detective Jack Bailey of the Bridgeport PD refused to comment."

Sweating, Donald stood mesmerized by the TV announcer. He opened his mouth, but no words emerged.

He gasped. "No. No." He gagged. Ripped off his glasses. Tossed them on the chair. "No. Can't be—" His stomach lurched. The meatball's spicy sauce rose to his throat. He dashed for the bathroom, tripping on the table, the can of beer and sandwich plunging to the floor. Made it to the john. Bent over the toilet just in time.

The TV was announcing sports scores when Donald staggered back to the living room and fell into the chair. He panted, wiped trickles of sweat from his forehead. Felt his glasses under his skinny butt. Scooched, retrieved the glasses from the scratchy fabric, put them on gingerly.

"Think. Think. What to do?" He'd call the cop station. Bridgeport or Skokie? Nah. No good. They wouldn't tell him anything. He grabbed the newspaper, still in its sleeve. Hands shook as he ripped it open, frantic. There is was. Bottom of page one. He read the article, noting more details than the TV news had revealed. The paper mentioned Bruce Welton's name as the second vic. Donald threw the paper on the floor.

He stood. Clenched his fists. Looked up. Yelled.

"No! No! Some bastard copied me!"

Chapter 30

Driving to work the next morning, Jack's mood fluctuated between upbeat and irritated. His near euphoria over his financial windfall was diminished by thoughts of Molly's rebuff. He refused to acknowledge he was humiliated, but logic told him he was overreacting. Things might work out between them, although given Jack's history with women, he doubted Molly would be a success. What the hell. Better off without her. Besides, she lugs heavy baggage, including alcoholism. Might be screwed up like the woman he hooked up with a couple years ago in Texas. Gotta forget those days. Now, he was about to become a rich man.

When Jack strolled into the bull pen, Sherk was at his desk drinking coffee.

"You're early," Jack said. "Everything okay? How's Erica?"

"She's fine. True, I'm on time this morning. Maybe Ms. LePere will notice."

"Who gives a damn?" Jack sat down. "Thought more about our talk with Abbott. Today we should interview all the guys, mainly the two he remembered from his school days with old Father McGarvey."

"Right. The priest probably messed with more than one boy. Curious if they'll act nervous like Abbott did." Sherk straightened his glasses.

"Yeah," Jack said. "Then see about getting their DNA. Depends how things go." He reached for his mug. "Gonna get coffee."

Too many thoughts crammed his brain. Tempted to tell Sherk about Buckley's offer, he knew he shouldn't say anything yet. How would he tell his family? His mother would faint. Or worse.

The break room smelled like strong coffee and warm blueberry muffins. Jack followed his nose to the coffee pot where Velda was pouring herself a cup. "Bailey, what's up with the latest murder? Vic was a coach I hear."

"You hear too much, Vatava. Keep your nose to the grindstone."

"Ha, always do. Tried to save you a muffin."

Jack noticed a measly half pastry on the tray, surrounded by crumbs. "Whaddya do? Eat the whole pan?"

Velda waved toward groups of cops sitting at small tables. "Those cretins got here first, the jerks."

Jack scooped up the remaining muffin in a napkin. "Seen Blondie yet?"

"Yeah, in the hall. In a sour mood. She needs a good lay."

"Vatava, I'm shocked how your mind works." Jack started for the door. "By the way, I agree." He stuffed the crumbly mess into his mouth and headed out of the room.

When Jack returned to his desk, he and Sherk studied the list of former students. Jack gulped his coffee. "Let's map out the closest ones and go from there."

"Right," Sherk said. "Let's see. Mark Percy lives in Bridgeport. Works at Testa Produce on Racine."

"Might be hard to get him alone. Better to get 'em at home, but don't wanna wait all day," Jack said.

• • • • •

Twenty minutes later, Sherk drove south of Pershing to the white, unadorned produce warehouse on Racine near Forty-fifth Street. Over 100 years old, the family-owned business supplied restaurants, schools, and other facilities with the freshest, tastiest produce in the Midwest, according to their marketing department.

When Jack and Sherk entered the building, a young, dark-haired woman of hefty proportions greeted them. "May I help you?"

After introducing themselves and assuring her that Mark Percy was in no trouble with the law, they followed her into a vast room with rows of multicolored fruits and vegetables in flat crates. Scents of citrus and rainforest filled the air, as they walked down the aisle to a back door.

The woman opened the door. "Hey, Josh," she called to a middle-aged man beside a truck. "Mark here?"

"Yeah, just a sec." He seemed to text someone. "Be right here."

The woman turned to leave. "He'll be here in a minute. Lucky he's not on the road yet."

"Must be a driver," Sherk said.

"What clued ya in?" Jack glanced around the parking lot where men in navy coveralls loaded boxes into semis. The trucks were bright blue with red lettering, with an image of a pineapple in a lower corner.

A robust-looking red-haired man trotted over. "Mark Percy." He held out his hand.

"Detective Bailey, Bridgeport PD." Jack flashed his badge. "My partner, Detective Sherkenbach."

Percy wore a long-sleeved denim shirt and black jeans. His smile was wide, and he exuded a hearty confidence. "What can I do for you guys?"

"Is there somewhere we can talk? Won't take long," Jack said.

"I'm due to pull out in a few minutes. Can we talk here?" Percy asked.

No one in sight. "I think that'll work," Sherk said.

"We're investigating the recent murder of Sister Anne Celeste from Nativity of Our Lord Church in Bridgeport." Jack watched him closely.

"Oh, yeah, heard about that. She was my fifth grade teacher back then." Percy tucked his phone in his pocket.

"Do you remember a Father McGarvey from that time?" Sherk asked.

"Oh sure. Father Dan. An okay guy. A little strict, but most were back then." If Percy were hiding something, he was a damn good actor.

"Were you an altar boy when he was there?" Jack asked.

"Nah. My mom wanted me to, but I was more interested in sports.

I said I didn't wanna, so she didn't fight me on it."

Jack nodded. "Did you ever hear anything negative about him?"

"Just rumors after he left about allegations against him. But nothing ever came of it far as I knew. Why? You think— "

"We don't know anything for sure, Mr. Percy," Sherk said. "We're questioning Sister Anne's former students when Father McGarvey was there."

Percy kept eye contact. "Yeah, I see. You think there's a connection to Sister's murder with Father Dan."

"We're exploring all the options." Jack figured Percy to be a dead end. "We won't take any more of your time." He handed the man his card. "Call if you think of anything more. Thanks."

"Okay. Wish I could've been more help." Percy turned. "I gotta run."

The men shook hands and proceeded on their separate ways.

Back in the car, Jack put on his sunglasses. "Didn't get a vibe he was involved."

Sherk drove away from the curb. "No. He doesn't fit the profile of an abused kid. Too friendly."

"Right," Jack said. "Confident, willing to talk. Doesn't seem like a kid who was picked on in school. Not like Abbott."

Sherk stopped at a red light. "You'd think a kid who attended Catholic school would end up with a higher job than a truck driver."

"Back then you didn't have to be rich to go to Catholic school. Hell, look at me. All of us went. Our church had a deal. Kind of a sliding scale."

"I see."

"Never checked, but heard truck drivers with seniority make pretty good money. Maybe I should look into that." Odd, for a second, Jack forgot his windfall. Took getting used to.

Their next stop was Armour Square, to check out Tom Chu, another guy on the student list. They found the office, drove around the block for a parking place, and trudged into a drab gray one story building. Lettering on the front window read Liu & Tang Tech.

"Liu must sell orange juice," Jack said.

"Ha, ha."

When Sherk inquired about Tom Chu, the receptionist said he was out of town and would return in a week.

Next they headed for Lawndale, northwest of Bridgeport. Sherk parked the car in a shopping strip and led the way into a T-Mobile store on Twenty-sixth Street. He asked a smiling young Indian man if he could speak to Joe Miller.

"Sorry, you just missed him," the man said. "He's off till tomorrow afternoon. One o'clock."

"Thanks," Jack said.

"You guys interested in our new model? Just came in."

Jack turned to leave. "Some other time."

"I'll take a look," Sherk said.

"Here's the best Smartphone of the year." The guy whipped out the device from the glassed-in display case. "I give you the Galaxy S III"

"If you're givin' it away, I'll take one," Jack said. "Come on, Sherk. Got work to do."

Quite a switch. Usually Jack was the slacker.

Heading south, they exited onto I-55 toward Midway Airport where Donald Sowder, the last man on the list, worked.

"How are your plans for the Germany trip coming?" Jack asked.

"Don't know yet. Erica has another round of chemo this Friday. She'll ask the doc about it then. May be too soon to tell."

"Yeah." Jack couldn't think of anything profound to say.

Ten minutes later, they turned into the main terminal of the airport. Sherk slid the cruiser into a spot under the gigantic parking structure. He and Jack made their way past people of all ages and sizes waiting, departing, standing, hurrying. Entering the building, they headed toward a customer service counter, where a uniformed older man stood tapping on his phone. Jack flashed his badge, introduced himself and Sherk, and asked to see Donald Sowder.

"Just give me a second here, fellas." He clicked several times, waited. "He's over in Area H, restricted, but not for you guys, ha ha. Here's a map." The man took a highlighter and traced their route to the destination.

"Shit, must be five miles," Jack said as they walked toward an escalator.

"The exercise will do us good. Wonder if Donald has a supervisor. Want to call first?"

"Nah. Better to catch him off guard. A boss may give the guy a heads up."

Flight announcements blared through the PA system as they passed magazine and snack shops, Starbucks, deli counters. The enticing aroma from a Cinnabon bakery floated through the air. Jack noticed a Chick-fil-A as they turned a corner.

"Let's stop here on the way back. I'm starvin'."

"Sounds good. They offer a Southwest salad that's quite healthy."

"To hell with healthy. I'm having the spicy sandwich deluxe with waffle potato fries. Gotta live a little, Sherk."

"A little or longer?"

Thinking of Erica, Jack didn't want to prolong this line of conversation.

After several minutes they reached Area H, where a uniformed airport official directed them to an office area across the entry space. An older man with a white billy goat beard sat at a desk staring at a computer monitor. A nameplate read 'Bob Wolfe'. He glanced up. "May I help you?"

Sherk made the introductions. "We need to speak to Donald Sowder. Are you his supervisor?"

The man's eyes widened. He began to stand, hands on desk. Jack said, "Don't worry. He's not in trouble. We're gathering information is all. Shouldn't take more than a few minutes."

"Well, ah, Donald isn't here today." Wolfe cleared his throat. "He called in sick."

"I see," Jack said. "Does he miss much work?"

"Hardly ever. Other than planned vacation days, Donald is never gone. Never been sick before that I can recall."

"Thank you, Mr. Wolfe," Sherk said. "We'll try another time."

The man coughed. "Yes. Yes. You could call first."

"Right." Jack turned to leave. He hoped Wolfe wouldn't call Sowder and tell him the cops came to visit. But telling Wolfe to keep mum would've made the guy more suspicious than he might already be.

Retracing their steps, Jack and Sherk stopped at Chick-fil-A. After devouring their meals of chicken and salad, they found their way out of the terminal. "Think we should surprise Sowder at home?" Jack asked.

"I do, even though we'll rouse him from his sick bed." Sherk unlocked the cruiser.

Climbing into the car, Jack said, "He's no more sick than I am. Interesting how the guy's a no-show at work right after the news stories break. Frickin' Skokie cops."

Jack dug out Sowder's home address and entered it into his phone. "Lives in Garfield Ridge, right in this neighborhood. Must take him all of ten minutes to get to work."

Sherk exited the airport and turned onto Central. At Fifty-fifth, he hung a left, and slowed down in front of a square gray building. He parked the car in the rear and turned off the engine.

Jack's stomach tightened. "Got a feeling about this, Sherk."

"You rely on instinct too much. Better to let your intellect guide you."

Jack bristled. "Yeah, yeah." Didn't need a lecture when his nerves were on edge.

The air was sunny and crisp as they walked from the car into the entryway. A row of mailboxes lined one wall. Jack squinted as he read the labels. "Here it is. D. Sowder. 3B"

A desk cluttered with file folders sat near the elevator. "Nobody around to screen us. Let's go." Jack punched the button.

They emerged from the elevator onto the third floor and found 3B several doors down the hallway.

Jack held his ear against the door. He heard a TV or radio. Men's voices.

No bell, so Sherk rapped. "Mr. Sowder?"

The TV stopped. Silence.

Jack rapped louder. "Bridgeport police. Open up. Just want to talk to you."

Nothing.

Sherk nodded at Jack. "Sowder, don't make us break the door down."

Nothing.

"Okay, you asked for it," Jack yelled. He pounded three times. Heard a click from the other side. Sounded like a lock.

The knob turned. Door opened a crack. No one visible.

Jack reached in his side holster and pulled out his Glock.

Chapter 31

Sherk edged away from the door and stood alongside the wall. Jack pointed his gun straight ahead. Across the hall a door opened, and a frowsy older lady stuck her head out.

"What the hell's going on? I'm gonna call the cops."

"We are the cops, lady," Jack snarled. "Get back in your room. Close the door."

"You sure you're cops?" She eyeballed Sherk. "Where's your ID?"

Sherk stepped toward the woman. "Ma'am, please go back in your apartment." He flashed his badge close to her withered face.

"Okay, okay, but that guy's harmless. Weird, but harmless." She stepped back and slammed the door.

Jack knocked one more time. "Come on, Sowder. Open up. Slowly."

"Let me see your badge." A tentative voice from inside.

Sherk held out his ID. "Mr. Sowder, we just want to talk to you. Won't take more than a few minutes."

The door opened several more inches. "I'm not feeling well. Can you come back tomorrow?"

"No we can't." Time for bad cop. Jack rammed in the door, and a thin middle-aged man fell backwards.

The man staggered and righted himself. "Hey, what are ya doing? I didn't do anything."

"Then you got nothing to worry about." Jack pointed his gun at the floor, noting the man's short, brown hair, thick wire-rimmed glasses. His faded red t-shirt and gray sweatpants loose fitting, rumpled. A faint musty odor hung in the air.

Sherk indicated a threadbare sofa. "Have a seat, Mr. Sowder."

The man dropped onto the couch. Sherk sat beside him, Jack stood.

"Why were you hiding, Mr. Sowder?" Sherk asked.

"Ah, I dunno. I'm not feeling well and I didn't know— "

"Yeah, you said that already. Called in sick from work." Jack slid his gun into its holster.

"You went to my work? You talked to my boss? Why? What do you want?"

"Slow down, Mr. Sowder." Sherk leaned toward the man.

"Donald. Call me Donald." He pushed up his glasses with a shaky hand.

"Okay, Donald." Sherk's voice softened. "Take a couple deep breaths. Try and relax. We have a few questions and then we're done."

Donald took a deep breath and appeared to calm down. He glanced back and forth between Jack and Sherk. "All right. What do you want to know?"

Jack took out his notebook. "Were you a student at Nativity of Our Lord School in Bridgeport back in the seventies?"

Donald's head jerked sideways. He rubbed his hands together. Kept rubbing. "Yeah. Back in grade school."

Jack sat in a chair across from the sofa. "Do you remember Father Daniel McGarvey?"

Donald's right eye twitched. "Ah, I'm not sure. I dunno." Pause. "Don't think so." His eyes darted to the floor, then the wall.

Jack studied the man. "I see. Don't remember Daniel McGarvey? Maybe the kids called him Father Dan?"

Donald sprang up. His hands flew to his throat. "No." Voice pitched higher. "No. I told you I don't remember the son of a bitch. I don't remember."

Sherk stood and touched the man's shoulder. "It's okay, Donald. We don't want to upset you. Please sit back down."

"I'm not upset." Loud, then softer. "I'm not upset."

"Would you like some water?" Sherk asked.

Donald stared at him. "Water? Ah, yeah. I'll get it."

Sherk followed Donald into the drab kitchen and watched him take a glass from a cabinet and fill it with tap water. The sink and counters were free of clutter with no unwashed dishes in sight. Fridge and oven shiny, gold colored.

"Why do you want to know these things?" Donald asked on their way back to the living room.

"There may be a connection between the priest and a case we're working on," Sherk answered as he and Donald returned to the couch.

Donald gulped his water. "Well, I don't know anything about that."

"About what?" Jack shifted closer.

Donald's eye twitched again. "About anything. Any case you have. I mean any crime that, ah, happened." He squeezed his glass with both hands.

"You're saying you know nothing about any crime? And what crime is that?" Jack saw the guy withering.

"No crime."

"No crime," Jack repeated.

"Stop it." Donald's voice rising. "You're messing with me. Messing with my head." He set his glass on an end table with a thud. "You're trying to—trying to—"

Sherk nudged toward the man. "Trying to what, Donald?" Voice soft, soothing. "What are we trying to do?"

"You're—you're—I dunno!" he yelled and leapt from the sofa. He covered his ears with his hands and paced back and forth. "You—you have to leave. Just go. Go! Now!"

• • • • •

Donald Sowder heard himself yell. "Leave. Get out!" Why wouldn't the buzzing stop? He paced faster. The high pitched buzzing in his head, relentless. "Stop. Stop." He was slipping down the hole. Same as before. Years ago. First the panic attacks. Thought he was better.

Now the cop's gentle voice. "Donald, please sit down. We're not going to hurt you."

Uncovering his ears, Donald stared at the cop who wore glasses, tall, thin, blond. Bet women called him handsome. He sank into the sofa, avoided looking at the other cop. Shifting against the armrest, Donald's hand shook as he touched his glasses, swiped at his brow.

"You okay, Sowder?" the other cop asked as he fiddled with his phone.

"Yeah. Don't feel good. Like I said, I'm sick." Donald glanced at the cop, whose black hair was sprinkled with gray. Why were his eyes piercing through Donald's brain? Wait a minute. He'd seen this guy before.

"Do I know you?" Donald asked. "Think I've seen you somewhere."

The nice cop chuckled. "Detective Bailey gets that a lot. People think he's Liam Neeson's doppelganger."

"Huh?" Donald paused. Frowned. "Maybe that's it. But—" He was still puzzled. Where?

"Bailey, you said? That's your name?"

"Yeah. Why?" Bailey put his phone away.

Donald shrugged. Something niggled at him. "No reason." He stared at Bailey, confused.

The blond cop said, "Now, Donald, before we leave, there's one more— "

"The funeral!" Donald jumped up, covered his ears again. Stared at Bailey, who looked surprised. "You. You were at the funeral. I saw you. I saw you." *Careful,* the voice said. *Careful.*

Bailey rose from the chair and stood in front of Donald. "Whose funeral, Sowder? What are you talking about?"

"Don't pretend. You know. Her funeral. Hers!" he yelled.

"Ah. You mean Sister Anne Celeste." Bailey squinted. "Yes, I knew her. Paid my respects."

The cop had a sly look on his face. Donald felt a surge of heat. Hot coals again. Buzzing in his head. "Oh sure. You think you can trick me? I'm not that dumb. You think I don't know why cops go to funerals?" His voice rose. "Do you?"

"You tell us, Donald," the blond cop said. "Why do we go to funerals?"

"To—to see if you can catch. Catch— "*Careful.*

"Catch who?" Bailey asked. His voice lower now. "Who do we want to catch?"

Donald took several deep breaths. He felt calm again. Smart. "I'm not saying any more. I know my rights. No more talking unless I'm under arrest and have a lawyer." He sat again.

Bailey looked at the other cop. "Bet he watches *Law and Order.*"

Careful. Careful. "Oh, you think that's funny? You guys are the stupid ones for— "

"We're sorry, Donald. We don't want to disrespect you," the blond cop said. Did he give Bailey a dirty look? "You knew Sister Anne Celeste from your student days?"

"Huh?" *Think. Think.* Do they know what he did to Sister?

"Yes, you attended her funeral. So she taught you at Nativity in grade school?" The nice cop smiled. A likable guy.

Very likable, trustworthy this blond cop. Soothing, like, like. No. No. Not like *he* was. The devil in sheep's clothing he was. But the other cop. Bailey. Villain. He must know something. Knows about Sister and how he—. Oh God, the buzzing, Louder. LOUDER. "Make it stop." Did he just yell that?

He felt a hand touch his arm. Blond cop bending over him. "Make what stop, Donald? Tell us. We'll help you."

Donald wriggled away. Jumped up. Paced. He sensed the cops looking at each other, maybe debating what to do. He was unraveling. Like ten years ago. Why did he skip his meds the last few months?

He heard a faraway voice. "Donald, why don't you come with us. We'll take you to a doctor who can help."

"No! No!" Did he yell again? He knew what they were doing. Tricking him. What do they really know? Poe's long-ago story penetrated his brain. Nervous, not crazy. The cop, the villains suspected him of the murders. Not the third one. Just two. They're making a joke of me.

Then Donald heard it. Thump. Thump. All their hearts. The nun.

The guy. They were here. *Careful. Careful.*

Someone took his arm. "Let's get a jacket for you. We'll get help, Donald."

He yanked his arm away. Shrieked. "You hear it don't you?" Thump. Thump.

"It's okay, Donald."

Sweat poured down his face. He threw his glasses on the end table. His eyes rolled back like a wild horse trying to break out of its harness. The villains know. They know. They hear. The thumping.

Donald let out a scream. "Villains! Pretend no more. Tear up the floor. I admit the deed. I admit it. But not all three. Not all three. Bastard copied me, he copied me!"

Drenched, shaky, he sank onto the sofa and rocked back and forth in a fetal position.

Chapter 32

Jack stared at Donald, then turned to Sherk. "What the hell does that mean? Villains, tearing up the floor? Guy's a wack job."

Sherk placed a hand on Donald's shoulder. "He's referring to "The Tell-Tale Heart". Poe. At the end, the narrator hears the beating of the heart of the old man that— "

"Yeah, whatever. Guy needs a straight jacket." Jack and Sherk gazed at Donald, who continued to rock, moaning softly.

Jack fished out his phone. "Called it in before. What's taking so long?"

Donald stopped rocking and looked up. He eyeballed Sherk. "Didn't do three. Just two. Just two. Prick copied me. Wait till I get him. Nobody copies me."

Sherk knelt on the floor next to Donald. Clear who the good cop was. "Donald, it's okay. Tell me about what two you did. What do you mean?" Sherk's voice calm, low.

Donald's eyes darted to the ceiling. "Why do you think I did three? Vengeance is mine, saith the Lord. The devil in sheep's clothes will burn in eternal damnation for the sins of— "

Wailing sirens interrupted his words. Donald sprang from the chair. "They're coming to get me. I tell you, I didn't do all three— "

Donald darted for the hallway and reached the bedroom when Sherk grabbed onto the man's shoulders. "Donald, turn around. Look at me. No one will hurt— "

"No. No." Donald tried to squirm from Sherk's grasp. "No." He looked wildly about the ceiling and walls. "Take thy beak from out my heart— ". He eyed Jack, who stood behind Sherk.

Sherk's voice calm. "Donald, we'll leave in a minute. Help is here— "

"Take thy form from off my door— "

"Come on, dude. Let's go," Jack said as he helped Sherk guide Donald to the living room. Two EMT's knocked on the door and walked in. They wore black pants and shirts with paramedic logo patches on the sleeves.

"Got a live one," the taller guy said.

Donald yelled, "Thy form from off my door— "

"Haven't heard that one," the other man said as he walked toward Donald and Sherk.

"Thy beak from out my heart." Donald sobbing.

The man patted Donald's upper arm. "It'll be okay, Buddy. Let's just— "

"Take thy beak from— "

"Yeah, I know," the man continued. He nodded to the other guy, who approached with handcuffs. Surprisingly, Donald did not resist when they quickly cuffed his wrists together in front. He gazed at his hands as if he understood rules must be followed.

• • • • •

Oh god, I can't stand the buzzing. Make it stop. And the raven. The raven claws hurt my back. I can feel them. Can't be. They'll take me away. Put me in a straightjacket like the cop said. Shouldn't have taken all the leftover pills. I knew they'd come get me. Nervous. Not insane. Just nervous like the storyteller. Like him. Not crazy.

"Take thy damn beak." Why is the room turning black? The black circle, the rim's fading in. Blacker and blacker. My legs turning to jello. No! Don't wanna faint.

• • • • •

Each EMT guy took one of Donald's arms and walked with him toward the door. "You got his ID?" one man asked, glancing at the detectives.

"Yeah." Jack handed him a wallet. "Just spotted it by his phone on the end table."

"Nevermore. Lenore. Nevermore take thy beak— "Donald's shoulders slumped, his head downward. "Take thy beak—" He whispered.

"Hey, it's okay, Buddy. On our way," the tall man said. He looked at Sherk. "Meet you at Mercy?"

"Yeah," Sherk said. "Want me to ride along?"

"Nah, he'll be okay. Winding down."

Donald's eyes rolled around in their sockets. "Oh god. Why hast thou forsaken me?"

The men shook their heads, looked at Sherk, and guided Donald through the door, holding onto his upper arms. Donald offered no resistance. "Forsaken me. Forsaken me."

Jack returned from the bedroom. "Found his keys. We gotta lock the door. One of 'em should work."

After a few seconds of trial and error, Jack found the right key and locked the door behind them.

Several people stood in the hallway near their apartments. "What's going on?" a young Latino man asked.

"I knew there was something about that guy," the frowsy lady said. "What happened to him? He's gay, ain't he? What did he do?"

"Everything's fine now," Sherk told the group. "Go back inside. Have a good night."

"Yeah, right. We can have a good night after that?" the lady rasped, and closed her door.

When they reached the elevator, Jack punched the button. Why were elevators so damn slow? Taking forever. Finally, the light flashed and pinged, the doors opened. Had a feeling this would be a long night.

• • • • •

Half an hour later the two men hung out on the second floor of Mercy Hospital waiting for Donald Sowder's exam to be over. "Want more coffee?" Sherk asked.

Jack glanced at his empty Styrofoam cup. "Nah, what I need is a shot of James."

"Maybe we'll get the tox screen results tonight," Sherk said. "I don't think he was drunk, but may have ingested some meds."

"Wonder how long he's been wacko." Jack tossed his cup in a trash can. "All that yakking about taking beaks from hearts and floor boards. And then the Bible stuff."

"Yes, Donald went way off the rails. Apparently obsessed with Edgar Allan Poe. He quoted both the 'Tell-Tale Heart' and 'The Raven'. He obviously couldn't be in that state most of the time, otherwise he couldn't hold a job."

Jack glanced at his watch. "Should be done by now. What's the hold up?" He walked to the nurse's station where a young black woman sat writing on a chart.

"Excuse me, do you know how long Donald Sowder will be with the doctor?"

The lady looked up. "No, Sir, but it shouldn't be too much longer." She smiled.

Jack wondered why he bothered. Always the same answer.

After ten minutes a thirty-something Indian man in a white lab coat walked toward Jack and Sherk, sitting in chairs near the nurse's station. "Detectives?"

The men introduced themselves to Dr. Nadeem Sodhi, who took a chair beside Jack. "We can talk here," the doc said. "No one around this time of night."

Sherk pulled out his notebook. "How is Donald, Dr. Sodhi?"

The doctor straightened the stethoscope around his neck. "He's calmed down. We gave him an injection of Haloperidol, and tested for drug and alcohol ingestion. He wasn't inebriated. Blood alcohol level was in the normal range. Tox results won't be in until tomorrow. We're keeping him overnight for observation. He became more lucid as the drug took effect."

"Can you tell us what he said?" Jack asked.

"He was incoherent the first few minutes. Babbling about evil deeds, some of it sounded literary, like fragments of quotations."

Sherk nodded. "Can we talk to him after awhile?"

The doc shook his head. "I'm afraid not. You can come back in the morning. He'll likely be assigned to a psychiatrist for a full workup. I'm the internist on call tonight."

Jack stood. "They got the insurance info from his wallet?"

"Yes." Dr. Sodhi rose from his chair. "His contact information was a father and sister. A social worker tried to reach them. Don't know if she was able to."

"We'd like to talk to her," Jack said. "She still around?"

"Not sure. You can check with the nurse," Sodhi said. "By the way, his DNA was sent to the lab. You can check in a few days." He glanced at his phone. "Excuse me. I'm needed in the ER."

After learning there was no contact with Donald Sowder's family, Jack and Sherk made their way out the hospital and rode to the station to retrieve their cars.

"Whew," Sherk sighed. "A long night. See you bright and early in the morning, Jack."

"Yeah, can't wait," Jack mumbled as he parked the cruiser and climbed out.

A chill nipped the night air as they walked to their cars. Jack noticed the silence. No people, no traffic. Just Sherk and he driving their separate ways into the darkness.

• • • • •

When Jack arrived home, he opened the kitchen door and got a smell of a suspicious, ammonia odor. He glanced around the floor and spotted a puddle of dog pee by the entry to the living room just as Boone trotted in.

"What did you do Buddy?" The dog gave Jack a mournful gaze. "Sorry. I know I was late. Won't happen again. Come on, let's go out."

Jack watched as the big dog scampered out the back and peed under an ash tree. The porch light cast shadows in the still blackness. Eerily quiet.

"Time for a beer," Jack said to Boone as they walked into the kitchen. "But first things first." He grabbed several paper towels and got busy.

He hadn't eaten since the chicken sandwich at the airport. Seemed like a day ago.

After opening a bottle of Sam Adams, he grabbed a bag of Doritos and plopped into his recliner. He noticed his landline answering machine blinking. Who could that be? Probably Ma. He pressed the button and listened.

"Hi Jack. It's Molly." His eyebrows rose. "Just want to see if you'd like to meet this week. I kinda left things hanging, so thought we could talk. See you. 'Bye."

"What the hell? Thought she gave me the old heave-ho." Boone stared at him with round, searching eyes.

"Too late to call now." He ruffled the dog's soft fur. "I'll never understand broads."

Chapter 33

Jack tossed and turned during the night, disturbing dreams penetrating his sleep. Images of Ireland, Karen and Elizabeth running in slow motion through green meadows with grazing sheep. Then blasts, turbulent colors of orange, red, deafening. A priest and Maureen sitting on a gold throne. "Holy Mary, mother of God. Pray for us sinners— "

Jolted awake, Jack sat up mopped his brow. He took deep breaths, lay flat on the bed. Hadn't had church dreams for ages. Finally willed himself back to sleep.

Next he heard his alarm buzzing. He staggered out of bed and gradually readied himself for the day. Felt like he'd slept all of two hours.

After a shower and breakfast, Jack listened to Molly's message again on his way out. Should he call later this morning? Texting might be better. Although he'd enjoy her company, he couldn't see a long term relationship in his future. Maybe he was too screwed up.

When he reached the station, the last person he wanted to see stood at his desk. Daisy LePere, fierce in a black power suit, crossed her arms under her too-perfectly shaped bosom.

"Bailey, glad you decided to show up and grace us with your presence. Unlike your eminent partner, Sherkenbach."

Jack resisted the urge to say, 'Don't screw with me, lady'. He plunked down at his desk. "Wonderful to see you too, Sarge. What can your humble servant do for you today?"

Her stare icy. "Watch the attitude. I heard about your episode with the Sowder guy last night. When and if Sherkenbach shows up, both of you come to my office."

Too tired for a clever retort, Jack gave her a mock salute. With pursed lips, she hurried away, rose perfume sickening the air.

Without warning, a sense of control and power enveloped Jack. He'd bide his time, and if he blew up at LePere, so be it. He could afford to get the hell out and not put up with her shit anymore.

On his way to the break room, he stopped by Gary Calvin's desk. Jack noticed the guy was decked out in a solid white polo shirt. "What's with the normal shirt, Calvin. The others finally in the wash?"

"Not your usual quality of sarcasm this morning." Calvin patted his carrot top. "Not that it's any of your beeswax, I have a funeral to attend later in Des Plaines. Friend of my mom's."

"So showing up in a shirt that says 'I Turn Beer into Pee—what's your superpower?' won't show proper respect for the dearly departed?"

"Not bad, Bailey. Where did ya see that one?"

"Some jerk at a pub. Who knows?"

"By the way, you should get the DNA on the Sowder perp in a day or two."

"Not a perp yet. Some confusion. Gotta wait and see."

Calvin typed on his keyboard. "I got the guy's contact info and work history. His mother's in Goldpine in the memory care unit."

"Trying to forget Sowder? Alzheimer's, a survival kit for a horseshit life."

"And my mother thinks I'm a cynic." Calvin turned to his screen. "Catch ya later, Bailey."

When Jack returned with coffee, Sherk was at his desk. "Morning, Jack."

"The blond bitch wants us in her office."

Sherk raised his brow. "She'll chastise me for my late arrival no doubt."

"To hell with her. We'll make it short. Gotta get to the hospital. Check out Sowder."

They made their way to LePere's office. The door was open.

"Hee-re's Johnny." Jack stuck his head inside, fake Joker grin pasted on his face.

"Not funny. Come in and sit down. Close the door."

They sat across from her desk. "Nice to see you showed up, Sherkenbach." Her smile fake as a nine-dollar bill.

"Yes, Ma'am," Sherk said.

"What's the story on Donald Sowder?" LePere smoothed her blond hair to the side.

"He went mental on us," Jack said. "Blabbed something about doing the first two murders, but not the third. Said a copycat smoked the coach in Skokie."

"Any evidence of that?"

Dumb question. She knew the answer. Sherk said, "We're waiting for DNA. No other forensic evidence so far."

"We're heading for the hospital now to see him," Jack said. "When and if we get done here." His sarcasm obvious.

"Cut the attitude, Bailey." She clicked her red nails on the desk. "Get on with it. Do your damn job. What you're paid for. Check in later." She waved them out of the room.

The men stood and Sherk opened the door. "Shut it on our way out?"

"Yes," she snapped. "Get this case closed, fellas."

In the hallway, Jack said, "You heard her. We'll close the case. Now." He couldn't wait for the day he told the old bag where to shove her case.

• • • • •

Jack and Sherk drove down Halsted toward Mercy Hospital. Gray clouds snoozed in the sky, but the air felt warmer than yesterday. Jack stopped for a red light. "Any idea why Sowder claims he didn't do the third murder? Can't recall if he mentioned the Bible verse."

"He referred to scriptures. 'Vengeance is mine saith the lord' and 'devil in sheep's clothing'. Actually, the verse is 'beware of false prophets coming to you in sheep's— "

"All right for god's sake. I'll take your word for it."

"Clothing, but inwardly they are— "

"Sherk, I swear— "

"Ravenous wolves. So Jack, it's technically not the devil in— "

"Lemme guess. Wolves. Gluttons at that. Now shut up already."

Sherk chuckled. "You're good for a laugh, Jack. Sure need one these days."

"Erica still feeling okay?"

"Yeah. She's not eager for her next chemo in a couple days."

They arrived at the hospital and parked in front. When they reached Donald Sowder's room, a young patrol cop stood by the closed door. "Hey, guys. Tim from the department. You're Bailey and Sherk."

"Can't argue with that." Jack wasn't surprised to see someone monitoring Sowder.

Sherk said, "Hey Tim. What's the update on Donald?"

"His dad stomped in early this morning demanding a lawyer. Said no one questions his son without the lawyer present." The cop took a gulp of coffee from a Styrofoam cup in his hand. "He's out getting a lawyer now. Doesn't want a court-appointed. A real loud mouth, but his son's ass is on the line."

"Think we can just talk to Donald without asking questions? "Sherk asked.

"Maybe. Nurse is in there now. See if she's done."

Sherk tapped lightly and opened it a crack.

"Yes?" a female voice asked.

Sherk stepped in. "We'd like to see Mr. Sowder."

A young girl in pink scrubs stood by the bed. "Just finished his vitals. He can talk a little. But no questioning. Okay, Donald?"

Donald lay propped halfway up on his bed, a sheet to his waist. A faded print hospital gown hung loosely around his chest. "You again. I don't have anything to say."

"We should wait for the doctor," the girl said. "Should be here any minute."

Following Sherk into the room, Jack said, "We'll only be a minute."

"No." Donald's voice rose. "I don't wanna talk to you."

"Okay, Donald." Sherk turned. "We'll wait." He followed Jack into the hall. "Don't want to upset him. We'll see what the doc says."

"Guess I'll go in," Tim said. "Looks like he's done with his exams for now."

"So you sit in a room all day. Boring job, but someone's gotta do it," Jack said.

"I get a break when the lawyer comes. Should be here another couple days," Tim said.

Sherk crossed the hall. "Let's wait for the doc, Jack. See what he says."

"And waste the morning sittin' on our asses? Docs never show up when they're supposed to. People die waitin' for 'em."

Sherk sat in a folding chair. "What else do we have to do except wait for lab reports?"

Jack grudgingly took a seat. "Fine. Think we should bother trying the other ex-students we missed yesterday?" He looked at his notebook. "Tom Chu and Joe Miller."

"Don't think so at this point. I'm thinking Donald's our man, except for his insistence about a copycat."

"Don't see it. The Bible verse, same paper, same writing, same drug, same everything that bumped off Sister Anne and Welton. No one else knows about the verse and drug unless— "

Sherk stared at him. "Unless what? You thinking what I'm— "

"Just a minute." Jack glanced at his phone. "Gotta take this." He stood and walked a few yards down the hall.

"Hey, Stu. What's up?" Jack had been expecting the call. He listened.

"No problem. At a standstill at the moment." Pause. "Yeah, that should work. In the middle of a case, but see you tomorrow if I can. Should know for sure by mid-morning. Yeah. Later."

Meeting with Stewart Buckley at the bank this week was lousy timing, but with all that dough, who gave a damn.

Jack returned to his chair and sat. Sherk said, "Any news?"

"Huh? Oh, nah, no news. Something else. Not important." He

needed to tell Sherk about his windfall sometime. But not now. Hadn't told anyone.

"We were talking about the third murder," Sherk said. "Oh, here comes someone."

"About time," Jack said.

An attractive middle-aged woman approached them holding a clipboard. She wore an expensive looking navy and white pants outfit. She smiled. "Good morning. You must be the detectives who were with Mr. Sowder last night."

"Yes." Sherk introduced himself and Jack to Dr. Kay Dunne MD. "I was called in early this morning to consult for Mr. Sowder."

I see by your ID that you're a psychiatrist," Sherk said.

Jack could imagine the lady was a damn good one. She had a soothing presence and a low, pleasing voice, as well as a self-assured demeanor.

She turned toward Donald Sowder's door. "Yes, I work with both in and outpatients. I saw Mr. Sowder earlier, and plan to do further testing. If you'll wait a few minutes, I'll talk to him and let you know if I feel he's ready to see you if his lawyer is present."

"Can you tell us anything from this morning?" Jack asked. "Was he still off his—ah, acting— "

The doc smiled. "Agitated. Incoherent?"

"Yeah, that's what I meant." Jack should elevate his vocabulary around pretty women.

"He was subdued during the night. Medication helped him rest. He seemed calmer this morning than last night." She tapped on the door. "I won't be long."

"Bet she's a good shrink," Jack said.

• • • • •

After fifteen minutes, Dr. Dunne emerged from Donald's room. "Let's walk down the hall and talk," she said.

They stopped in a small alcove at the end of the hall, away from the hubbub of people. The doc smoothed her honey brown hair.

"Mr. Sowder is still agitated and paranoid. We're transferring him to Rush for testing, hopefully this afternoon. I can share a few of his behaviors. Now we're allowed more leeway to reveal patient medical issues with law enforcement." She paused. "He claims he, quote, rectified the sins of two devils, but not three. He says he's doing God's work by ridding the earth of evil against children. He also rambles Bible quotes, but he does not present as psychotic."

"So he's not schizophrenic," Sherk said.

Dr. Dunne shook her head. "No diagnosis at this time. The buzzing and heartbeat he said he heard last night were symptoms of major panic attacks, which he's experienced previously. He was hospitalized ten years ago for major depression and paranoia. He has not kept up with his meds."

Jack nodded. "Did Sowder say anything about a priest abusing him?"

"He alluded to priests in sheep's clothing and damaging altar boys. He referred to himself as Humpty Dumpty that no one could fix, that he was beyond repair."

"What does this mean for an arrest?" Sherk asked. "I assume the confession at his apartment wouldn't hold up since he was not in his right mind."

"I agree. I'm afraid it may take awhile to determine if Donald can be tried in court."

Jack grimaced. "I've seen my share of scum of the earth, but I still can't shake off what these perverts do."

The doctor smiled. "As they say, when you stop caring, it's time to quit."

"Guess so." Jack wanted to quit, but not because he didn't care about defenseless people. He had other reasons.

Sherk glanced at his watch. "We've done all we can for now. Thanks for your time, Dr. Dunne."

Outside, the wind had picked up, blowing chillier air. Jack's phone buzzed on their way to the car. "Yeah." Pause "No shit. Right." He clicked off, turned to Sherk.

"That was Skokie. Found dandruff specks on the coach's body.

DNA doesn't match his own or the previous samples from the nun and Welton scenes. Doesn't prove a copycat, but a strong indicator. Crap. We gotta rule out Sowder, even though we both think he's clear of the third vic. Let's assume for now, that there is a copycat."

Back in the car, Sherk drove toward the station. "As we said before, the copycat knew about the Bible verse. Has to be someone—"

"Someone leaked it. Or someone—" Jack hated to think of an inside job. Always messy when it's one of your own. Hell, did he even want to know?

Chapter 34

"Or someone knew and acted on it. Someone who did the deed," Sherk said.

They arrived at the station and made their way into the building. "Let's grab a bite. Figure out what to do next," Jack said.

Settled in the break room dining on vending machine sandwiches and cokes, they talked about the dilemma of an inside job for the third murder. Cops hate the idea of one of their own breaking the laws they're paid to serve and protect. Truth be told, good cops sometimes give the rules a nudge, plant a little weed in a guy's pocket so he's arrested for a worse crime you know damn well he's committed. Jack had known dirty cops. Money the usual motivator.

"I'm convinced Sowder's DNA will match evidence from the first two bodies. Guy's a nut job, but I bet he's right about a copycat."

Sherk took a bite of his ham and cheese sandwich. "Yes, and remember the coach's scene was compromised by the cops who nosed around before CSI got there."

"Yeah," Jack agreed. "Could've been their dandruff left. Need to remind 'em of that small fact." Good thought, but there was still room for doubt. "Someone had to know about the Bible verse."

They finished their lunch and were on their way to the bull pen when Chub Nesbitt ran into them in the hallway. "What's the latest on the nut—ah, the mentally disturbed suspect?"

Jack cleared his throat. "Nothing's clear yet. Sowder wasn't of sound mind when he confessed to the first two murders. Has a lawyer, but we're gonna try for an informal interrogation. My trusty ESP says Sowder just offed the first two vics. He's transferring to Rush for further psych evals."

Nesbitt grimaced. "Stay on it." He strode away. Jack bet the cap caught the drift of an inside job for the third vic. No wonder Nesbitt was pissed.

"Guess we'll keep the Skokie dandruff call to ourselves?" Sherk asked.

"Yeah. We gotta think on it," Jack said as they entered the bull pen. "Something's staring us in the face. Don't know what it is yet."

They ran into Velda Vatava on their way to their desks. "You guys gonna arrest the Sowder guy? Heard he pulled a Cuckoo's Nest on you last night."

"Don't believe everything you hear, Vatava," Jack said as he sat.

"Right," she said, patting her permed hair. Her voice lowered. "What worries me, Donald, is how your poor mother is going to take this."

Sherk said, "Sorry, Velda, I have no idea what you're talking about."

"It's her lame attempt at humor. Quoting from the movie. You know, Nurse Ratched." Jack scoffed. "Your quotes, Sherk, are a cut above hers."

"Ha," Velda retorted. "I can quote Shakespeare too. 'To thine own self be true' and all that."

"A lucky guess, Vatava. Moving along, we got work to do." Jack opened a file on his desk.

She chuckled. "I can take a hint. See ya later."

"That woman knows everything," Sherk said.

"Yeah, about office gossip."

After twenty minutes of getting nowhere with case speculation, Jack said he needed a break and decided to contact Molly. Maybe she'd had a bad day when she brushed him off. He returned her text, recommending the White Lion again for their meeting, since the place was convenient for both, and the food good.

A few minutes later, Molly texted back, suggesting they meet later around 6:30 for drinks.

Fine with him; his social calendar was a vast wasteland.

• • • • •

Jack arrived at the restaurant early. He and Sherk had spent the remaining afternoon spinning their wheels. Possibilities of a fellow cop doing the third murder made little sense; a connection between someone at the station and Coach Grant Adams would be a huge coincidence. Jack didn't believe in coincidences, but nothing fit into place. He decided to focus on Molly and the potential of a relationship. God knows, a rarity in his life.

Jack told the hostess he'd wait in the entrance area for his other party. Since he disliked crowds, he was happy to see mostly empty tables. After several minutes, the door opened and Molly strolled in. Damn, she looked good.

"Hey, Jack." She took his hand and gave him a half hug. He caught a hint of lavender as he stepped close. Her smooth hair looked shorter, both sides curved over her ears.

His heart skipped a beat. "Same place as last time okay?"

"Sure."

The hostess led the way to a secluded booth in a corner. Jack indicated Molly sit first, then scooched in beside her. The décor was minimalist, with dark wood, red leather booths, and a modicum of wall hangings. A middle-aged waiter greeted them and asked for drink orders. The guy was half bald with wide-set eyes that bulged like a frog's. Molly ordered a Shirley Temple, Jack, a Guinness.

Jack took in Molly's white shirt and black and gray patterned jacket. Was it animal print? What did he know, but it looked fashionable to him. Her green eyes sparkled.

After making small talk about the weather, work, and Sister Anne, the waiter returned with their drinks. "Will you be having anything else?" The poor guy did resemble a frog.

"Not right now," Molly said. "Maybe later."

Jack held up his beer glass. "Here's lookin' at you, kid." Upper lip pursed against upper teeth. A pretty decent Bogart if he said so himself.

Molly laughed. "Not bad." She took a sip of her drink and set it down. Her smile faded. She eyed Jack. "I know we don't know each other very well, but I felt a connection when we were here a couple weeks ago."

"A week, but who's counting?" Jack hoped this was leading somewhere promising. "Yeah, you could say that."

"I've thought a lot about things since then, and I'm gonna go out on a limb here and be honest. At our age, we've been around the block a few times, and I wanted to tell you where I stand on goals and things. I'm not into the relationship games that younger couples play."

Oh God, this didn't sound good. Not ready for a commitment. He took a swig of beer. "Okay, I'm listening."

His phone buzzed. "Sorry. Forgot to turn the damn thing off." He glanced at the screen. His mother. Figured.

Molly smoothed her hair. A blue topaz ring sparkled on her right hand. "Anyway, I think we both have issues. I mean, they're manageable, but issues. Maybe somewhat broken in places."

This was getting heavy. "Just a minute here—" What was she? A shrink?

"Sorry, wait." She held up her hand. "I want to finish and then you tell me what you think."

She was moving too fast. Felt his cheeks flame. Hoped he wasn't blushing.

He shrugged. "Sure thing."

"I don't mean to say we're both too screwed up, but you know I'm a recovering alcoholic. Off the wagon last month. A constant battle. I'm prone to depression as well, so you see, I'm no bargain."

"Molly, everyone has— "

"I know, but I'm hoping to find someone to be with on a steady basis. Not looking for marriage. Just someone to be with. As a friend and lover, and—now this is the hard part— "

"Ready to order anything else yet?" The guy snuck up on them.

Jack wanted to bare his teeth at him. "No thanks. I'll let you know." Didn't mean to snap. Oh well.

Molly took another sip. "Some people can be friends. Companions to travel with, all that. But I'd want more. And—I can't have that with you, Jack."

His heart raced. "You're moving way too fast, Molly. We haven't even— "

"I know we haven't slept together. But I know what's coming. It's happened before. You can't help it, but you're—you're still in love with Karen. I don't know if you'll ever be able to love anyone else. I'm not blaming you of course— "

Jack scoffed. "Well, this is a new one. Pardon me, but you have some balls telling me how I tick. What my future is. How I feel about anything. I didn't know you were a licensed shrink and— "

"Oh, Jack. Please don't be angry." Tears blurred her eyes. "I can tell when a man has a lost love he can't get over. You can just tell. And I'm certain you are still entwined with Karen, whether through guilt or— "

"Now I've heard enough. You have no idea—" His voice rose. She'd overstepped into his private thoughts. Struck a nerve. The guilt.

"Right, I have no idea what Karen was like except she must've been one hell of a woman to capture your heart, Jack."

"You don't know the—" He wasn't about the break his code of silence about Karen. That was sacred territory.

"And furthermore, before you walk out in a huff, I cannot and will not compete with a ghost." She sounded frustrated that things were going south.

Jack flinched, drained his glass and slammed it on the table. Several people at a nearby table stared. He didn't give a damn. He shifted himself out of the booth and stood. "I'll pay the tab on the way out." He leaned close to Molly's face and said softly. "I'm outta here. Better luck with your next patient."

Hmm, that went well, Jack told himself as he walked out of the restaurant after throwing down enough cash at the hostess station to cover the bill. Heart thumping, he climbed in his Beemer and burned rubber to get the hell out of there and away from that pompous broad forever.

How could he have misjudged her? Her words still reverberated with him. Could she be right? Maybe he'd never find anyone to be with. In disbelief, he felt a lump in his throat. He stifled the urge to bawl like a baby. What was happening to him? Wish he could talk to someone. Needed to vent. But no one available for that unless he looked up his old shrink from years ago. The image of Sowder's doc, Kay Dunne flashed in his mind, but nah. Never happen.

After Jack arrived home, he lowered himself into his chair with a shot of Jameson with Guinness chaser and a bag of Doritos. Felt like the wind was kicked out of his balls. His answering machine blinked, but probably his mother. Ignore it. If it was Molly calling to apologize, forget that.

The beacon in his dismal life was the money he acquired from Buckley. Hell, the meeting was tomorrow already. How time flies when you're getting crapped on.

Willing himself to compartmentalize Molly and all women, he thought about the case and how he and Sherk needed to get their shit together. Another thought crossed his mind. What if the coach's killer thought Jack was getting too close to the truth? Could Jack's life be in danger?

Chapter 35

Jack slept surprisingly well after drinking enough to put most men under the table the night before. Guess the booze kept nightmares at bay. Still licking his wounds from Molly's unfair treatment of him, he drove to the station in a foul humor. He realized his life was full of gray areas, but in her case, she was wrong, he was right. Wouldn't take long to forget about her.

He didn't care that the clear sky promised a refreshing spring day, nor about the birds who warbled from budding trees. Determined to focus on the Bible thumper copycat, Jack arrived at the station ready to face the day. A recollection from yesterday popped into his brain. What was it? Damn, couldn't come up with it.

On a brighter note, he was eager for his afternoon appointment with Stewart Buckley. Should be a life-changer.

When he reached his desk, Sherk greeted him. "Ready to face the day?"

"Am I ever?" Jack grabbed his White Sox cup. "Right back. Donuts?"

"Day-old cookies." Sherk held up a half-eaten oatmeal raisin.

Several minutes later, Gary Calvin called out. "Bailey, over here."

"Got something interesting?" Jack walked to Calvin's desk.

"Always do." He held out his chest. "Just got this."

The geek's gray t-shirt showed a couple Crayola's above words printed in black, *I have neither the time nor the crayons to explain this to you.*

"Damn, dude. Getting worse by the day." Jack took a bite of cookie. "Ugh. Dry."

"You don't understand the nuances of sophisticated sarcasm,"

Calvin said. "Anyway, f-y-i, your wacko guy is now in the psychiatric unit at Rush. Here's his contact info."

"Thanks. I guess." Jack took the note. "Anything else?"

"What's your take on a copycat? Think Sowder is talkin' crazy? Any evidence?"

"You ask too many questions, Calvin. Besides, you should've heard everything by now through the internet or grapevine, both the same."

Jack gazed at him. "By the way, how was the funeral yesterday in Des Plaines. You grow up there?"

"Yeah, why?"

"Just came to me." The memory Jack couldn't grasp earlier. "That's where the coach worked back in the nineties."

Calvin eyeballed Jack. "The coach?"

"You know, Grant Adams, the third vic in Skokie."

"Oh. That coach. Thought he grew up in Skokie."

Jack gulped his coffee. "Nope, lived in Des Plaines back then. Taught at a high school there. Maybe you went to the same one. You have all the info, cuz you forked it over last week."

Calvin clicked his keyboard, moved the mouse, looked at the screen. "Yeah, here. Carver Central High. Adams was a history teach and coach."

"You go to that school?"

"No. That place was a pit. I went to Niles West."

"You ever play Little League?"

Calvin stared at him. "No. Did you?"

"Nah. Sissy stuff. Gotta run." Jack walked off and could feel the guy's eyes piercing through his back. Maybe there were such things as coincidences. Lots of people live in Des Plaines.

When Jack returned to his desk, he replayed his conversation with Calvin to Sherk. "That's a coincidence all right. I wonder why Gary didn't mention he grew up Des Plaines when we first heard it. You'd think he would've unless— "

"Yeah, unless," Jack said.

"I'm no psychiatrist, but I don't see Gary as the perpetrator."

"Yeah, but he has the tech know-how to pull off the details like getting the drugs and syringe used on the coach, not to mention knowing about the verses."

Sherk shuffled some papers. "Our hands are tied until we get DNA on the dandruff. Hopefully it'll match Donald's. Then we know his copycat rantings are definitely delusional."

"I'm gonna call Skokie and tell 'em to run the dandruff DNA on the two cops and whoever else was screwing up the coach's crime scene. They better get their asses in gear."

Sherk busied himself with paperwork while Jack made the call. A couple minutes later, he hung up.

"That was quick," Sherk said.

"Got right to Rossi, aka Vito Corleone himself." He resisted the urge to assume the accent. "He's sure the two cops at the scene would be happy to give their DNA, and he'd let us know. Get the idea he wants his department to shine and ours to suck."

Sherk pushed up his glasses. "You're a little paranoid."

"And you're a little naïve. For a German yet. You of all people should be wary, suspicious. Trust no one."

"Ah, Jack. 'Suspicion always haunts the guilty mind'." Sherk looked smug. "Henry VI."

"Sherk, if I didn't sorta like you, I'd kick ya right in the ass."

"No doubt, Jack. No doubt. Now let's get busy."

The next couple hours they spent on phone calls and paperwork. Regarding Donald Sowder's status at Rush University Medical Center, one of Chicago's finest, Jack learned Sowder was in testing and would not be available for a supervised visit until the next day at the earliest.

At noon, Jack told Sherk he had an appointment and didn't know when or if he'd return. Sherk looked puzzled, but Jack wasn't ready to talk about meeting Buckley. Save that for later. Maybe never.

After avoiding everyone in his path on the way out, Jack reached the parking lot and climbed into his Beemer. He entered the address of the Parkway Bank & Trust in Park Ridge in his GPS. He should have time to grab a quick sandwich from Jersey Mike's Subs before meeting his former father-in-law at the bank. He drove up Halsted to 55, then took the 90 interchange toward Park Ridge, the usual familiar route. Sunny skies and light traffic made the drive easy.

Jack had arranged to meet Buckley and his friendly banker, the trustee of his portfolio. Buckley had mentioned the funds would be in a trust and doled out in increments of something over 200K per year, which to Jack, was big bucks. Jack knew his brother Andy, CPA in Arlington Heights, was on board to manage finances. Jack thought himself a quick study, but was smart enough to know when he needed an expert. What did he know about high finance?

● ● ● ● ●

That evening Jack lounged in his recliner, Boone at his feet. He'd met Buckley and the trustee of his at the bank, and gone over the details with a fine-tooth comb. Jack lost track of the papers he'd signed. After an hour, his was brain saturated with information; he couldn't wait to get home and knock back a shot or two. Buckley had suggested they stop for drinks and dinner to celebrate, but Jack begged off. Needed down time to process his new financial status. Now he regretted turning Buckley down. After all, the guy just made Jack rich.

"Mum's the word," Andy had said, when Jack mentioned he wanted to hold off telling the family until sometime in the future. How would that go over? Meanwhile, he had a killer to find. Or from the looks of it, more than one.

Chapter 36

Still in a daze from his newly acquired wealth, Jack drove to the station the next morning determined to crack the damn case. No surprise, the first person he ran into was Daisy LePere sashaying down the hall.

"Bailey, good to see you right on time." Why did she have to wear that damn rose perfume?

"Sarge, full of good humor as usual." Jack continued on his way.

"Just one minute. What about the case?"

"What about it?"

"Cut the attitude. What's Sowder's situation?"

Jack sighed. "Transferred to Rush. Had testing yesterday. We'll try to see him today."

LePere brushed the shoulder of her white silk jacket. "What's the latest from Skokie?"

"DNA doesn't match other two stiffs. A couple cops might've screwed up the scene before CSI got there. Lookin' into it." He didn't tell her about the dandruff. Didn't want her words of wisdom.

"Think it's a copycat or is Sowder blowing smoke?"

"Don't know yet, Sarge. Gotta go." He turned to leave, surprised she refrained from trying to stop him. Perhaps she sensed something in his demeanor. A self-assuredness. She marched off without a word.

By noon no significant developments in the case had arisen. The Skokie DNA on the dandruff should be ready by Monday, according to a detective Sherk spoke to.

"I'll call Sowder's shrink. Doubt if he'll be ready for visitors, but won't hurt to try," Jack said. He placed the call and after several minutes of waiting and listening, hung up.

"Pay dirt. We can see him at three this afternoon for a supervised interview." Jack had expected delay. Lawyers in cases of competence like Sowder's usually cooperate with the cops, figuring they'll provoke the client into going off the rails, thus indicating a no-trial. That decision would be determined by the court at a later date, after muddling though red tape. A guy whose title Jack forgot, gave him directions to the appropriate building and unit.

Sherk stood. "How about lunch at Shinnick's? Then we'll head out."

"I'll even spring for it." Hell, he could now buy the whole frickin' pub if he wanted.

• • • • •

After a leisurely lunch and chatting with Charlie, bartender extraordinaire, the men drove up Thirty-first Street, turned right onto Loomis and headed north. Traffic wasn't too thick off the freeways, so they made good time. They zig-zagged onto Ashland and drove north to the sprawling hospital complex of Rush Medical Center on Congress Street.

According to Sherk, the venerable facility, built in 1837, houses one of the first medical colleges in the Midwest. "Very impressive, Jack. Rush's physicians and scientists are involved in hundreds of research projects."

"Glad Sowder's in good hands," Jack replied. "Sure is a hodge podge of buildings."

"Yes, obviously evolved over the decades." Sherk indicated the mammoth steel gray high rise with semi circles of upper floor windows jutting out. "I have no idea what architectural design that is."

"Dunno, don't care." Sherk missed his calling. Maybe an architect rather than professor.

Jack secured a designated parking space, and followed the contact guy's directions in the rat's maze of walkways and corridors. The interior was bright and modern, obviously one of the newer buildings, or towers as they were called. After taking the elevator to Donald Sowder's floor, they showed their badges to the nurse manning the station and proceeded to Room 405. When Sherk rapped on the door, a woman's voice said, "Just a minute."

The door opened and a young Asian nurse smiled at them. "Are you here to talk to Mr. Sowder?"

"Yes, Ma'am," Sherk said, as he and Jack held out their ID's.

A dark haired thirty-something man sat in a chair under a window. He wore a white dress shirt and a burgundy tie. "Hello, I'm Fred Dodge, Mr. Sowder's attorney."

Jack and Sherk introduced themselves and shook hands with Dodge. Donald sat in a chair beside the bed, dressed in a blue t-shirt and sweatpants. His pasty skin and droopy mouth accentuated his forlorn look.

He adjusted his glasses. "We meet again."

"Hi, Donald," Sherk said. "It's nice to see you."

"Wish I could say the same." He gave a half-hearted smile.

The nurse indicated two chairs for Jack and Sherk. She leaned in and whispered, "He's under medication. Will be relaxed."

A standard hospital room, the space was surprisingly large with few decorative touches. A small table with recording equipment sat in front of Dodge.

The nurse asked, "May I offer you water or coffee?"

Jack and Sherk accepted water, which she poured from a pitcher into glasses. She topped off Donald's glass, and Dodge waved her away.

"I'll leave you gentlemen to it." She smiled and left the room.

"If everyone's ready, let's start," Dodge said. "As you know, Donald will speak with you here in my presence. His medical team advises against transporting him to law enforcement headquarters. He's been read his rights." The man looked at Sherk and Jack. "Understood?"

Jack nodded. Sherk said, "Yes, Sir."

Dodge reached over and turned on the tape recorder. He spoke the date, time, place, purpose, and people present for the interview.

"Okay, Donald," Sherk began. "Why don't you tell us a little about yourself. Your job. Family."

Donald shrugged. "I work at Midway Airport as you know. Do some software design. Support."

"What about family?" Jack asked.

"My mother's in Goldpine Home. She has Alzheimer's. Goes in and out." He circled his forefinger near his temple. "My sister's younger than me. Lives in Oak Lawn."

"What about your father?" Sherk asked.

Donald's eyes twitched. "Yeah, he's around. Still lives in the Bridgeport house."

"Do you see him much?" Jack figured there was a problem with the old man.

"Nah. He's busy with stuff." Donald shifted in his chair. "We don't have a lot in common." He took a drink of water.

Jack wanted to get to the point, not have this turn into a therapy session, but knew Sherk preferred a gradual transition to put Donald at ease.

"So you don't share common interests with your father?" Sherk asked.

"No. He wanted a macho son. 'Go into sports. Be good for you. Get your nose outta them books. Come on, let's shoot some hoops.'" Donald's mouth shrank into a prune.

Jack glanced at Dodge, who wore a poker face. "What about your school days back at Nativity Church?"

"What about them?" Donald looked at him through squinty eyes.

"We know you may not want to revisit those years, Donald, but school was difficult for many people," Sherk said. "You're not alone."

"Right. Guess I'm the classic example of the kid who got bullied. That's a big deal now, isn't it? 'Put a stop to bullying', and all that." He looked at the floor. "Didn't help back then."

"Look, dude, I know it's tough, but you gotta talk about the damn priest some time. What did Father McGarvey do?"

Donald shook his head, evidently resigned to come clean with the truth. "You no doubt know what he did. I don't wanna talk about that son of a bitch. Wolf in sheep's clothing. The devil in sheep's clothing is the truth of it." He took a gulp of water.

"Donald, I know it's difficult, but please look at me." Sherk waited for Donald to make eye contact. "You can rest assured other boys were victims too. Not just you."

Donald looked down. "I-I didn't wanna be an altar boy, but my mom insisted. Good Catholic boys and all that. At first I really liked Father Dan. He was so nice to me. Spent time with me. I was special, he said. *Donny, you're special in God's eyes. God loves you. He shows his love —* "

During the next several minutes, Donald talked about Father McGarvey's asking him to do special favors, keeping him after Mass, telling his parents that Donny was exceptional.

"He told me I deserved love and respect. Spent time in McGarvey's quarters. *Others don't appreciate you, Donny. Your talents.* Then in the sacristy where I learned more. More — "

"Learned more what, Donald? What did Father McGarvey teach you?" Sherk asked gently.

Dodge shifted in his chair, eyes on his client. "I don't think — "

Donald waved him away, gave a raw, bitter laugh. "I supposedly learned about doing God's work. How we should grow up to help God, you see. *Like me, Donny. I show you God's love. Love you don't receive from the world. The world doesn't love you Donny. But I do through God. Here, let me show you.*"

Jack felt a chill. Then rage toward the scum priest and others like him. Fuckin' hypocrites, preaching Christianity. Donald stared at his hands. The nurse was right. He seemed medicated all right.

"What about the nun? Sister Anne Celeste?" Jack asked.

"Ah yes, the good Sister. Sister Anne. Much adored." Donald glanced at the ceiling. "She did nothing. Nothing. She could've reported him." His voice rose.

"Was she in the sacristy, Donald? When Father McGarvey — "

Donald squirmed. "The door was ajar. She peeked in. She saw. Saw what he did." Donald's voice squeaky, like it needed oil.

"I'm sorry, Donald," Sherk said gently. "No need to explain. Did she say anything? Did the priest see her?"

Donald rubbed his hands. "She didn't say a word. Looked right at me. Think the bastard heard something. He turned around as she closed the door. But I know damn well he saw her."

"Then what happened?" Jack's voice quiet.

"Bastard stood up in a hurry. Said he had a meeting he forgot. Told me to go home. *Remember what we talked about Donny? Our secret. It's a sin to break a secret. People don't understand the ways of God.*

"You must've been upset at the Sister for turning a blind eye. I sure as hell would have," Jack said. Hard to keep his emotions in check.

Dodge cleared his throat, gave Jack a hard look.

Donald hung his head. "I always liked Sister, but afterwards I was ashamed. Embarrassed. That all came out ten years ago in therapy. But I thought she'd save me. Do something. Tell a bishop or someone. Things would change. But—but— "

"Did the priest hurt you again, Donald?" Sherk asked.

"No. Not me. But I know he hurt a couple other kids after that. Then he left. Was sent to another parish." Donald grimaced. "That's what churches do. You know that. Send 'em on to another place so they do it again. The gift that keeps giving. Ha ha."

"So Sister Anne didn't help you." Sherk sighed. "The ultimate betrayal. A cliché, but brutally true."

"You wanted to get even with those who abuse children," Jack said. "Can't say I blame ya."

"Careful, Detective," Dodge said.

Donald squinted, paused. "I dunno. The idea of doing God's work. Wiping out evil against children. Started growing in me. Maybe— "

"Donald, I'd advise—"

"No, I wanna get it out. Something happened inside my brain. Read about a little boy who—you know. Was in the papers last year. Something snapped in me."

"And by now the McGarvey prick's dead, good riddance," Jack said. He caught Sherk's glare. Dodge shook his head but said nothing.

Donald drained his glass. "Yeah, looked him up online. Maggot city. But someone had to atone. Atone for the sin of the Father. The nun was as guilty. She turned a blind eye. She had to pay."

"Then Bruce Welton." Sherk rose and refilled Donald's glass.

Dodge put his hand on Donald's arm. "Donald, again I'd advise you— "

"No. Let me talk. That scum Welton. On the registry. So easy to find. Messed with that little boy. Someone's gotta save the world from that vermin. At least I could start."

Sherk nodded. "The coach in Skokie— "

"No." Donald's demeanor changed. Sat straight. "I told you. Somebody else did that asshole. Not me. Didn't know the son of a bitch." He stared at Jack. "A copycat who knew about the Bible verses. Wasn't in the papers. Who'd know?" Donald's eyes glinted. "An inside job?"

"We're working on that, Donald," Sherk said.

Dodge turned off the tape recorder. "I think we're done here. I'll— "

"Ha. Wouldn't that be something?" Donald cackled. "One of your own bumping off pedophiles?"

That would be something, all right. But who?

Chapter 37

By 6:00 Jack and Sherk were back at the station, exhausted from the afternoon with Donald Sowder. They'd gleaned solid information, which amounted to an unofficial confession of the first two murders. Time would tell whether Donald was fit to stand trial, if he'd remain at Rush or remanded to jail or prison. Jack figured the man would end up at Rush or another psychiatric facility, especially if he convinced himself and others he was doing God's work in ridding the world of evil against children. Although pleas of insanity, mental deficiency, disorder, disease, you name it, were difficult to prove in court, Donald might beat the system.

Flopping into his desk chair, Jack called Nesbitt, who had left for the day. "I'll try his cell tonight, update him then."

Sherk nodded his agreement. "Let's file our paperwork on Donald and call it a day."

"Yeah. I'll try Skokie, but not holding my breath on the dandruff results." Jack made the call, and sure enough, no word yet.

The bull pen was quiet with few cops or staff around. Jack stood. "I'm outta here. The CYA garbage can wait till Monday."

"Go ahead, Jack. I won't be long. Have a good weekend." Sherk turned his attention to his computer.

Jack always felt like a slacker next to Sherk. A real pain at times.

"Come on, man. Erica's probably keeping dinner warm. Get your butt home."

"In a few minutes," Sherk said.

• • • • •

By 9:30, Jack was relaxing in his recliner when the phone pinged a text message. Damned if it wasn't Molly. Tempted to ignore it, he gave in and read, 'I'm sorry Jack. Was out of line. Please text or call me'.

"Don't think so, baby," he said to Boone. "Not gonna happen." The big dog blinked his wise brown eyes in response.

Several minutes later the phone rang. Hoping it wasn't Molly calling, he checked and saw his mother's name on the screen. Shit. Now what?

"Yeah, Ma. What do you want at this hour?"

"Hello to you too, Jacky. Called your landline earlier. You must've worked late," she chirped.

"What's up, Ma? No time for small talk."

"Okay. Okay. Tommy's coming for lunch tomorrow. I want you to come too."

Jack sighed. He pictured his mother in her pink robe, hair in curlers. "Guess so. Around noon?"

"Yes, that's good. We'll have a nice chicken— "

"Okay, Ma. It's late. Turning in. G'night." He clicked off. Knew he was grouchy, but she was used to him. Wouldn't take it personally.

• • • • •

Clouds swept the sky Saturday morning, and made way for the sun by noon. Jack needed to talk to Andy soon about financial advice, but that could wait. The case was gaining momentum, and he was impatient for the dandruff DNA results from Skokie.

Around noon he arrived at Maureen Bailey's house. "Come in," she called as Jack unlocked the front door. "Taking the casserole out."

A scent of chicken and spice glided in the air as Jack stepped in. "Smells good, Ma."

"Come sit in the kitchen. Tommy should be here in a minute." Maureen wore a loose blue top over black pants. A gold Celtic harp hung on a chain, resting in the center of her ample bosom.

"Lookin' good, Ma. Didn't have to dress up for me."

"Ha. Just came from Saturday Mass. No time to change." She

fluttered about the room.

"Your blue blouse matches your Maureen O'Hara Irish eyes." Jack attempted a brogue.

"Shows how much you know, smarty pants. Her eyes are green."

"Eye, blimey, sorry you weren't the mither of a bishop."

"Here's Tommy thank God. No offense, Jacky, but your accent needs work."

Tommy joined them in the kitchen, and soon they gathered at the table laden with chicken casserole, soda bread, green salad with boiled egg slices and tarragon dressing, and a bottle of Blarney red.

Jack uncorked it and poured three glasses. "This the wine Andy ordered you for Christmas?"

"Yes, straight from County Cork." She paused. Bowed her head and waited for her sons to do likewise. "Bless us, oh Lord, and these Thy gifts which we are about to receive from Thy bounty through Christ our Lord. Amen." All three hurriedly crossed themselves. The ritual was a habit ingrained in their childhood. Jack gave it no thought. Ma's house, Ma's rules.

After finishing dessert of pineapple upside down cake, the three sat in the living room drinking coffee.

"Andy said he'd come over in the next couple weeks to look through your father's box of things. Maybe he'll want stuff for his kids." Maureen brushed imaginary lint off the arm rest.

"You're sure hung up with that box," Jack said. "Nothing in there but old papers."

She scoffed. "They may be old to you, but they could be valuable some day. Your father went though a lot during the war."

"He wasn't the only one, Ma," Tommy said. "Plenty of men got-"

"Easy for you boys to say. You never had to go. You have no idea."

"Yeah, but not everyone came back and took it out on their families." Jack was tired of putting the old man up on a pedestal.

"Oh pooh. You had a good life. Everyone spanked kids in those days." Maureen sipped her coffee.

"Spanked? You call getting the belt on your bare ass spanking?"

Jack said.

"Take it easy, Jack," Tommy said. "I got it worse than you and I'm not complaining."

Jack looked at his mother. "I know. Ma got plenty herself, but she won't admit it."

"He drank because of that damn war," Maureen said. "It wasn't his fault."

"Come on, Ma. Admit it. Bet he belted you too. Just out of sight."

"Jack." Tommy's voice rose. "You never saw anything like I—" His voice trailed off.

"Like you what?" Jack said.

"Enough. Both of you. I'm not gonna drag your father's name through the mud. Doesn't do anybody any good now."

They sat in silence until Tommy said, "Yeah, let's leave the past where it belongs."

"Right." Jack drained his cup and stood. "I gotta get going. Lots of work."

"Are you getting anywhere on the nun's murder?" Maureen asked.

"Ma, you know I can't say anything about an ongoing— "

"I know, I know. But you'd think your own mother— "

Tommy smiled. "Not even you, Ma. I'll stay a little while. Help you clean up."

"Ah, my good son." Maureen glanced at Jack. "Used to be you, Jacky."

Jack gave Maureen a rare hug. "Love ya, Ma. Thanks for the grub."

• • • • •

Later in the afternoon Jack's phone buzzed. The call he'd been waiting for.

"Jack Bailey." He listened. "No shit. You sure? Right. Keep ya posted." Clicked off and called Sherk.

"Heard from Skokie. The dandruff DNA wasn't a match for the

cops at the Grant Adams scene. Not in the system. Don't know about Sowder yet. Assuming there is a copycat, we're lookin' for someone who knew about the Bible verses." Jack paused. "Gotta call Nesbitt. See about getting samples from everyone on the squad. Rules are always changing."

Jack listened to Sherk. "Yeah, right. Could be dispatch, any employee, cop or not. God, what a pain in the ass that'll be."

After hanging up, he thought about the headache trying to get all employees of the PD to give DNA samples. The rules of demanding cops to submit their DNA kept changing. On a voluntary basis, the guilty one would refuse, but others may too, for reasons of privacy and such.

After dialing Nesbitt's two contact numbers outside the station, Jack had no luck reaching the captain, and left a message to return the call. Maybe he's playing eighteen holes. Perfect golf weather.

He'd dump the case in the cap's hands. Jack was sure Sowder didn't do the third murder, and without forensics, he had no clue who the copycat was. Someone who knew the Bible verse was the perp's calling card. Someone smart enough to leave no prints or anything else except a little dandruff. Someone who could access a syringe and the somulose. Someone they probably ran into every day. Who the hell was it?

Chapter 38

It occurred to Jack that the coach's killer could be someone other than a PD employee. What if someone blabbed to a spouse, a friend, or a cousin's Dutch uncle?

Chub Nesbitt returned Jack's call several hours later. He told Jack to wait until Monday morning when they met with Sherk. Meanwhile, the cap would research protocol on DNA and consult with his cronies in other Chicago departments. Needless to say, Nesbitt was not happy.

Jack spent the rest of the weekend doing as little as possible. Thoughts of Molly floated in and out of his brain. Wondered what Karen would think. Could he have overreacted when Molly told him in so many words he was too messed up to get involved with? Maybe her words were true. There would never be another Karen, but couldn't he have a woman in his life? The idea of quitting his job and flying off somewhere grew more tempting by the day. He could forget the case. So someone was bumping off pedophiles. Could be worse.

• • • • •

Monday morning Jack and Sherk sat across from Nesbitt in his pristine office. The cap scowled. "Preachin' to the choir here, but always a bitch when you suspect one of your own." He furrowed his wide ebony brow. "Talked to a few of the brass, did some research. Bottom line is we can't force our employees to submit their DNA. But we can check backgrounds. Did that before hiring."

Jack knew what was coming. He nodded and Sherk sighed.

"So you guys get busy looking for red flags. Start with male cops first, then staff. The priest, and other two vics all preferred young boys, so a woman wouldn't have motive. Or if your gut tells you somethin' start there. Look for connections to Adams, mainly in Des Plaines when he coached Little League. Don't rule out Skokie though."

Sherk adjusted his glasses. "What about privacy from prying eyes, Sir?"

"Gettin' to that. We're setting you two up in the conference room upstairs. Larson from HR is ready with your lists, directions, whatnot. He'll get you going."

"Okay, Cap." Jack stood. "You know I don't know about computers other than my own stuff."

"That's why the tutorial from Larson. By the way, he's clean. Checked him first. Then me." Nesbitt rose from his chair. "You can eliminate us from the usual suspects."

Was the cap serious? Playing it safe, Jack said nothing.

• • • • •

Within two hours, Jack and Sherk, ensconced in a meeting room, hunkered over their computer screens. The aroma of black coffee drifted in the air. Jack took notes during Larson's instructions, not trusting his directions to memory. Sherk, no problem.

"I'm gonna do Calvin first," Jack said after Larson departed the room. "I like the guy, but he did grow up in Des Plaines."

"Good," Sherk agreed. "He's the only caution light we've seen, so I'll start with the cops, alphabetical order. Alas, there is no joy in Mudville."

"Ha. 'Casey at the Bat' — an easy one for a change."

"Very good, Jack. But a depressing aspect of our job. Suspecting one of us."

"Right." Jack began his search, punching in keywords, grunting now and then, writing in his notebook. Working in an enclosed space was strange, with no one milling about chattering, interrupting, strolling in and out of the bull pen. Helped his concentration, but he felt closed-in. Several minutes later, he murmured, "Shit."

"Find something?" Sherk asked.

"Maybe. Calvin didn't go to the coach's high school in Des Plaines like he said. But got into trouble a couple years before he graduated Niles West High. Nothing serious until a drug bust at a party. Did community service. Happened again at a graduation party. This time he's fined, community serve, and mandatory rehab. Did that at Gateway for three months for cocaine addiction. Then went to Oakton Community for a couple years. Got a tech degree. Then hired on here."

"Not an immaculate resume," Sherk said, "but nothing ties him to Adams unless he lied about being in Little League."

"Yeah." Jack was already tired of the search. "I dunno. Something doesn't mesh. Can't pinpoint it."

"Let's soldier on then."

Sherk was annoying as hell with his stiff-upper-lip attitude.

Ten minutes later the call came they'd hoped for. "I knew it," Jack said.

He punched off. "Sowder's DNA isn't a match for the dandruff. Yay to him for using Head and Shoulders."

"Good news. Now we can soldier— "

"You said that already. I got it the first time."

"You're a quick study."

Half an hour later, Jack stood and stretched. "I'm starving. Let's have lunch. Get outta this room. Need some air."

Sherk agreed. "Sure aren't having any luck thus far. Unless Gary pans out somehow."

They headed for Nana's, a popular restaurant down the block on Halsted, a short walk from the station. The café featured American and Mexican cuisine, along with organic food on the menu, which pleased Sherk. Jack couldn't stand the stuff.

Later in the afternoon Jack strolled to the break room; the coffee machine upstairs was empty with no one on hand to brew more. He used Styrofoam cups since his trusty White Sox mug was at his desk. He wanted to avoid the bull pen and the inevitable questions about the copycat progress.

Carefully balancing coffee for Sherk and himself, he threaded his way out the door. He was about to press the elevator button with his elbow when Daisy LePere appeared.

"Need help, Bailey?" She pressed the button with her finger, red nail polish shining in the light.

"I'm good, Sarge. You can go on wherever you're headed." Her perfume about knocked him out.

"Actually, I was coming up to check on you and Sherkenbach. I hope you've made some progress."

Bitch. The doors opened and they stepped into the elevator. "Pretty much status quo. We're doing fine on our own."

"Trying to get rid of me, Bailey?" The doors reopened and Jack followed LePere into the hallway to the conference room. She let herself in without knocking. "Sherkenbach, nice to see you at work for a change."

Sherk looked up from his monitor. "Excuse me, Ma'am?"

"Just what I said. You're late most of the time around here."

"That's bullshit and you know it," Jack growled and placed the cups on the table spilling coffee on his hand. "Need someone to pick on? No kids at home or anyone else to bully?"

Sherk said, "Jack, it's— "

"No it isn't okay." Jack glared at LePere. "Give the guy a break. He has enough to worry about at home without your— "

"Watch your mouth, Bailey. You've crossed the line here." She threw her shoulders back. "I'm going to your superiors one last time."

"Lady, I have no superiors. Especially the likes of you." He stood facing her, adrenaline rushing to his head.

Her eyes were slits. "Well, we'll see about that." She stomped out of the room and slammed the door, nauseating perfume drifting in her wake.

"Good God. What have you done?" Sherk looked rattled. He stood and removed his glasses.

"Nothing I haven't wanted to do for a long time with that frickin' bitch."

"Your job's on the line, Jack. Control yourself."

"Fuck the job. I'll explain later." His heart pounding, he told himself to calm down. "Let's finish this son-of-a-bitchin' list and get the hell outta here."

"All right, Jack." Sherk took a drink of coffee. "We'll probably be done in half an hour. But you still shouldn't have — "

"Quit worrying. Believe it or not, I know what I'm doing."

They worked in silence. Jack found it difficult to concentrate. He'd had enough of LePere's uncivil treatment of Sherk. Downright mean-spirited, bullying. He'd been on the brink of telling her to go screw herself, and admitted he wanted to belt her. Didn't recall having a strong urge to hit a woman. First time for everything.

An hour crept by before their work was complete. "Nothing popped out. No flags," Jack said. "Let's report to the cap and get outta here."

Sherk stood and cleared his paperwork. "Nothing important that I saw. Found it interesting to read the resumes. Where our colleagues came from and so on."

"I guess," Jack muttered. He gathered his files and left the room with Sherk, heading for Nesbitt's office.

After they reported their findings to the captain, Nesbitt said, "I'll talk to Calvin tomorrow. He's probably okay, but need the alibi for his whereabouts on — " Nesbitt glanced at his papers. "Oddly enough, the coach's murder happened April Fool's night or early next morning."

"Okay, Cap," Jack said. "Don't think he's our copycat either, but gotta rule him out."

Nesbitt stood. "You two look beat. Enough for today."

Someone knocked on the door. "Yeah," Nesbitt called.

Daisy LePere burst in, face flushed. She seemed surprised to see Jack and Sherk. "Chub, I'm glad these two are here. I need to talk to you about Bailey. Couldn't get here sooner."

Jack scowled and rose from his chair. "Yeah, Cap, she has lots to say, so we'll be on our way."

Sherk pushed back his chair and started to rise.

"Hold on a minute," Nesbitt said. "Maybe you guys need to stay. I'm sure we can settle this — "

"All due respect, Cap, I doubt that." Jack turned toward the door.

"For once I agree with Bailey," LePere's voice high pitched. "He overstepped his boundaries for the last time a little while ago. He — "

"Yeah, yeah," Jack said. "Insubordination, Cap. Guilty of that."

"Now just a damn minute here — " Nesbitt clearly pissed.

"Bailey's at the end of his career here." LePere's hands on her hips. Blue silk shirt outlined her probable boob job.

"For crissakes, Daisy, calm down. This isn't a fuckin' school yard. We all need to act — "

"You've got to fire him, Chub. He went way too far. He told me-"

"Fire me?" Jack's voice rose. The dam burst. "Fire me? Guess what, bitch, you can't fire me. I quit!" He stepped toward the door. Turned and glared at LePere. "Been wanting to say this for months. Take this job and shove it up your ass!"

He stomped out the door, turned and glanced at Nesbitt, forehead shiny with sweat. Sherk's mouth hung open like he'd had too much Novocaine. LePere's eyes, marbles.

"And take that fuckin' perfume you wear and flush it down the crapper."

Jack glanced at Nesbitt. "You'll have my resignation in the morning."

Chapter 39

Jack swore he heard his heart thumping. Reminded him of Sowder's going off the rails the other night at his apartment. Racing out of the station, he ignored several co-workers, and climbed into his car.

When he arrived home, he let Boone outside for a quick pee, then called him back in. Jack poured a couple shots of Jameson and sat at the kitchen table. "Sure did it this time, Buddy," he told the big dog who sat by the chair.

Needed to decompress. Alone. He knocked back the shots and then concocted a sandwich of sausage, lettuce, and mustard, carried it into the living room along with a Sam Adams, and flopped into his recliner.

He switched on the TV news, ignoring his buzzing phone. Didn't want to talk to anyone. He'd call Sherk later and apologize for leaving him in the lurch. He owed his partner that much. Nesbitt would no doubt try and talk him out of resigning, then assign Sherk a new partner who would be easier to work with. Maybe someone normal.

An hour later, Jack checked his phone. Messages from Nesbitt, Sherk, Maureen, Calvin. Didn't listen. Another text from Molly. He imagined news of his stomping off the job spread like wildfire through the squad, even though no outsider had witnessed the event. Screw 'em all. After guzzling another beer, he flopped into bed.

"Sweet dreams," he told Boone. The yellow hound turned in two circles and settled on the floor at Jack's side.

• • • • •

Dawn brought no light through the wooden blinds in Jack's bedroom. Groggy, he bumbled into the bathroom. His head felt like a bowling ball. Recalling yesterday's events, he groaned, shucked off his boxers, and turned on the shower.

After breakfast, he bit the bullet and called Sherk, feeling guilty he hadn't called him last night.

"Hey, guy." He put the phone on speaker and sat at the kitchen table. "Got a minute?"

"Sure, Jack. Eating breakfast." Good old Sherk. Didn't sound pissed.

"Sorry. I'll call ya later."

"No, that's fine. Erica's in the den with the kids getting ready for the school bus."

"Well, ah, don't know where to start. Look, sorry for bailing on ya, man. Leaving you holding the bag, the old bag, that is." No chuckling from Sherk. "Anyway, it's been building up a long time. Should've come clean with ya, but— "

"Jack, you can probably go in and explain to Nesbitt—you need to think about your future. Besides, I don't want to lose you as a partner, and I hate to see you throw your career down the toilet. What about your resume?"

Jack cleared his throat. "That's what I should've told ya. I don't need to worry about another job. Not for awhile anyway. Too long to go into now, but I want us to get together this week and I'll explain."

"Jack, you don't owe me any explanations. I— "

"Yeah, I do. I want to. You've put up with my shit for two years. Been a loyal partner." Jack wasn't used to emotional conversations.

"Okay," Sherk said. "You coming in today to see Nesbitt? If you're determined to carry through with this, and you want help clearing out your desk, I can do that much."

"That might be good. Lemme think about it. Get back to ya. I'll email my resignation to the cap this morning. Don't wanna run into that bi—you know. Don't wanna face anybody in the place. Hate goodbye's."

"Right, Jack. Nesbitt told me after you left to keep your walking-out news under wraps, but somehow word got out. Gary knows. Asked me for details, but I said I couldn't say."

"Yeah, Calvin called last night. I haven't called back. Don't know what he wants."

"Right. Thanks for calling, Jack. Hang tight."

"Call ya later, dude. Hi to Erica if she's still speaking to me."

They clicked off. Jack was relieved he could skip going to the station this morning. He'd probably need to go in sometime. Maybe sign his resignation papers. Who the hell knew.

Outside the sky spit raindrops against the window panes, so Jack knew Boone would turn down a walk. He spent the gloomy morning writing a letter of resignation on his laptop and sent it to Nesbitt. The cap called, making sure Jack was serious about leaving the job.

"I'm sure we could negotiate with— "

"Thanks, Cap, but it's been brewing a long time. I'm positive it's the right move. Thanks for everything. Appreciate it." They clicked off. Lucky the cap was such a sport about the situation. Bad timing too, zeroing in on the serial killer.

Jack made a list of people to contact, including his brother Andy, Tommy, his mother. Soon his mind wandered far from the job and murders. He thought about his finances. Maybe he'd contribute a chunk to an animal shelter in Karen's memory. She'd loved dogs. Might even open his own shelter. Or add a unit to an existing one. Lots of possibilities.

Around noon Gary Calvin called. Jack answered. "Yeah, Calvin. What's up?"

"About to ask you the same thing, Bailey. Is it true what I hear?"

Jack wasn't about to lie to the guy or anyone else. "It's true. Been a long time coming."

"Man, I know you and LePere didn't see— "

"Don't wanna interrupt, but is there something else you're calling about?"

A moment of silence passed. Calvin coughed. "Actually, yeah. Look, man. I've thought about it and I really want to talk to you. In person. Private."

What the hell. Jack wasn't a cop anymore. "I guess. Wanna come over tonight?"

"Yeah. Got your address. How 'bout six?"

"That'll work. See ya then."

● ● ● ● ●

At 6:00 on the dot, Gary Calvin showed up at Jack's front door, Boone barking a healthy welcome. "Hey, guy." Calvin bent down and ruffled the big mutt's fur. "Old Yeller himself."

"Eaten yet?" Jack asked.

"Yeah, grabbed a burger on the way. Got caught in the rain. Can use a beer though." No wonder Calvin's red mop was damp and curlier than ever.

"Guinness or Sam Adams?"

"Sam. Prefer my brew cold."

They settled in the living room with their beers, Boone plopped down by Jack's feet.

He replayed his departure scene from yesterday while Calvin listened with an occasional 'yeah'. They spoke of department politics and general office gossip until Calvin said, "Look, Bailey, I know you're wondering why I'm here, so I'll get to it. First, the reason I'm here is because you're no longer with the department. Not a cop. Not in law enforcement."

"Can't argue with that. Another drink?"

Calvin nodded, and Jack retrieved two beers from the kitchen.

"Okay, here goes, but first, this is totally confidential. I need your word on that, Bailey. Otherwise I'll leave. Won't put you on the spot." He took a swig.

Jack figured what was coming. Sure, he'd keep it to himself. "Yeah, you have my word. I have a feeling I won't be shocked."

Calvin cleared his throat. "Well, I lied to ya before. I did know Grant Adams." A bitter laugh. "Only too well. Joined Little League when I was about ten. Adams was one of the coaches. Long story, but at first, a friendly, nice guy to kids like me. Chubby red-haired nerd, parents forced me to join. You know, 'good for you to play a sport', 'make new friends', all the usual bullshit kids like me hear." He paused. Took another swig.

Jack's jaw tightened. Said nothing.

"Anyway, the guy gives me special jobs to do for him. Then the season ends and we go on a retreat. Overnight at a campground. Not gonna go into details, but that's when it happened. I wasn't the only one. Knew it was wrong, but said nothing to nobody. Afterwards, I had a feeling in my bones my mom knew something happened. Could tell somehow. She never brought up playing baseball again." He paused.

"Take your time," Jack said. Anger rose in his chest against these sick bastards.

"So fast forward to high school. I'm miserable. Life sucks. Make friends with other losers who accept misfits like me. So I get into weed. Then coke. Get busted. End up in mandatory rehab. By then I'm pretty fucked up." Calvin stood. "Where's your john? Beer goes right through me."

Jack pointed the way, and when Calvin returned, Jack asked, "Want some Doritos and another brew?"

"Sure, why not?" Calvin rubbed Boone's back, waking the dog up. "Oops, should let sleeping dogs lie—more ways then one."

Jack placed a bowl of chips on the end table and handed Calvin a beer. "Didn't have to get so fancy, Bailey."

"Thought you'd be impressed with the bowl. Don't eat outta bags around here." Yeah, right.

Calvin sighed. "Ah, where was I? Oh yeah, rehab. At Gateway."

Jack didn't indicate he knew this from the background check.

"So I meet other people, group sessions, the usual. I make a friend, older, who had been messed with as a kid. From a family member. Worse then me. Went on longer. I'm the lucky one—only happened once." He snorted. "Always someone worse off."

Jack wondered why the rehab talk, but he kept silent.

"Another long story, but this friend I make, stays longer than me. By the way, I'm straight. Just unlucky with women."

Jack held out his bottle in a mock toast. "Join the club."

"So we keep in touch. I go to Oakton, take tech classes. First time in my life I'm successful at something. End up getting hired at the PD about ten years ago. Told them about rehab right off. Gave me a second chance. Then my pal needs a job. Thinks the PD sounds good. Gets hired a few months after me."

"Oh, who's that? He still there at the PD?"

"Wait a minute." Calvin held up his hand. "Fast forward again to the Bible thumper case a few weeks ago. Sure, I'm curious as hell about who's killing off pedophiles. The thought occurred to me over the years."

"Understandable," Jack said.

"Then when I hear about my old coach Adams, I'm like 'what the fuck?' The assumed Bible thumper copycat must be someone the coach screwed with. But how did he know about the Bible verse? And why the nun? And the Welton guy?"

Jack stared at him. "Huh?" Was Calvin saying he wasn't the copycat?

"Then when I hear the dandruff DNA from the coach scene isn't a match to the first two, I'm like freakin' out." Calvin gazed at Jack. "Then the clincher. Sherk tells me today that Sowder's not a match for the new DNA either. It's a copycat all right. Only one person it could be. Someone who knew the perp's calling card of the Bible verse. Someone who hated Adams. Someone who knew Adams ruined my fuckin' life. Someone who saw the perfect opportunity to get revenge for me. Someone who'd kill for me. Who is that someone? My pal in the Bridgeport PD."

Chapter 40

"Jesus, Mary and Joseph." Jack hadn't used his mother's expression for decades. He was confused, shocked. "You're saying your pal from rehab's the copycat?"

Calvin eyed him. "You thought it was me, didn't ya?"

"Can ya blame me?" Jack paused. "Sorry, man, but I don't know shit these days."

Calvin rose and walked toward the door. "I'll leave you be, Bailey. Enough for one night."

"Wait. You gonna tell me who it is?" Jack couldn't even take a stab at the answer.

"Nah. Won't happen. I promised. No one ever cared about me like this friend, bumped off the scum who ruined me. I won't betray that kind of loyalty. It's one secret I'll take to my grave, Bailey. Only evidence is the dandruff they can't match yet. And you know, they can't force us to submit our DNA."

"Right on that." Jack still confused, shook his head. "I've never seen you hang out with anyone at the station. Can't even make a guess who it is. You're like me. We got no friends."

Smiling, Calvin reached for the door. "Me and my pal decided a long time ago. Don't hang out at work. Better that way. Didn't want our drug history coming up in workplace gossip. Easy to overhear stuff in that place."

"Maybe it's best I don't know." Jack held the door open. No rain in sight.

The men shook hands. "See ya, Bailey. Keep in touch."

Jack knew they wouldn't. Just something people say.

• • • • •

Jack's brain was on overload. Who could the copycat be? He and Sherk would've seen someone's drug and rehab history other than Calvin's in their search. Nothing showed up. Guy probably hid that part under the radar. Could've skipped time gaps in the resume. He'd let it go for now. Sick of thinking about it.

Jack stayed up late, but couldn't get a decent sleep. Still took Ambien. He'd considered contacting his former shrink about resuming his meds for the PTSD that plagued him several years ago, but he tried to convince himself he was coping well. Some may debate that assessment.

• • • • •

The next morning after his shower and breakfast, his phone buzzed. Chub Nesbitt asked him to stop in and sign a couple papers.

"Can't do it by email?" Jack balked at darkening the doors of the station again.

"Afraid not, Jack. It'll be your exit interview as well. All bureaucratic bullshit, but what can I say?"

"Yeah. I'll sneak in sometime this afternoon."

He clicked off, walked Boone around the block, and called his brother Andy. Their conversation lasted half an hour, with Jack arranging a time to bring his financial files to Arlington Heights and discuss managing the portfolio. Jack had a learning curve ahead of him, but Andy would be a good instructor. He needed to tell his mother and siblings before long. How would they react?

Sherk called and offered to bring Jack's desk contents over around noon. Hopefully, they would remain friends. He needed all the pals he could get. He wanted to tell Sherk about Calvin's conversation, but he'd promised to keep it confidential. And now he wasn't a cop on the case, even though he was still mentally invested in it.

His phone pinged another text from Molly. Why wouldn't she

give up? Maybe he was too quick to take offense at her criticism of him. He still felt dumped on. Perhaps he should take a hard look in the mirror. Then again—

Boone trotted to the front door when the doorbell woke him up from his nap on the floor. He yipped with excitement. "Hold on, big guy. You know who this is."

When Jack stepped onto the porch, Sherk stood holding a large cardboard box.

"Don't just stand there. Come in." Jack took the box and carried it into the kitchen. He dropped it on the floor with a thud. "What the hell's in here? Bricks?"

Sherk smiled. "Files, papers, few books and pamphlets. I wasn't sure about some of it, so toss what you don't want." He fished out Jack's White Sox mug. "I knew you'd send me back if I forgot this."

For the first time, Jack felt a twinge of regret. "Too bad. Kinda liked the job if it weren't for that— "

"I know. But close one door and open another. You never know what opportunities— "

"Spare me the psychobabble. At least I won't have to listen to that anymore."

Sherk laughed. "Have to admit, Jack, I'll miss you. Got assigned to Chuck Wells until further notice."

"He's an okay guy. Can I make you a sandwich?"

"No thanks. I had an early lunch. Now tell me about your plans."

They sat in the living room, Sherk with a soda, Jack with a beer, and he talked about his financial windfall and plans for a charity in Karen's name.

"That's great, Jack. Quite a legacy. You can travel now too, which brings me to an idea I have in that regard." Sherk removed his glasses.

"Erica talked to her oncologist about traveling to Germany in June. He advised against it and wondered if I'd consider going with a friend or relative." He paused. "That's where you come in, Jack."

Jack was confused. "What?"

"Erica's folks can stay with the kids during the trip dates. About nine days. She begged me to go. She said I haven't seen my family in Munich for years, and she'll be fine. We're optimistic about her recovery or remission or whatever we can get." Sherk took a drink of soda. "So I'm thinking, why not Jack? You've never been to Germany. We'd have a great time. You could meet— "

"Whoa, man. What makes you think— "

"Why not? Now you're financially well off and aren't working."

Jack sat, speechless. He couldn't think of a valid reason not to take the offer. "Let me think about it. Caught me off guard, dude. Don't know what to say."

"First time for everything." Sherk put his glasses on.

"Smart ass. I'll get back to ya. You said you had airline tickets already."

"Yes, I'll get Erica's ticket canceled for medical reasons, and book a reservation for you. We'd be all set. You'll enjoy my cousins. They're just like me."

"No comment. Gotta tell ya, things are happening too fast. Every part of my life is changing."

"Change is good, Jack. I find it very exciting. A trip to Germany. Look at it this way. You'll be doing Erica a huge favor. Don't know anyone else I'd want to go with."

"You're a lousy liar, Sherk, but I appreciate it."

They said their goodbyes with Jack promising an answer on the trip in a day or two.

• • • • •

At 2:30, Jack snuck in the door of the station hoping to avoid running into anyone. He made it to Nesbitt's office unseen and signed the prerequisite exit papers. The cap asked Jack about his future.

"I can finagle a good reference if you want a transfer. I know you, Bailey. Truth of the matter is I'd ditch LePere but there's family bullshit, as you know through the grapevine. I never said that, though."

"Said what?" Jack shook Nesbitt's hand and departed the office for the last time. He glanced around corners on his way out, thankful no one appeared. Almost at the door. He no sooner grabbed the handle when he heard a woman's voice. "Hey, Bailey, trying to make another escape?"

Shit. Almost a clean getaway. He turned. "Vatava, what are you doing on the loose? Don't you have real cops to harass?"

She laughed, her rosy cheeks like apples. "Heard you left us for bigger and better things. You know you broke my heart."

"Wasn't meant to be, Vatava. Now if you'll excuse me, I have a retirement to plan."

"I'm on the way to my car. Forgot something. But we can sneak over to Shinnick's for a quick one."

Jack scoffed and opened the door for her. "Age before looks." He waved her outside.

"Says who?" As she passed him, he caught a whiff of woodsy fragrance. Better than that rose crap of LePere's. Then he saw it. On the shoulder of her dark brown pantsuit. Something clicked. A floodlight moment. Nah, can't be.

"Hate to admit it, but I'm gonna miss ya, Bailey." Outside they faced each other.

"Yeah." Jack gazed at her. Blood rushed to his head. He reached out, touched her shoulder and gave a small sweep with his fingers. "Nice fabric, but you might think about a good dandruff shampoo."

Her smile faded. Eyes turned to coal. Stared at him. Jack could read the question in her eyes. She blinked several times, looked to the side. Her words barely audible.

"Gary Calvin is like the son I never had."

She turned and walked toward her car.

The End

View other Black Rose Writing titles at www.blackrosewriting.com/books and use promo code PRINT to receive a 20% discount when purchasing.